LIES, *Love*, AND *Breakfast* AT *Tiffany's*

LIES, *Love,* AND *Breakfast* AT *Tiffany's*

PROPER ROMANCE®

JULIE WRIGHT

SHADOW
MOUNTAIN

To all the women who work in Hollywood,
and in other creative endeavors, who are making
the changes needed to have their creativity
and voices heard and recognized.

Library of Congress Cataloging-in-Publication Data
Names: Wright, Julie, 1972–   author.
Title: Lies, love, and breakfast at Tiffany's / Julie Wright.
Description: Salt Lake City, Utah : Shadow Mountain, [2018]
Identifiers: LCCN 2018010591 | ISBN 9781629724874 (paperbound)
Subjects: LCSH: Motion picture producers and directors—Fiction. | Man-woman
    relationships—Fiction. | LCGFT: Romance fiction.
Classification: LCC PS3623.R55 L55 2018 | DDC 813/.6—dc23
LC record available at https://lccn.loc.gov/2018010591

Printed in the United States of America
LSC Communications, Harrisonburg, VA

10   9   8   7   6   5   4   3   2   1

Chapter One

"I'm not going to let anyone put me in a cage."

—Holly Golightly, played by Audrey Hepburn
in Breakfast at Tiffany's

Audrey Hepburn was haunting me. She had been ever since I was a child. Not in the literal sense. No wispy spirit trailed behind me everywhere I went or anything like that—at least, I didn't think so—but we were connected, Audrey and I, because she died from cancer on the same day I lost my right eye to that same monster. She had been sixty-three; I was five. Likely the connection wouldn't have been all that remarkable except the TV from the nurses' station across the hall was loud, and the news coverage focused on one story.

The one story where Audrey died.

My five-year-old mind feared I would be cancer's next victim. After all, it had already taken my eye. And it had taken a woman the nurses had loved well enough to cry over.

"She was an amazing woman," said one nurse.

"And so brave," said another.

I imagined cancer lurking through the dark hallways and sneaking into my room to steal my life like it had stolen hers. People say I shouldn't be able to remember that day so clearly because I was so little, but I bet if they had lost an eye, the details would stick out in their memories, too.

The surgery was not the most frightening part of losing my eye. The scariest part was when night came and the hospital noise quieted to whispers. I imagined cancer hiding under my bed or behind the monitors that glowed and beeped in the dark. With only half my vision available to me, how was I supposed to see when cancer attacked? Every noise from the hallway or squeak from the frame of my own bed sent my heart rate speeding enough that nurses came in to check on me. I was glad to see them come and devastated when they left again.

Alone in the dark, I thought of Audrey. In my mind, I pictured a beautiful woman in long, white, glowing robes. I gave the ghost woman a sword and a shield and imagined her at the foot of my bed, keeping watch over me. The ghost of Audrey conjured by my imagination battled the cancer lurking in my closet and under my bed. She fought back death for me.

Only then, with this picture of a woman guarding me firmly fixed in my mind, did I finally go to sleep.

Thankfully, cancer didn't collect anything more from me than the eye. But I still worried—even when the doctor released me from the hospital. Later, when she fit me with my prosthetic eye, she asked me what I was going to name it.

"Name?" I asked. "Why would I name an eye?"

"It will make it personal to you so you'll take better care of it."

I didn't know exactly what she meant, but coming up

with a name was easy. "Audrey," I said. The name of my midnight protector.

Though I slowly grew out of the idea of Audrey as my guardian angel, Audrey-the-eye remained my constant companion.

Audrey-the-eye went through many iterations over the years as I grew and had to upgrade to larger models. When I was twelve, my parents gave in to my tantrums and let me get a version with a star-shaped pupil.

That was the year Grandma commented that it was fitting for me to want a star for my eye since I'd named my eye after a star.

When I asked her what she was talking about, she explained that Audrey was a movie star—not just an eye, not just a random person who died from cancer. She wasn't even *just* a star. She had been *the* star. The one woman to teach other women how to be.

"She taught us to reach for the moon in a way that would make the moon want to reach back," Grandma had said.

"Sounds like a horror film, Grandma."

Grandma had glared at me. "Don't be sassy."

She was perturbed that I had the audacity to name an eye after Audrey Hepburn when I didn't even know about her movies. So for my twelfth birthday, I got a starry eye and an education on the film *My Fair Lady*. The movie had the longest beginning of nothing but names and music that anyone had ever been forced to endure, and I almost sneaked out of the living room, but Grandma had zebra cookies baking, so I decided to stick around until they came out of the oven. The credits finally ended, and actors bustled out in front of the camera, hit their marks, and froze.

I froze, too, standing in front of the television, mesmerized by the scene cuts, the music, and the smudged flower girl. It was the first time I noticed camera angles and how the movie cut from one actor or actress to the other.

Grandma and I stayed up late to finish the film, and I left Grandma's house with bloodshot eyes—well, *one* bloodshot eye, since I only had one—but perfect vision. I knew what I was going to do for the rest of my life. I was going to make movies, and it was all because of Audrey.

Which was why I felt like I could blame her for my mess of a life when, years later, I landed a job as Portal Pictures' newest assistant film editor, and things weren't as awesome as I'd hoped. Audrey-the-ghost-protector had become Audrey-the-poltergeist-getting-me-into-trouble.

I sat in the editing studio and checked the digital wall clock, the one patterned after Portal Pictures' first science-fiction film, and tightened my mouth to keep from saying something that would make Grandma scowl at me.

He'd said he'd meet me here so we could go to the sound studio together.

He'd promised he'd be on time today, and though common sense told me that *that* was a bald-faced lie, I'd held out hope.

When I received an out-of-the-blue text from Ben Armstrong, who had been my boss when we'd worked together at a much smaller film studio, asking me how it was working with the illustrious Dean Thomas, I wanted to write, "I wouldn't know, since he's a serial no-show." What I actually sent was, "Great! Thanks for helping me get this job! You'll never know how much I appreciate you helping me get this chance."

And I did appreciate it. My career meant everything to me. I wanted to climb until there were no mountains left. I wanted to make films that mattered—ones that had staying power in the minds and hearts of audiences everywhere. I wanted to make movies like *My Fair Lady*. Like the hundreds of other movies that inspired me through film school and kept me inspired even after job hunting had become awful. But now that I'd landed a job—with Ben's help—at a high-profile studio, it felt like I was babysitting, not creating iconic films.

Sending the text decided it: Dean Thomas was going to show up today because I did not want my text to Ben to be a lie.

I pushed back from the editing panel and stood. "Let's figure out where you've gone off to this time, Mr. Thomas." I was only twenty-seven years old, and the phrase "I'm too old for this" played on constant repeat in my head.

I marched to where Adam, Dean Thomas's personal assistant, sat at his desk and guarded the way to the boss's office. As soon as Adam saw me, his face flushed as red as his hair, and he put up his hands as if to defend himself from my attack. "I swear I reminded him, Silvia."

I jabbed a finger at the closed door. "Is he even in there?"

Adam stood, apparently anticipating that I was about to barge in uninvited. He stepped in my way. "He *is* in there, but he's busy."

"Busy with what?" I kept my voice to a whisper-yell.

"The only thing he has to do is the stuff *I've* been doing for him and the stuff *you've* been doing for him. Between the two of us, he's completely unnecessary. We should fire him."

Adam frowned in confusion. "But he's the boss. And I don't know what he's doing. He just told me he wasn't to be disturbed."

"Are you kidding? We're supposed to be meeting the sound director today. Dean said he'd be there for this meeting. How do you think it looks when I have to tell these people that their film editor is too busy to meet with them?"

Adam shrugged. "Take good notes."

I'd never punched someone before, but Adam was treading on dangerous ground with me. I glared as hard as a one-eyed woman could glare. "You do know that when I asked Dean if we could have a post-production assistant because I saw we had it listed in the budget, that he told me *you* were the office assistant and that I was to use you. Do you want to be the one to *take good notes*, or do you want to step aside so I can fetch Dean?"

Adam moved.

I sucked in a deep breath of courage, knocked on the door, and then entered before he could tell me to go away.

Dean had his head bent over his laptop. I could see the way his dark hair was thinning on top, revealing a shiny scalp under the carefully combed lines. He looked up from his laptop and growled, "Adam!"

Adam poked his head around the doorframe.

"What part of 'I'm not to be disturbed' did you miss?"

I cut in before Adam could speak. "I'm sorry, Mr. Thomas, but we have a meeting with Bronson, the sound director." I added Bronson's job description because Dean's blank look indicated he had no idea who I was talking about. Of course, he had to know Bronson, but Dean's increasingly erratic behavior meant I couldn't depend on anything. "He wants to discuss the musical score we've planned."

"If we've already planned it, what's there to discuss? You have my notes. Surely you can manage the follow-up meetings without me holding your hand."

I refused to look away from his challenging gaze. The fact was, I did have his notes. And they were useless. Which meant that it was a good thing *I* had taken copious notes during our last meeting with Bronson. Dean had spent the whole time drawing stick figures shooting each other or stabbing each other. I tried not to read anything into the art, but when I mentioned the stick figures to my friend Emma, she bought me a can of pepper spray to keep in my purse. Just in case.

"Bronson's asked to speak with you directly, sir. And we're also supposed to visit the set today to talk to the director and the script supervisor. They'll be waiting for us at the video village. I was also wondering if we could let the DP know the slate isn't getting its fair share of screen time. Some of the shots are too dark to see it properly, and it would be great if we could get more of the slate in the shot."

"You don't bother the director of photography with slate details, Sara. Call the assistant cameraman. I'm sure you have his number—or do I need to get that for you, too?"

"It's Silvia, sir. And I *do* have the number. I *have* called the assistant cameraman, and the slate is still a problem. If you could mention it—"

Dean narrowed his eyes at me as he lumbered to his feet.

"Look, new girl, I've worked with these guys for a lot of years, and the slate has never been an issue before, which means the problem is likely not with them."

I shut my mouth with a clack of teeth before I said all the things in my head. New girl? Really? He called me *new girl* even though he'd just heard me say my name? And for him to imply that the slate fault was mine?

But at least he was standing. That was movement in the right direction.

I forged ahead. "Also, with production under way, the DIT is sending the raw footage dailies faster than I can process them. Have you thought any more about the second assistant film editor position we discussed last week?"

"DIT?" Adam whispered to me.

"Digital imaging technician," Dean answered, proving he was listening to at least one of us. "Look, I know you're new, which means you're still trying to figure out my processes, so listen up. I'm not someone who gives in to the idea that an assistant needs an assistant. The redundancy is ridiculous." He slid his jacket off the back of his leather chair and shrugged into it.

I should have let the conversation go. He didn't like to be contradicted, but he wasn't helping with the dailies at all. I was the assistant, which meant I was there to assist someone else and not do the job entirely on my own. "But the budget allows for—"

He pinned me to the spot with a single sharp glance before he resumed fixing his jacket collar. "Budget? Just because something is budgeted doesn't mean it's needed. Don't be frivolous with other people's money. *You're* the assistant, which means we don't need another assistant, because we already have one. If you don't like it, maybe this won't work out for either of us."

I closed my mouth again. But this time I kept it closed. At least Dean was walking in the direction of the sound studio. I had to celebrate the little things.

When we got to the studio, Dean held out his hand to Bronson and flashed a smile I barely remembered from when I'd had my interview with the man. I swear that interview was the one and only time Dean Thomas had ever really looked at me. Dean gave Bronson a one-armed hug and clapped him on the back. "Good to see you, good to see you!" Dean never used Bronson's name, which made me wonder if he really didn't remember. He never seemed to remember mine.

Bronson had us listen to a variety of needle drops that he felt added to the emotion of the film before he took us through a full list of the sound effects he intended to use. He'd marked the script for each sound cue.

"At our last roundtable, I also took some notes of some sound effects I thought might work really well for the mood Danny said he wanted." I offered up my iPad.

Bronson was excited to see my notes and to hear my ideas. He played with the sound board to create a few of the sounds I suggested then nodded and scribbled some notes of his own. Together, we talked about some of the more creative Foley work we'd heard throughout our careers and laughed at how something like a chair scraping back on a cement floor could create a monster growl.

Dean laughed along with us and added suggestions of his own that sounded like he was being unique and original at first, but when analyzed, were simply different ways of re-stating something Bronson or I had already said. I tried not to sigh at that, or at the way he chummed with Bronson as if they were good friends.

Going to the actual set was more of the same. Dean shook Danny's hand like they were long-lost brothers. "Danny, it's so good to see you. How's filming going? The weather re-schedules haven't seemed to hold you back any."

He'd only known about those delays in exterior shots be-cause I'd told him.

Danny laughed, his brown hair spiked up in a way that was both stylish and whimsical, which matched his personal-ity. He was a director who was easy to get along with as long as your vision for his movie matched his vision.

Dean had a knack for making it seem like his vision was in perfect alignment.

The problem was he had no idea what Danny envisioned because he'd never worked on any part of this project so far. Not one part of this film had Dean's stamp of approval on it. Not one scene had any mark of Dean Thomas and his edito-rial work. I doubted he had even read the script.

I realized Dean wasn't going to step aside and allow me to take part in the conversation, so I stuck my hand out and said hello.

"Hello, Silvia, nice to see you," Danny said. He then turned to Dean and said, "You trust this girl with a whole lot of responsibility. She's been meeting with us regularly and seems to have a good handle on what she's doing. Girl's got a sharp head on her shoulders. It's a pity she's an editor.

She'd have made a great actress with eyes like that. She's got Audrey's eyes."

I started at the reference. It was something my grandmother said often. My mom and dad said it on occasion. Every now and again, even strangers mentioned my eyes. But in the movie business, the place where Audrey Hepburn would be most recognizable, few people ever mentioned my dark, slightly olive-shaped eyes, and even fewer made the comparison. It made me laugh when people told me I had Audrey's eyes since one of my eyes was named Audrey. If they only knew.

"Thank you, Danny, but I realized a long time ago that my acting skills were nonexistent," I said. "I do my best work after the filming has been handled by the professionals."

He waved away what he looked at as false modesty. "Anyone can be taught to act, but you can't teach someone to have eyes like yours. You're either born with it or you're not. You, Silvia, were born with it."

I didn't bother telling him that I might have been born with it, but I didn't get to keep it for very long since one of those eyes he admired so much went missing two and a half decades earlier. If he couldn't tell a glass one from a fake one, who was I to correct him?

"Have you seen her movies?" Danny asked. "You should do some research on her. You really do look like her."

I *had* seen her movies—or several of the major ones, anyway. When I was a film student, they were homework, but my relationship with Audrey had become complicated over the years. Yes, I had named my eye after her, but when I thought of her, I could still remember the fear of the phantom cancer lurking in my hospital room, a fear that had never quite gone away.

"I hear she was great," Danny continued. "You know, they say she used to bring chocolate for the entire cast and crew while on set, paid for with her own money."

"Really? I didn't know that." I gave a laugh. "Sounds like someone I could be friends with."

"Or sisters, with eyes like that."

Dean shook his head and stepped forward enough to put himself between Danny and me. "Now don't go giving the new girl a big head," Dean said. "The last thing I need is a starlet hoping for a big break. I need someone who can work seriously."

"You've definitely found that. All Silvia does is work. You guys are keeping up with the dailies nearly as fast as we're sending them. Between your team and Bronson's team, things are going well. You cannot know how much I appreciate that."

Dean smiled, but he didn't make any sign of agreement regarding my work habits. He also didn't comment that his team was a one-woman show.

Danny continued, "I really need you guys to keep up the pace."

Dean made a joke about taking away my breaks and lunches, which irritated me enough to need a distraction, so I turned to the sound mixer and gave him my most apologetic smile. "I hate to ask this, but could you do me a favor? The walkie-talkies are getting too close to the mics during filming and creating pops in the sound. They aren't too bad, and I was able to scrub them out of the raw footage for the last two days, but it's a lot of detail work. I'm worried I might not be able to clean them out in the future. Could you tell the crew to keep their distance from the set during filming? I know they need their walkies, but it could be a real issue if we don't take care of it now."

The sound mixer nodded and said he'd talk to the crew.

"Cheese thirty!" A woman from craft services brought over a tray filled with fruits, cheeses, and crackers, and left it on a stand near Danny's director chair.

Danny and Dean, deep in conversation, didn't seem to notice the food.

I edged closer. I wanted to hear whatever they deemed important enough to discuss in such hushed tones.

Danny's creased brow and firm jaw let me know he was giving Dean a stern talking-to. "I'm bringing this up because of what Silvia mentioned about the walkie pops. I know you're working hard. Silvia keeps in good contact with us as we're doing the dailies, but Christopher has made this clear: we can have no more interruptions. Karl-Erik's skimboarding accident was a delay we couldn't afford. The first cut pretty much needs to be a final cut. The studio won't allow any further delays."

"A final cut on the first round is ridiculous," Dean said. "Nobody expects that. Postproduction is just as important as filming. You gotta ask yourself, do you want it fast, or do you want it right?"

Danny's hands splayed out in helplessness. "I hear what you're saying, but Christopher is adamant. He expects it both fast and right if you want a job."

Dean stiffened. He didn't like being threatened. I didn't like it either. My job was on the line, too.

Danny shook his head, making his crazy hair wave back and forth. "It's not my place to say this to you, but it's better to know what Christopher is thinking. I like knowing where I stand. I figured you would want the same."

"Sure. Sure," Dean said. "Thanks for the heads-up."

Danny clapped his hands together and said, "Well, now that that's settled, let's enjoy cheese thirty! Then we can look at today's footage."

Christopher showed up soon after and confirmed everything Danny had said. Only Christopher was far less friendly in the message delivery.

On the way back to the studio, Dean ground his teeth together and stayed relatively quiet. Relief flooded me. If Christopher and Danny expected final-cut quality on the first pass, Dean would have to involve himself in the process. He'd step up and take some of the work off my shoulders.

We passed through the guardhouse and parked the car, and Dean exited the vehicle without a word.

"Mr. Thomas?" I said, hurrying to catch up with him. I mentally rolled my eyes at myself calling him "Mr. Thomas" and "sir" as if he was someone to respect. But in my short time working with him, I knew this man—or at least I understood his type. He clung to the old Hollywood ways where women were to be looked at, not looked up to. It was past time for that to change, in my opinion.

He opened the glass doors leading into the studio. I barely squeezed through before the doors swung closed; Dean hadn't bothered holding them open, even knowing I was right behind him.

When he made a right turn to his office instead of left to

the editing studio, I called out to him. "We have a lot of work to do if they want a final cut in a first-cut time frame."

He didn't even glance back to me. "Yes, *you* do."

"Mr. *Thomas!*"

Realizing I'd pretty much yelled at him, he stopped and turned in my direction. "Do you have something you need to say to me?"

I had lots of things I needed to say to him. I wanted to say that he was a misogynistic monster. I wanted to tell him his lazy behavior disgusted me. I wanted to explain that stealing the hard work and ideas of others and passing them off as his own made him a vulture.

Instead, I said, "Do you intend on taking part in this film at all?"

He stepped closer, close enough I could see the bloodshot eyes of a man who'd hit the bottle too hard for too long. "I did my part. I hired you."

I lifted my chin, my chest tightening with the anger that burned through my entire midsection. "And you believe that's enough to earn your name in the credits when they roll?"

His chin came up as well. He stretched his neck and squared his shoulders. With a breath that looked like he was about to unleash a torrent of anger in my direction, he turned left in the direction of the editing studio.

I closed my eyes and balled my shaking hands into fists before following him. Round one to me.

The sad thing about rounds was that winning one didn't mean anything in the grand scheme of things.

A couple weeks later, with Dean still being hit-and-miss on coming into the editing studio, and me finding I actually hated working with him on the days he did show up, we had a blowup because I needed him to sign off on some of my scene choices, but I was insisting he actually see the footage first. He was hungover and angry.

"You know . . ." His gravelly voice had lowered to a tone that sounded dangerous. "I've often found that those who are dependent on the opinions of others are fairly weak. Show me any assistant film editor, and I will show you a man who would jump at the chance to work without someone breathing down his neck."

I caught the insinuation. A *man* wouldn't be bothering him with the trivialities of the job.

But I wasn't bothering him with trivialities. This job belonged to him. My job was to assist him.

I lowered my voice to match his tone. "So you're fine with me doing my job *and* yours?"

He narrowed his eyes. "I resent you saying that."

"I resent doing it. So I guess that makes us even." Holding my ground with him looming over me in my personal space took all my effort. I thought about the shooters and stabbers he drew when he should have been taking notes, and wondered why he was so angry all the time. "I'm actually surprised you don't want to do your job." The statement alone would have definitely earned me a sharp reprimand had I let him respond. "At some point, you had to have cared. You wouldn't have moved into this position if you hadn't been good at your work. So what's the problem here? What happened to you?"

His nostrils flared, and his eyes widened at my unmistakable belligerence. "You don't know anything about my life or my work. Just do what you're told if you want to still have a job!"

With that, he fled the office.

I sank into my chair, wishing I'd become a carpenter or maybe a private detective or even a lion tamer, because working in Hollywood was a nightmare.

The problem with my particular nightmare was that there was no leaving. I would never be able to wake up to a more pleasant reality. No one ever told me that Hollywood came with no exits. They never mentioned that I could drown in Hollywood dreams. For me, making movies was an addiction stronger than any other known substance. All I had ever wanted was to be a part of making films that were like Audrey's *My Fair Lady*.

Which was why this was all her fault. I slammed my fist on the table, took a deep breath, and got back to work.

Because hate it or love it, I had a deadline to meet. I was a strong, independent woman who'd somehow managed to be put into a cage with bars forged of ambition and fear.

Thanks for nothing, Audrey Hepburn.

Chapter Two

"I could have danced all night, I could have danced all night, and still have begged for more."

—Eliza Doolittle, played by Audrey Hepburn in My Fair Lady

Over the course of the next couple of months, nothing improved with Dean. I did his bidding while he brooded all red-eyed and sullen in the background like the Emperor in *Return of the Jedi.*

I really missed working with my old boss, Ben. The original Star Wars trilogy was one of Ben's favorites, and whenever I heard the words, "You will never find a more wretched hive of scum and villainy," I never thought of the Mos Eisley spaceport; I thought of the iconic white Hollywood sign situated near the top of Mount Lee overlooking Los Angeles.

No one working in Hollywood would argue the point. Instead, they would likely nod and smile that indulgent smile of an uncle watching his favorite niece and nephew claw at each other in some scathing brawl where one of them would likely get shanked by a shard of whatever family heirloom had been shattered during the course of the fight.

Then the uncle would shrug and say, "We are what we are."

As I stood at the entrance to the hipster club Burnout, stared into the harem-styled décor, and felt the music pounding from the floor, through my feet, and into my bones, I thought of the Hollywood sign.

I wanted to punch that imaginary, indulgent uncle.

The woman of *My Fair Lady* wouldn't recognize the Hollywood of today. Or maybe she would, which would be sadder still.

"Silvia!" Adam yelled in my ear over what sounded like K-pop with a Hindustani vibe pulsing from the sound system. "Where do you think he'll be?"

I shrugged. The task of finding Dean Thomas shouldn't have been too hard. Adam and I had already made it past the bouncer, who'd been pretty chill about letting us in, all things considered. The problem was that there were so many bodies writhing on the bitty little dance floor and between the tables that finding any one individual would be all but impossible.

From my vantage point at the top of the stairs, I could see the crowd pretty well, but I'd have to enter that crowd to find Dean. Having only one eye meant that I was completely blind on my right side. Any kind of surprise, good or bad, could come from that side, and I would never see it coming. This meant that all surprises were bad surprises. A horde of humans guaranteed surprises.

But we couldn't leave without our boss. Dean had to approve the end credits and make the final cuts, but he had skipped out of his responsibility to his job, to the studio, and to me. Again.

For months, I had been the one forced to make lame excuses as to why Dean had become the serial no-show.

I was the one who scoured through the footage dozens of times to be clear on what would work best for pacing and what needed to be trimmed away. I was the one who met with the sound editors and music directors and made decisions Dean had to be strong-armed to sign off on.

But this first cut?

A full week had gone by where he'd promised every day to show up and finish the film.

Today was the last day, his last chance before we presented the cut to the director and producer in the morning. And yeah, I didn't love that the review was being held on a Saturday morning either, but I wasn't the one hiding out in a club on a Friday night, ditching my responsibilities. In four months, Dean had managed to avoid any semblance of real work. He'd dumped everything on me.

And I was sick of it.

"We should split up to find him," I yelled, but Adam shook his head.

"I'm not going anywhere in this place alone. What if someone spikes my drink?"

I grunted at him and rolled my eyes. "You're a guy. No one is going to roofie you."

"It's a new world. Everyone gets roofied now."

I stared at him in disbelief. Was he serious? I mean, yeah, the guy was on the smaller side and probably wouldn't win in even a minor scuffle, but was he really worried about such a thing? "Then don't drink anything," I finally said. "It's not like we're here for fun."

Adam stayed glued to my side, making it difficult for me to pick through the people and tables. I felt like shoving at him to give me some space, but if the guy was worried about laced liquids, he would definitely be a run-to-HR kind of person.

I wished Adam hadn't been the one I'd been stuck with while finishing edits all night. Adam spent a lot of time complaining that Dean had yet to get him an audition in Portal Pictures' most famous TV series: *Gray Skies*. Dean Thomas apparently didn't keep promises to anyone.

Which was why we were scouring Hollywood's club scene for him.

"There!" I shouted and pointed to where Dean sat at a table. His salt-and-pepper roots were starting to show, which meant he was late with his salon appointment. None of the other older men in my personal circle were salon-going kinds of guys. They accepted their gray hairs and face wrinkles with grace and dignity. From all of our personal interactions together, I'd learned Dean didn't do anything without a fight—not even grow old.

Dean drummed his fingers on the table as if he waited for someone or something. He sat alone, so now was the best time to approach him and get him out of the club and back to the studio so we could all go home and get some sleep.

I stepped on more than a few feet as I rushed to reach Dean before whoever he was waiting for could return and act as interference.

"Mr. Thomas!" I nearly fell onto the table since Adam

didn't stop when I did, and he ran right into me. "Thank heavens we found you!"

He turned red-rimmed eyes on me. For several seconds, he just stared as if unable to reason why a woman was knocking into his table and shouting at him. Then some light of familiarity dawned in those burned eyes. "Sara?"

I ground my teeth together, took a few breaths that weren't actually very cleansing considering the smoky atmosphere, and said, "It's Silvia, sir." How many times would we replay this conversation before he decided my name was worth remembering?

A slow smile crawled over his lips. "Right. Silvia. The new girl."

"That's right." Agreeable behavior would win the day. At least that was the lie I told myself as I smiled back at him and nodded as if talking to a child. When did a person no longer qualify as the new employee? I'd been with Portal Pictures for four months. It felt like long enough to simply be Silvia Bradshaw: assistant film editor.

"You're actually very pretty."

This didn't feel like a compliment.

"He's drunk," Adam said with a scoff.

Also didn't feel like a compliment, but for entirely different reasons.

"I have my car outside, sir. Why don't we get you back to the studio so we can get the final edits done on *Sliver of Midnight*? Then we can get it all signed off and turned in on time." I spoke slowly and clearly to try to cut through the fog glazing over his unfocused eyes.

"Do you dance, Sara?" he asked.

I would've sighed, except that would've required me to take a deeper breath and fill my lungs with more smoke.

I didn't answer, refusing to allow him to sidetrack the conversation into meandering nothingness. "Are you ready to leave, sir?"

"I'm ready to dance!" He used the table for leverage as he shoved back in his chair. The table knocked into my thigh hard enough that it would probably leave a bruise. I gasped, then coughed. A woman with a major cancer phobia did not belong in hazy dance clubs.

He was on his feet and making sloppy grabs for my arm, which I avoided until Adam nudged me in Dean's direction. "Just dance with him, Silvia, so we can get out of here."

I glared at Adam, gratified when he shrank back. Maybe he'd think twice before encouraging bad behavior.

I turned to Dean. "Sir, it's time to go—"

But he already had my hands locked tightly in his as he swung them wide in rhythm to the music. He leered at me, and I shuddered. No wonder his wife insisted on a male secretary for her husband. He tugged my arms, forcing me to follow as he led us away from the tables and farther into the crush of bodies in the middle of the room.

"You're a good dancer!" Dean declared with a grin that looked manic. Like he had any idea if I could dance or not, since he was dragging me all over the place, not caring that he used my own momentum to knock me into other people who were on the dance floor with us. Without being able to see the right half of the room, I couldn't avoid anyone.

"Sir!" I tried to get his attention, to force him to focus on me with enough clarity to see reason. "If we don't meet this deadline, it will be our jobs. They can't push back the release date. We need to get back to the studio."

"I can't hear you, Sara," he said. "Music's too loud!" He swung me out, letting go of one of my hands so that I had to flail wildly in an effort to regain my balance.

Hands on my hips caught me and righted me on my feet again. I turned, expecting to thank Adam for paying enough attention to keep me from falling and being trampled by the writhing mob of dancers, when I realized my rescuer was someone else entirely.

Someone I both loved and hated to see.

Loved because Ben Armstrong was my friend, and seeing him made me feel like I finally had some support coming from somewhere. Hated because Ben had helped me get the job at Portal Pictures, and now he would witness how badly I was handling it.

"Ben!" Shouting his name was all I could do before Dean pulled me back in.

As I spun away, I saw a woman in a spangly dress the exact shade of ice-blue as Ben's eyes standing next to him. Not that anyone could see his eyes in the muted lights of Burnout. But I knew Ben's eyes. We'd worked side by side for three years at Mid-Scene Films. And now he was here? On a date? Oh, no.

But rather than joining the throng of dancers or going back to find a cozy table somewhere, Ben wove through the crowd to follow me. "Are you okay?" he shouted above the music and tossed a worried look from me to Dean.

"I'm—" I was about to say *fine*, but that wasn't true. I had a drunken boss who wanted to dance instead of do his job.

"Back off, pal," Dean growled and yanked me to the opposite side of him, away from Ben.

I apologized to the guy whose shin I accidentally kicked in the process and turned back to where Ben had been, but the pulsing crowd had already swallowed him. Dean reeled me close again. He pulled me tight, wrapping his arm around my back, which thankfully freed up one of my hands.

People crowded against us. Even without seeing them, I felt the press of them against me, their energy and heat searing from my blind side. Anything could be in a mob like that.

Crowd claustrophobia kicked in—hard-core. I could handle a lot of things. I could handle my boss being a sexist jerk. I could handle humiliation every now and again. But crowd claustrophobia? No.

I dug my fingers into Dean Thomas's hand and held on tight. Turning, I headed for the edge of the mass of people. I needed out of the crowd. If I had to punch my way through every single person—even the ones outside my field of vision—I was getting out, and that stubborn, horrible man who employed me was coming with because I wasn't leaving without him.

Think of meadows. Wide-open meadows with lots of fresh air and light and space. Think of open space, Silvia. I chanted this over and over in my mind as I dragged the dead weight that was Dean behind me. By sheer will, I broke through the mob's inner circle and more easily moved through the fringes.

Dean continued to jiggle behind me as if he was still dancing. His behavior definitely counted as a deviation from all the times he barely acknowledged me. I waved my hand in the air to allow him to believe we really might be dancing instead of taking part in an exit strategy.

I finally got him back to the table where Adam still waited. I gave Adam—and the drink in his hand—a sharp look. "What are you doing with that? I thought you were scared of getting roofied. You don't have time for drinks. We're leaving!"

The words had an immediate effect on Dean. He yanked his hand from my grip and shook his head. "I'm not leaving!"

Well, so much for getting him to the car peaceably. Thanks for the assist, Adam.

"Crowd claustrophobia kicking in yet?" Ben appeared from out of the crowd again.

He'd been in a packed elevator with me once when I'd been stuck in the middle and incapable of really moving my head to see the people on my right. Naturally, the experience blew into a full panic attack. Ben knew how well I handled hordes of people, how not seeing them entirely frightened me.

I nodded in answer to his question. "Yes, but we're not staying, so I'll be okay."

I wanted him to know he didn't need to rescue me from my fear or pat my shoulder for an hour while I tried to settle my breathing into something normal. He'd done it once before, but I never wanted anyone to have to do it again. The fact that Ben had ever witnessed me in a full panic still embarrassed me.

I looked Dean sternly in the eye. "Mr. Thomas! We are going back to the studio. I have a car waiting."

Ben's eyebrows shot up with sudden understanding of why he found me in the middle of a crowded dance floor in a trendy club with a guy who was absolutely too old for this scene.

Adam hurried to swallow whatever he'd ordered. Chances were good that he'd told the waiter to put it on Dean's bill, not that I cared. It served Dean right to have to pay. If I could've put something on the bill, like a pizza or a box of donuts, I totally would have.

"Time for drinks!" Dean slurred as he all but collapsed back into his chair.

I tried to hold him up and propel him toward the door, but the man's six-foot-two frame compared to my five-foot-six won. Instead of helping me, Adam waved a waitress over to take a drink order.

"We're not getting drinks!" I insisted.

"Sure we are!" Dean countered as he threw an exaggerated wink at me.

I did not want to interpret what that wink might have meant.

"Dean Thomas!" Ben said over anything anyone else might have been about to say. "I love your work."

There it was. The most magical thing anyone in the business could hear: praise.

Dean stopped leering at me long enough to send a lopsided smile in Ben's direction. Ben's date smirked at how easily Ben conquered the situation. I would have smirked, too, except I knew the situation was far from conquered. Getting Dean's attention was one thing. Keeping it long enough to get him into the car was another.

And though I appreciated Ben's help, this was my problem.

"Ben, I got this. You and your date can go enjoy your evening," I said.

Ben, not listening to me at all, scooted Adam out of the

seat he occupied next to Dean and took Adam's place. "The scene changes and pacing on *Mysteries of Cove* were nothing short of genius."

Dean nodded with slow, deliberate motions. "Right? I told JJ those cuts were what the film needed. He argued the whole time. But I was right. All the reviews mentioned the pacing. Called it art. Art!" He burst out laughing. Dean's head lolled back, so he was looking up at the ceiling. "I'm an artist."

"Definitely," Ben agreed.

So did I, actually. Dean had done some pretty great work in the past, which would make his current decay incredibly sad if it didn't tick me off so much.

Ben tossed me a reassuring smile.

Ben's date caught the smile and turned her full attention to me. She looked me up and down in an obvious show of measuring my worth. She narrowed her eyes, and then shrugged a bony shoulder and, with a sniff, looked away.

I frowned, not liking that I'd been so quickly dismissed as not valuable.

Granted, I was in a club where everyone dressed to impress, and I happened to be wearing a T-shirt from the premiere of one of the first films I'd ever edited. A very small premiere. Of a very small film. Which tanked. I still wore the shirt. I also had on black yoga pants and a pair of old Toms; I wasn't even wearing socks. And where Ben's date had hair that shined with a dark luster, my hair probably looked like a brown oil slick since it hadn't seen the inside of a shower for days.

Based on that, Ben's date's assessment of me might have been fair, but still. Ouch.

I shook my head and refocused. His sparkly date had

nothing to do with my presence in the club. I was here to get Dean Thomas back to the studio. The end.

Ben still had Dean talking, chumming and schmoozing like some executive producer wooing the most sought-after talent.

Adam ordered himself another drink. I glowered at him and shook my head. He quickly turned away and pretended not to see. Ben's date ordered a drink as well, but Ben either didn't notice or ignored it so he could keep Dean talking.

"Hey," Ben finally said, "I'd love to see more of your work, man."

Dean nodded. "You will. You *will*. I have lots of new films coming up. The light stays green in my studio."

I hated when Dean said that. It didn't even make sense, since he didn't have the power to green-light anything. He could only make a film when someone else gave the green light and someone else did the filming.

"Great!" I said enthusiastically like I was trying to talk a toddler into handing over his candy. "Why don't we all go to the studio, and you can show Ben what you're working on now?"

Or what I'm *working on,* I amended in my head.

After four months of dealing with Broody Dean, dealing with Drunk Dean demanded a different skill set—skills not in my possession. I understood him when he was sullen, but this goofier version of him caught me off-balance.

Ben nodded, understanding my motivation to get Dean out of the club, and getting on board with it. "I'd love to see what you're working on right now. That would be amazing!"

"Su-ure!" Dean slurred. "That's a good idea. Gotta get to

work anyway. My assistant's always nagging at me. She never shuts up." He squinted at me. "Hey! That's you!" He started laughing.

"Yep," I agreed. "That's me." I flagged down the waitress to settle the bill. I somehow talked Dean into signing the credit card slip, and then Ben hoisted Dean up and supported him with an arm around his shoulder.

"Let's go back to the studio. You can show me what you got going on," Ben said.

His date finally spoke up. "I thought we were dancing tonight."

"I'll come back as soon as I get him settled in the car."

She nodded, her silky dark locks falling forward. I fought to keep my hands from reaching up to pat at my own hair shoved back into a ponytail. I tried not to feel like a moldy old mop next to her.

"I'll come right back." Ben flashed his date a smile, but she didn't sit around waiting for him. She followed along with our procession to the parking lot. Ben held Dean's right arm, and I held his left. Adam trailed behind us, up the stairs and out the door.

At the car, Dean refused to get in. He wanted to talk to Ben some more. I rubbed my eyes, wishing I had a normal boss. Seeing Ben reminded me of how nice it was to work for a responsible, amiable boss. I missed it more than I'd realized.

"I should go with you," Ben said, lowering his lips to my ear so only I heard.

I shook my head and whispered, "You're on a date, Ben. I'm pretty sure you leaving with a different woman would be a deal-breaker."

The spangly date must have sensed the gist of the conversation, because she sighed and said in a kinder voice than her body language implied, "It's okay, Ben. Even if you manage to get him in the car at this end, how will she get him out at the other? I get that you need to go." She smiled at me. "It's okay. Ben will be miserable if he doesn't help. It's against his nature." She turned back to Ben. "If you can get back in the next hour, great. But if not, don't worry about it."

Ben gave her a hug and kissed her on the cheek. "Thanks for understanding."

She shrugged. "I know you'll worry if you don't go. We can catch up some other time. Let's just make sure that our 'some other time' is soon, okay?"

The moment between them would have been sweet, one of those scenes where the sound editor would have amped up the romantic music and the director would have made sure the close-ups were perfectly framed as they surveyed each other in this moment of service and sacrifice. It would have been sweet, except Ben's date had to dodge Dean, who'd decided kisses were for everyone and tried to land one on her lips.

"Not for you, buddy!" she said, sticking a warning finger in his face and shooting him a look that was both withering and warning at the same time.

I admired her. Not only had she made a legitimate sacrifice, but she was also right. I'd never get Dean out of the car again once we hit the office.

"How will she get home?" I asked Ben, giving him one last out.

"She has her own car," he said. "We met here."

"What about your car?"

"I'll get it later. No big deal." He turned back to Dean. "C'mon, Dean. Come show me where the magic happens." Ben opened the car door, and gestured for Dean to get in. Ben kept his hand between Dean's head and the frame of the car, and then scooted in next to him in the back seat before Dean could get any funny ideas about getting back out again. Adam took shotgun, and I slid in behind the wheel after handing the valet a generous tip for letting the car stay in the front.

Sometimes, I really felt the inconvenience of having only one eye. It made it harder to split both my focus and peripheral vision between the road in front of me and the rearview mirror. "Thank you," I mouthed when Ben caught me looking at him and our hostage, and not at the road.

Ben smiled and clapped Dean on the back. "I could totally go for some coffee right now—how about you, Dean? A little coffee sound good?"

"Coke and rum," Dean answered. Then he laughed long and loud.

Adam drummed the dashboard in front of me, and the noise made me want to shout at all of them to be quiet.

Instead, I said over my shoulder to Ben, "I'm sorry about your date."

Ben shrugged. "Don't worry about it. But it would make me feel better if you kept your eye on the road."

I laughed, which made Dean cackle even more. "Don't panic, Ben. You're safe," I said.

My assurance must have not been very assuring, because Adam halted his drumming fingers. "Wait. Is he seriously worried? Are you a bad driver?"

"She's not a bad driver. She's a cyclops," Ben said. "Silvia only has one eye."

I saw Ben grinning at me in the mirror, and he motioned with his finger for me to look forward again.

Adam looked at me in horror. "What? One eye? Is it even legal to drive with only one eye? Why didn't you say anything? I could've driven!"

As if I would have let Adam drive after he knocked back at least two full glasses of unidentified alcohol.

Ben laughed. "Don't sweat it, buddy. Your chances of dying in a car crash over the course of your life are one in a hundred and fifty-eight, regardless of who's driving."

"What?" Adam checked his seat belt. "Is that true? One in a hundred and fifty-eight?"

"Eight. Eight . . . Eeee-iiiight . . . That's a weird word," Dean said. "It doesn't sound anything like it's spelled."

Adam ignored our boss and his word dilemma in the back seat as he continued with his own breakdown. "Those are terrible odds. How would you even know such a thing?"

Ben shrugged. "Well, statistics aren't an exact science, and they vary based on circumstances. You know: inside the vehicle versus outside the vehicle, that sort of thing."

"Eeee-iiiight . . ."

Adam sucked in a deep breath and muttered, "I think I'm walking from now on."

"Your chances of dying as a pedestrian are one in six hundred and forty-seven. So while the odds aren't as high, it's not like walking makes you immune to kicking the bucket."

Adam swiveled so he could look at Ben directly. "Who are you? Why do you even know that? Who knows stuff like that?"

"What?" Ben said, seemingly unconcerned by Adam's panic. "You never wonder about your own demise? You never stay up at night thinking, 'How is it all going to end?'"

"No!" Adam insisted. "I stay up at night wondering how to get ahead and how to achieve my goals."

I would've bet money Adam stayed up late wondering how he could bribe or poison his way into an acting gig. It was the reason he took the position as Dean's assistant. We all took our points of entry into the business wherever we could find them. Adam's question reminded me of a movie quote, however, so I ignored his alarm over my having only one eye and smirked in the mirror at Ben. "So, Ben. *How's it going to end?*"

Ben smirked back, recognizing the tone in my voice as the invitation to the movie quote game we'd played during the years we worked together. "Too easy. *The Truman Show.*"

We spent the rest of the ride slinging quotes and guesses to each other. Adam didn't join the game because he was too busy telling me to keep my eye on the road. Dean tried to play but guessed that everything came from a John Wayne movie.

We arrived at the studio gate, where I flashed my ID at the guard and Dean screeched "Eeee-iiiight!" out the window. Dean's appearance was the only reason the guard didn't check Ben's ID. Once we were, finally, parked in my assigned spot, the light at the end of the tunnel seemed to shine brighter. I even started to believe it might not be a train.

"A little coffee, and we'll be right as rain," Ben repeated to Dean several times as he helped him out of the car and up the steps. Adam didn't offer to help or to hold the door until I rolled my eyes at him and commanded him to keep the door propped open so we could get Dean through.

Adam gasped. "You really do have only one eye. Only one rolled! That's awful!" He made a retching sound when I rolled my eye again. What a lightweight.

We settled Dean onto the studio's bright orange, incredibly modern, and even more incredibly uncomfortable couch, and I went to make coffee. Ben left Adam in charge of keeping Dean busy and followed me to the studio kitchen. From behind us, I heard Dean shout, "We're supposed to be dancing!"

Ben leaned against the counter as I pulled out the pods of coffee and chose the one I felt would produce the strongest results.

"Never thought I'd live to see the day when you were on a dance floor in a crowd thick enough to be a moving game of sardines. You hate dancing."

I pushed the pod into the coffee maker. "I hate it even more now." I was lying. I actually loved dancing, loved moving with music, but *going* dancing? *That*, I hated. Going dancing required you to endure mob-like conditions where surprises from the right were likely and body odor a definite.

"And all those people?" Ben continued. "When I first saw you out there, I thought you were going to have a full-blown attack and pass out or something. You told me crowds made you feel like you were literally being blindsided. I was actually worried, Sil."

I put a mug under the spigot and looked up to meet Ben's serious gaze. "Desperate times called for desperate measures." I rubbed at the skin around my glass eye. It had been a long day.

"Are you okay?" he asked.

I smiled, showing all my teeth. "Of course I am."

He straightened and crossed his arms over his chest. "You

know what I mean. I didn't help you get this job so you could be miserable. I got it so you could—" He blinked and gave himself a slight shake. "Are you happy here?"

"It's a stepping-stone," I said, adding a splash of an energy drink to Dean's mug—a little liquid pep that would hopefully bring him to full capacity sooner. "But happy? What's happy, Ben? Dean—who is currently incapacitated—is supposed to go through an entire film and provide feedback on choices that *I* had to make because *he* didn't. And in less than ten hours, he has to meet with Christopher and Danny with a product that is as close to perfect as possible. *Christopher and Danny!* Can you imagine?" I lifted my eye to the ceiling as if looking for divine intervention.

Ben, of course, could imagine. Christopher and Danny were the producer-and-editor dream team. Working on one of their films was an unbelievable opportunity. If Dean hadn't fallen under the control of his addiction, he would've realized how important this chance really was. The chance was certainly important to me.

I picked up the oversized coffee mug and blew across the top of it so the coffee wouldn't be too hot for Dean. He'd probably chug it, and I didn't want to ice down his scalded esophagus later.

"Dean's barely done anything on the film. I've been covering for him for over three months. I've done all the work while he leaves early and comes in late, but if anything goes wrong, I'll be the first one under the bus."

"You could explain . . ." He trailed off, recognizing the truth of the situation. Hollywood talked a lot about being progressive, but it was still a world where only one or two out of a hundred scriptwriters were female. Things were shifting, but waiting on a glacial-slow shift tested the mettle of the most determined women in the field.

"So am I happy?" I closed my eyes to get some moisture into them. When I opened them again, I gave Ben another smile—a real one this time. "I will be. And even with all the crazy of this, I still appreciate your help in getting me this job. I know, ultimately, it's exactly what my career needs. And you know my career means everything to me. So thanks, sincerely."

We stood for another microsecond or two before Ben said, "I should probably get back to Alison."

"Right . . . your date. You can take my car." I nodded and turned to lead the way out. After all, I had to get back to Dean. It was time to get to work.

But upon approaching the orange couch, Adam shook his head. "Our patient has flatlined."

"What?" My eyes flew to Dean, whose eyes were closed. I would've believed he'd actually died except for the snore that rose up from him. "He's just sleeping," I stammered. "We can wake him up. We can get him to drink the coffee and get him to finish the edits and sign off on everything. This will still be okay."

Adam never stopped shaking his head. "Sorry, Silvia. It's just not going to happen."

"Nice attitude, Adam," I snapped. Not that he was wrong. Dean Thomas was pretty much unconscious, and I had nine hours and thirty-six minutes before the film presentation. I guess we were all done dancing for the night.

Chapter Three

"When you sell a fake masterpiece, that is a crime."

—Nicole Bonnet, played by Audrey Hepburn

in How to Steal a Million

Of course, I tried to wake Dean up.

I called his name, shook him, splashed ice water on him, clapped loudly next to his ear. I stopped short of dumping his hot coffee on him—though I did think about it for a fraction of a second. I immediately felt guilty and was glad I hadn't vocalized it. No need for Ben and Adam to know what kind of monster they were dealing with.

Besides, I'd already taken the satisfaction of slapping Dean across the face. The red handprint on his cheek proved I hadn't held back. Though I couldn't be sure the slap was meant to wake Dean or satisfy my own frustration. At least it achieved one of those purposes.

Dean snored on. No matter what I did, his mouth hung open in his own blissful cocoon of slumber while I went into full panic mode.

Ben must have recognized the signs, because he didn't leave to meet up with his date. He took off his jacket, hung it over a chair, and pulled me back to the kitchenette.

He opened the fridge and rummaged through it until he found what he was looking for. He held up a can of Dr Pepper and grinned at me. "I knew if you had access to this fridge, you would keep it stocked for personal emergencies." He pulled out a plastic cup from the cupboard and filled it with ice. He cracked open the can and poured it over the ice with a familiar fizz and crackle that made me actually feel better.

"Drink this," he ordered.

I did as directed, then I set the cup on the counter and hung my head in my hands. "I'll just have to turn it in as is and hope for the best."

Ben moved closer and rubbed his hand over my back. "You're selling yourself short, Sil. I know you. I know what your work looks like. You've got mad skills and great vision. It's why you got this job. Any director would be grateful to have you on his team."

"Or her," I countered, meeting Ben's gaze. "Just because only seven out of every hundred directors are female doesn't mean it doesn't happen."

"Or her," he agreed. "The point is that you're good at what you do."

"Art can't be made in a vacuum. It needs collaboration. It needs checks and balances. You were a huge part of what helped make me great. I don't have that here. At least, not enough of it."

"That's patently false. You're amazing without anyone's help. But in spite of that, you still have me. I'm here. I'll stay.

Let's look over the film, and I'll give you an honest critique. Just like old times."

Relief, gratitude, and guilt all hit at the same time, which made my eyes leaky. "That's way too much for me to ask."

"It's a good thing you didn't ask then, isn't it?"

"What about Mid-Scene's noncompetition clause? You could get fired."

"Right. Because you would totally tell on me. C'mon, Silvia. If I can't trust you, then I can't trust puppies."

His analogy made me frown. "But you can't trust puppies. They'll eat your shoes the first time you turn your back."

Instead of responding to my observation, he fixed me with a stern "You're in trouble, young lady" look. "When was the last time you slept?" He grabbed my chin, tilting my face so he could see the left side.

I couldn't answer because I honestly didn't know.

"Did you even know your right eyelid is practically glued shut? It only does that when you've reached your exhaustion limit."

I both hated and loved that Ben was a good enough friend that he knew such lame yet important details about me. I hadn't known it was shut. Since I couldn't see out of my right eye, the lid had a mind of its own and took advantage of the situation.

"I'll sleep when this is all over," I promised. "I'll sleep a lot."

"Good. Because lack of sleep doubles your chances of dying from heart failure or stroke. So let's get you some rest sooner and not later, okay?" He shoved away from the counter and waited for me to lead the way to the editing suite. We stopped to check on Dean and Adam, and I left Adam with strict instructions to keep a fresh cup of coffee ready every fifteen minutes.

"Every fifteen minutes?" Adam whined.

I shot him a look that shut him up. We both knew Dean would never drink from a mug prepared too far in advance. Dean was a snob when it came to his hot beverages.

"Those pods are expensive," Adam groused.

I bent low so I could look Adam in the eye. I worked to make my eye muscles pull up my right eyelid so I wasn't pirate-squinting at him. "I don't care if we go a million dollars over budget in coffee expenses. If he wakes up, you are to force him to drink a fresh cup. If he and I get fired because we screw this up, you get fired, too. And we both know re-entry to any studio is nearly impossible. So help me hit a home run, okay?"

Adam nodded. He actually looked humbled, which made me feel guilty for threatening his job, but not guilty enough to apologize. It was a tough day for everyone, and we all had our lumps to take. Well, all of us except the snoozing princess passed out on the couch.

With that out of the way, I led Ben to the place that was both my battlefield and playground.

When I unlocked the door to the editing suite and let him inside, Ben whistled. "I have never felt deprived at Mid-Scene Films until this moment. Look at those monitors! Look at your panel. Oh! Your headphones!" He touched everything, oohing and aahing over every component visible.

I smiled. "I haven't even turned anything on, yet. The hardware is nice and all, but wait until you see the software."

Ben sighed with the envy and awe I had felt when Portal Pictures first interviewed me. Entering the modern steel-and-glass fortress hadn't intimidated or impressed me, no matter how vogue it looked. I didn't fall in love until I met the editing suite.

"Fire it up. Show me what I'm missing," Ben said.

The laugh that had been about to bubble out of my throat froze. "I can't let you help me with this," I said, pulling my fingers away from the power button.

"Proprietary?"

"No . . . well, *yes*, but this is a lot to ask you to do. It's not fair to you. And I need Dean's signature to show he's approved everything. Even if you look at the film, you can't sign off on anything."

"But I can review it, make sure you dotted all your i's. Then, we get Dean to wake up in a few hours, have him sign off on the final cut, and maybe even have him sober by ten to do the presentation."

"That's just it. *We* can't. You can't be here at ten. You can't be here after eight when the weekend staffers show up. If anyone sees a film editor from a competing studio here, they'll go crazy."

Ben blew a raspberry at me and flipped my ponytail so my hair hit me in the face. The smell was not awesome. I really needed a shower. "Right, like Mid-Scene Films could compete with Portal Pictures. You guys compete with Sony and Fox."

I bumped him with my shoulder. "We do not."

He bumped me back. "You're closer to them than we are

to you. But your argument has been made and accepted. I'll be gone before eight. So we'd better get started."

I'd given him every out possible. If he chose to stay, well . . . I was glad he'd chosen to stay. We got started.

Ben almost wept when he put on his pair of headphones and claimed he'd never be able to go back. I poked him in the shoulder, but he'd already quieted and become the serious Ben I knew so well from the few years I'd worked under him at Mid-Scene Films.

This was how a critique always went. He'd review the entire work in silence, saving all comments for when the screen went dark again.

I checked the time on my phone, but Ben put his hand on mine and lightly pulled my phone away. He couldn't do his job properly if we were clock-watching and not screen-watching. He was right, of course, so I refrained from looking at the digital wall clock, too.

We watched the movie together from the title screen of *Sliver of Midnight* to the credits. His face stayed passive the entire time.

I hated that he could do that. I was a laugh-out-loud and cry-out-louder person. Some of my friends refused to go to movies with me because they said my on-display-emotions diminished their viewing experience. Emma actually admitted to being embarrassed by my raucous laughter.

The credits rolled. He waited until the very last before finally turning his attention to me. His eyes were glassy, the teary kind of glassy, the kind of glassy I'd never seen before in Ben.

Was it possible he'd felt touched enough to cry? I mean,

yeah, sure *I* cried after viewing my final product the first time, and I likely would have gotten emotional this time, too, if I wasn't already so keyed up with nervous terror. *Sliver of Midnight* was a beautiful story. The director had handled it perfectly. But Ben never got emotional.

I strained to not look at the time, but I didn't really have to. I knew the film was exactly an hour and thirty-eight minutes long. We had just under six hours to polish and perfect it.

We might as well have had six minutes for all the good it would accomplish.

But I didn't say that out loud. Instead, I waited for Ben to process and file, rearrange and rethink. I didn't even harass him for getting emotional since the compliment of that emotion was all mine.

He cleared his throat and said, "Silvia, I know that, in your heart, you already know this, but . . . this is some of your best work."

I released a shaky bark of laughter. "What?"

"No, really. This is good. Better than anything you ever did while working for me, and you know I loved what you did for me. So you've either been honing your skills or the equipment really made up the difference." He laughed at his joke and shook his head. "The cuts you made that were interruptions of one conversation but segued into other, entirely different, conversations are nothing short of genius. You must have spent days on that alone to make it so seamless. The fact that you kept the emotions high and tense during those shifts is astounding. You're staying invisible, which is an art form within an art form. I bow to your skill. The student has become the master."

Ben pushed back his chair and actually did bow, which made my cheeks burn and my eyes get leaky.

Ben's smile faded into concern. "You're crying blood, Sil."

I reached for the tissue box I kept handy in every workstation where I spent more than a few minutes a day. The thing about fake eyes was they got messy sometimes. "Awesome." I dabbed at the corner of my eye and sighed. "The socket's probably irritated from the lack of sleep. Water builds up behind the eye and makes me cry demon tears."

"Cyclops tears," he corrected.

"I never should have told you that's what my friend calls me." I flipped some of the buttons on the panel to bring up the lights.

"Don't I qualify as your friend?"

"It's almost two in the morning, and you're still here. Yes, you qualify."

"Good, then that means I get cyclops rights. It's only fair."

I shook my head and wiped my eye until I was sure it had finished embarrassing me. "So, aside from telling me I'm amazing—critique?"

"There were a few jokes where you came into the scene too early and left too late. It affected the timing—especially when those jokes were meant to lighten some serious tension. Remember what I said about timing?"

"It ebbs and flows. You can feel it in your chest likes waves coming in and out." I repeated his favorite lesson. It was how he explained the magic of intuition—a thing he insisted could not be taught. A film editor either had it, or they didn't.

"Right. Everyone can feel timing, but you happen to be lucky enough to feel it stronger than most people. So if you shave . . . here . . . and here—now watch." He adjusted the sliders on the panel for a few moments before the film began to play again.

We re-watched the scene. He was right. I could've kicked myself for not catching the error on my own. We spent the next few hours sliding through the scenes, edging parts in, taking parts out, rearranging the order of certain shots, slipping in second-team footage in places I hadn't considered before. We worked at a pace Superman would have envied. Ben was like a magician.

"I wish we had time to watch it again," he said, clicking his pocket watch open to glance at the time. It was a full-on Doctor Who replica, complete with the Gallifrey writing on the case. Ben was nerdy and old soul all wrapped up into one.

"I'll invite you to the premiere," I said.

He gave me a sidelong look. "Really?"

"Sure. You should be able to see your masterpiece."

"Nope, not my masterpiece. This will be known as the work of Dean Thomas."

I laughed and leaned to the side of the panel between several of the sliders. "But we'll know who the real geniuses are. You can be my date."

Ben swiveled in his chair to face me directly and put his hands on my knees to stop his chair's momentum. "You and me? On a proper date?"

I laughed under the intensity of his stare. "Fine. We'll even go to dinner first. After all, you've earned it."

Ben smiled, though it looked forced. "Right. Earned. Like a cookie or a sucker." He slid his hands from my knees to his own. "Have you ever thought about—" He broke off, squinted at me, then shook his head.

"What?"

"Nothing. Never mind. I'm tired and delirious." He rubbed his hands on his knees and drummed his fingers.

"I so get delirious. Thanks, Ben. For everything. I do believe *you*, in just a few hours, did a better job than what Dean could have done if he'd been around for the entire time."

"I've seen Dean's work. He's brilliant when he's actually doing it, so I accept your compliment."

"He used to be so good at what he does," I said, not meaning to excuse my new boss by pointing out skills he chose to no longer use. "He seems to be pulling away more every day. He's slipping."

"Well, he'd better sober up soon, or the slip will end up in a free fall."

"True. I want to loathe him for being the worst boss in the business, but it's hard to pass judgment when I don't really understand the guy. Because, who knows? People often turn to substance abuse because they want to fill the holes inside their souls. I don't know what's going on in Dean's life, but chances are good that it didn't come from him having a really great day."

Ben rolled his head from one side to the next. "And that's why I think so well of you. You try to see the reasons for everything, which includes allowing people to have reasons for acting reprehensibly. But don't forget that he *has* acted reprehensibly. It doesn't matter what the guy's got going on, the reality is that he overworked you, left you in a bind, and should be slapped for it."

I smirked. "Well, I *did* already slap him."

"Do it when he's awake next time. He deserves it."

We both laughed, which felt good after our grueling night of intense collaboration. Ben had given up a lot to help me.

"I'm sorry about your date," I said.

"Don't worry about it. The night I got was worth giving up the night I'd planned." Ben stretched his way to a standing position. "I'll make it up to her."

I couldn't say why, but I didn't love hearing that. Sure, the first part was fine, but the second part made me bristle— proof that I was not exactly rational. "Where do you know her from?"

"Film school. She's an old girlfriend. We reconnected on Instagram, and she's been trying to get in touch in person for a while now. Last night was our first time together in a few years." He rubbed the back of his neck. "It seemed like a good idea to get together and gauge our compatibility."

I stood as well and began shutting down the equipment. "What made you break up the first time?" The question should have sounded like non-nosy, non-concerned, just-curious idle conversation. But to my ears, it sounded like a catty way to remind a guy that he already didn't choose that girl and had no business looking to try again. I didn't mean any of it in that way but worried that was how it sounded to him.

He either didn't notice the snark or he was too tired to call me on it. "We were young. She had her own ideas about how relationships worked and failed to imagine that I could have any opinion in the matter."

I laughed and did a final sweep of the room before we

left. "I bet that didn't go well for her since you have an opinion on everything."

"True that." He offered me his fist. I pressed my knuckles to his in our job-well-done fist bump that we had used as our victory dance for the last few years at Mid-Scene Films. I shut the light off, and we left to go check on my sleeping boss.

Dean still snored the sleep of the cluelessly guilty. Adam slept on the floor near the couch. He had yanked one of the throw pillows off the couch to use for his own personal pillow and had drooled on it liberally. Someone would either have to take it home to wash it, or—more likely—I would just throw it away. Adam's mouth hung open but, surprisingly, no sound came from him. The horrible noise rumbling through the room was all Dean.

The room smelled like old coffee, unwashed feet, and fetid alcohol. I'd need to open a window or two—or all of them.

I wrinkled my nose. "Sleeping people stink."

Ben nodded his agreement and pulled the neck of his shirt over his mouth and nose. We made our way to the kitchenette where I'd abandoned my purse. I didn't want my personal items in a public space and needed to haul it to my office before everyone started showing up for work.

"It doesn't look like Adam got Dean to drink any of the coffee," Ben said. Thirteen full cups of coffee lined the counter. Ben grinned at me, and, altering his voice, said, "Excuse me, miss; there seems to be a mistake. I believe I ordered the large cappuccino. Hello!"

"*So I Married an Axe Murderer*," I said. Ben high-fived me for getting the movie quote right.

Adam hadn't bothered to empty the mugs or wipe down the coffee maker. Once I woke him up, I would insist he be a grown-up and clean up his messes.

I dug through my purse until my fingers wrapped around the cold metal of my keys. I pulled them out and offered them to Ben. "You'll need a ride out of crazy town."

"I can call for a driver."

"You could. Or you could take the easy, fast way out." I jingled my keys. "I can swing by your place later to pick it up."

"How will you manage that without a car?"

"I can get a ride."

He narrowed his eyes at me, making the ice-blue in them seem positively frigid. "From who?"

I shook my head and rolled my eye. "My friend Emma is coming into town. You remember her, right?"

He nodded and leaned over me as if trying to intimidate me. "Is she already coming into town, or will you have to arrange all this after I'm gone?"

I didn't back down from his leaning. Honestly, the guy was such a worrywart. "We're going to dinner. Take the keys. Take my car. I'll see you tonight." I jingled my keys until he finally took them.

I then folded my arms around him. He seemed surprised and froze as if not sure what to do. "It's called a hug, Ben. It works best when you hug back. It's when you take your two arms and put them around me and then squeeze. You can squeeze a lot if you're really happy to see someone or are leaving them and going to be missing them too much to let go."

"I know how a hug works, Silvia."

"Prove it. Put those arms where your mouth is."

Slowly, his arms came up and encircled me. It was then that I noticed how nice he smelled. I'd worked for three years in close proximity to Ben, but I had never really been this close. There was a time or two I thought he might have asked me out, but Mid-Scene Films had a pretty intense no-fraternizing-with-your-coworkers policy. After a while, romantic notions ended, and we settled into the steady friendship that made us who we were.

Which is why me even noticing how good he smelled felt out of place. Ben was my friend. That was it.

But dang, that friend of mine smelled good, like an orange spiced with cloves and sandalwood—citrusy, musky, and masculine all at the same time. I pulled away and blinked rapidly at thoughts that must have been provoked from going forty-eight-plus hours with no sleep.

I dropped my arms abruptly, stepped away, and patted his shoulder. "Glad to have been able to train you on the finer points of hugging. Let me know if you ever need a refresher course—"

I cut off, feeling heat flare to my ear tips. I'd just said that out loud. I'd invited him back for hug seconds in the flirtiest way possible. I needed sleep. I needed *days* of sleep. I would apologize after that—when I could be sure of my own coherence.

He didn't respond to anything I said, which made sense. Ben wasn't a flirty kind of guy. He wasn't a hugging kind of guy either. He was the kind of guy who memorized the morbid stats of mortality and who loved classical film with the devotion of a religious zealot. He was the guy who had memorized the dialogue from more films than most people

ever saw in their lifetimes. I didn't dare try to make any determination of how uncomfortable I must have made him feel.
Instead, I smiled brightly and shrugged. "You saved my bacon
tonight. I totally owe you."

"It was no big deal."

I started walking him toward the hallway. Our time was
ticking. He had to make a quick exit, unless we wanted to
explain why an editor from a different studio was here doing
Dean's work. I shuddered at the thought. "It's a huge deal.
Your creative efforts will have someone else's name on them.
We can't ever tell anyone. Is working incognito going to sting
later?"

He shook his head and lowered his voice now that we
were in the commons area where the two sleepers snoozed
on. "No. It was good practice. It made me rethink a few
of the things I could do for the film I'm currently working
on. Practice never hurt anyone." He looked down at Dean.
"Time to wake him up."

"Let's get you safely exited first. Chances are good he
won't remember you were here. It'll make it easier to hide the
crime."

Ben chortled softly. "Crime? What crime? Yes, I can see
it now—'I find the defendant guilty of committing art. Life
in prison. Glass of unfiltered water, white bread full of gluten
and preservatives. No TV.'"

"You know what I mean. I need him to sign off on this.
He might not if he knows you were the creative genius."

Ben passed the couch and kept his steady pace in the direction of the glass doors that led to the also-glass lobby. Even

though he obediently walked in the right direction, he gave me a look out of the corner of his eye. One I recognized well.

I shot it right back at him. "Don't give me that snide-ways look of yours. It *is* your work, not his."

"At seven forty-five in the morning, I can snide-ways look at whoever I want," he said. "It's not my creative genius. It's yours. This was all you, Sil. I just built on what was already there. What I did was the equivalent of adding a few potted plants to a newly built palace."

"Well, whatever it is, it's our secret." I held my pinky out to him the way Emma and I always did when we wanted an agreement to be binding.

He smirked at my offering before he linked his pinky in mine. "Our secret," he agreed.

I nodded and walked him out of the personal office area and down to the main floor lobby, where the guard who worked the day shift was taking his post. I waved at him. "Hey, Nathaniel!" I called and tried to put some cheer into my tone.

"Silvia! Good morning! What are you doing here so early?" Nathaniel, being the good guard that he was, eyed Ben closely, likely memorizing details in case he needed to pick him out of a lineup later.

"Just working. Dean and I had to finish cuts on a new film. He had a few friends over to show off our work."

Nathaniel nodded. "Oh, right. Dean's up there, then?"

I nodded and hurried Ben faster through the revolving door to avoid further scrutiny. Allowing Nathaniel to believe that Ben was one of Dean's friends made him less likely to bring up the fact that anyone out of the ordinary had been in the office at such an unusual hour.

Hitting fresh air filled me with a new surge of energy. I pointed down the row of parking spaces to where my car sat alone. Portal Pictures people were not early-bird people. They were come-into-work-as-late-as-you-can-get-away-with people. "I'm parked right there."

"I know," Ben said. "I wasn't drinking last night, so parking information wasn't hard to hang onto."

I smiled and then frowned. "Thanks again. There's no one else I'd rather perpetrate fraud with than you."

He did his snide-ways look again. "You take all the fun out of it if you're going to feel guilty. Besides, we didn't do anything wrong. There was no crime."

"Right. No crime," I echoed.

He gave me a salute. "Wake Dean up, slap him again if you get the chance, and get this presentation over with so you can go home and get some sleep."

With a return salute, I promised I would obey.

Ben folded himself into the front seat of my compact car and drove away.

I frowned. No crime?

Then why did I feel so guilty?

Chapter Four

"I don't care how you treat me. I don't mind your
swearing at me. I shouldn't mind a black eye;
I've had one before this. But I won't be passed over!"

—Eliza Doolittle, played by Audrey Hepburn in My Fair Lady

I stood on the curb for a long time waiting. For what, I didn't know. With a sigh, I made my way back to the office. I stood over the other cohorts in my night of criminal mischief and gently shook Adam's shoulder. "Adam," I whispered. "Time to get up." I kept my voice low and bent down close to his ear so Dean wouldn't wake up yet at the noise. Not that I thought Dean would wake up to anything. The guy was practically a corpse.

Adam snorted awake and bolted upright, almost knocking into me. I dodged him and backed off fast in case he was one of those people who woke up delirious and violent.

I put my finger to my lips and pointed at the still-sleeping Dean.

Adam finally reached consciousness enough to slide his body along the floor so he could stand up without knocking into Dean. "I was just resting my eyes," he said, his voice still thick with sleep.

Not likely. The drool on that pillow was the work of at least two hours . . . probably longer. Plus, I'd told Adam to make coffee every fifteen minutes. If the cups on the counter were any indication, he'd only made it through three and a half hours before succumbing to the siren call of the sandman.

Not that he could be blamed. "It's fine," I said. "I appreciate you staying. Hopefully when this is all done, we can get back to our regular lives."

It made sense to be nice to Adam. After all, none of this was his fault, and he had been willing to stay and help, which was more than anybody else would have done in similar circumstances.

Besides, I still had to give Adam the unpleasant news that he had to clean the break room while I woke up Dean.

Adam took the news better than I expected. Oh, sure, there was whining and grumbling, but he hung his head when he realized I wasn't his mom and had no intention of giving in on the point.

"Oh, and Adam? Dean will need another cup of coffee." I shot a glance to the couch. "Better get him a glass of ice water with a freshly squeezed lemon—and add a squirt of those liquid vitamins and a splash of apple cider vinegar. He's going to need to hydrate quickly."

Once Adam left, I stared down at Dean on the couch. This was going to be a long day. "Mr. Thomas? Mr. Thomas, it's time to wake up."

His snoring stopped, but he only smacked his lips together and rolled over as if to try to get back to a deeper sleep.

With a grunt, I shook his shoulder. Seriously? He'd slept all night. He got more sleep on the couch than I usually got on a regular night in my bed. I was not going to feel sorry for him. And I certainly wasn't going to let him sleep any longer. He had to at least watch the film before he presented it. If he wasn't going to sign off on it, then he would have to be the one to ask for an extension. He would not make me the fall guy for a delay.

"Mmngh." He swatted at me to make me go away.

"Mr. Thomas! Dean!"

Though his eyes didn't open, he rolled to his back and sighed in a way that let me know I'd finally made contact.

"What do you want, Sara?" he asked, still not opening his eyes.

"My name, sir, is Silvia. Silvia Bradshaw." I tried. I really did. But the frost in my tone could not be hidden. It was one thing for him to call me by a different name when he was out of his mind with alcohol, but now? He was just being belligerent.

"That doesn't answer the question of what you want." His shut eyes tightened as if speaking hurt his head. Chances were good he had a hangover. If I'd had less self-control, I would've done something mean like scream at the top of my lungs in his ear.

As it was, I spoke softly and slowly. His understanding was imperative to us both. "You have a meeting with Christopher and Danny this morning at ten. You're supposed to present *Sliver of Midnight*."

I sat on the arm of the red chair opposite the couch and waited to see what his response would be. I was no longer worried about the quality of my work. Ben had declared it my best and then improved on that best. The cut was clean and as close to final as humanly possible.

What interested me now was Dean's reaction to a now-impossible-to-ignore deadline.

He remained lying on his back with his eyes closed for the several moments it took his cloudy, muddled head to translate my words into something that made sense to him. Then his eyes snapped open.

There you are, Mr. Thomas, I thought.

He squinted against the light, his hangover evident. "That's today?" His hoarse voice reflected the horror that I felt was appropriate, considering the circumstances.

"Yes, Dean. That's today." It was the first time I'd taken the liberty of using his first name. His old-school Hollywood attitude never left room for me to speak informally to him, at least not while he was sober and quasi-lucid.

The old-school Hollywood attitude no longer mattered to me. I had created the product without his help or input. That put me on equal enough terms to be on a first-name basis.

He sat up slowly, holding his head while trying to shake it at the same time. "No. It can't be today. It's next week."

Adam returned with a coffee in one hand and the water mixture in the other. Dean reached for the coffee first, but I got to it before he did. I swiped the coffee and handed Dean the water mixture. "Here. I had Adam make you a hangover helper. Drink this. Then you can move on to your coffee."

He squinted at me. I couldn't tell if it was because of the light or if he was trying to glare at me. Either way, he took the water concoction from my hand and drank.

"That tastes terrible."

"Probably," I agreed. "And yes, the meeting is today."

He put the water cup on the table and reached for the coffee, which I relinquished. "But we haven't really worked on it, yet." He looked like he might throw up. I motioned to Adam to get him a garbage can, just in case.

"No. *We* haven't. But *I* have. It's done. I just need you to watch it and sign off on it and present it to Christopher and Danny."

He narrowed his eyes even more as he looked me over, apparently unconvinced by what he saw. When he opened his mouth to speak, I decided if he called me Sara one more time I was going to take Ben's advice and slap him again.

Instead of saying anything, he checked his phone, likely to get a concept of time, put his coffee cup to his lips, drank it dry, handed the cup back to Adam, and said, "I'll need another of those. And another of that nasty drink, too."

Adam peeked at me as though ownership of his services had transferred to me. I nodded my approval, and he scurried off to do as told.

Dean noticed the exchange and grunted. "Looks like I'm going to have to retrain my assistant. So, Silvia Bradshaw, let's go watch our movie." He lumbered to his feet, cringing with each movement, and then added, "Let's keep the volume on low, though, okay?"

I didn't respond but followed him to the editing studio, where I occupied the same seat I'd had the entire night. Dean may have gotten my name right, but his calling the creative effort I'd spent over three months working on "our movie" grated on me.

I brought the studio back to life, adjusted the panel sliders, and hit play.

Unlike Ben, who was entirely passive when viewing a film, Dean grunted a lot. The grunts might have been good noises. They might have been bad noises. They might have been the grunts of a man who only knew how to make caveman sounds. There was no way to tell for certain. But I'd spent four months being called the wrong name, ignored, and left to my own devices. If his grunts became anything more negative, I would punch him in the trachea. I wasn't dirt under Dean Thomas's feet. This job was supposed to be a "wish on a star, dream come true" for me. There was supposed to be pixie dust and blue fairies and maybe even a godmother or two because why not?

Instead the job was a lot of lonely.

There was no collaboration like I'd expected to find in a larger studio. The studio was too divided into various projects. There wasn't any feeling of apprenticeship or mentoring between Dean and me.

Quitting wasn't an option. Where would I go? My career meant too much to me to just walk away. Sure, Mid-Scene Films would probably hire me back, which, given everything, sounded pretty good.

But it was ridiculous. Why would I ever want to go backwards in my career? I wanted to move up, not back down.

I thought about it as I watched the fruit of my labors play out on screen.

Who would ever go back to subpar equipment and outdated software? Or return to an office that was done in a brown decor that dated back to the seventies?

The answer was easy. Anyone who knew Ben would want to go back.

Benjamin Armstrong. Seeing him again, spending a night with him in intense collaboration and creativity, reminded me of all that was awesome about Ben.

Ben and his serious eyes that looked like ice in the shade and his dark hair that always had the look of being finger-combed because he ran his hands through it when he was thinking. And Ben was always thinking. I'd missed his habit of calling things "proper" when they were the way he felt they should be, the way he knew bizarre trivia, and the way he stayed calm even when everything else in the world felt like it was beyond repair. He'd shown up at the club and immediately turned the crazy into something rational. He'd stayed with me rather than leaving me to fend for myself. He'd worked *with* me.

I wondered why we hadn't hung out more since I'd left Mid-Scene. Except Ben had acted strangely toward me at the last, which made being around him hard. He'd been the one who pushed for me to get the job with Portal Pictures. And when I got the job, he'd acted unhappy. It insulted me that he couldn't be happy for me and the new opportunity presented in my life.

Who wanted to be around people who couldn't be happy for their friends' successes?

The whole situation, now that I thought about it, was proof that stupidity didn't end with adolescence. Grown-ups got to be stupid, too. Considering the circumstances in hindsight made me wonder . . . who was the stupid grown-up in our scenario? Me? Him?

"This will work." Dean's voice cut into my thoughts.

"What?" Had he been talking long to me? I had no idea since I'd zoned out, thinking about jobs and Ben and possibilities.

"This version of *Sliver of Midnight* will work just fine. There are some changes I would make, obviously, if we had time, but . . ." He checked his phone. "We really don't have time, do we?" He slapped the counter and pushed up out of his chair. "This will work." He looked a lot better than he had when he'd first entered the studio. What kind of mess had he expected to walk into?

"Will you put your digital approval on it then?" I asked.

"Oh. Right." He sat again and moved his chair to the main computer where he entered his password to verify his digital stamp of approval.

While he finalized his signature, I asked, "What changes?"

"Hmm?"

"You said there were obvious changes you'd make if we had time. I'd like to know what those changes are."

He flustered and floundered before cutting off the conversation with an abrupt, "It hardly matters. There isn't time." He loaded the first cut onto the company server so we could access it from the theater and stood. "We need to get going if we're going to be on time."

I agreed, but after looking at him standing, there was no denying the man looked rumpled and a little on the homeless side.

"Dean?" I said as he moved toward the door.

He turned to me. "What?"

"Do you keep a change of clothes in your office?"

He lifted his eyebrows as if to send a warning that I had better tread carefully, but as I pointedly looked at his clothing, his gaze followed mine and his brows knotted above his nose. He grumbled something that might have been agreement and bustled out of the room as if I'd caused him a terrible inconvenience.

I made a mad dash to my own office and pulled a long sweater off the back of my chair. It was a nice sweater and would cover up a lot of the grunge of my own outfit. I grabbed my notebooks and phone in case I needed to do any scheduling or messaging. Adam, as Dean's personal assistant, should have been coming with us, but when I'd exited my office and went to wait by Dean's office, I noticed Adam's desk remained conspicuously empty.

Knowing Dean would be another few minutes, I checked the kitchen, which was a graveyard of abandoned cups. Adam, the little miscreant, had ditched his post and his duties and left the work for me.

Shrugging, and forcing myself to accept that Adam was not my personal responsibility—and neither was the kitchen—I returned to Dean's office to wait.

Dean tossed open his door, nearly throwing me into cardiac arrest, and nodded at me as if to say, "Well, let's get on with it."

I pushed off the wall that had been holding me upright and led the way to the studio golf cart that would take us to the theater.

Christopher and Danny were already there. A small entourage of assistant directors and other people who were pivotal to the future of the film hovered near them.

Dean greeted them with firm handshakes and big smiles. It was only because I was watching closely that I noticed the tightening around Dean's eyes when Christopher boomed out a hello that must have hit all the pains of a hangover. Good for Christopher.

When Dean failed to bring me to the attention of the directors and assistants, I put out my hand to Danny. "It's so nice to see you again!" I said warmly.

Danny was my favorite of all the people present—at least of the ones I knew. His light-brown hair looked like he'd toweled it off after stepping out of the shower and it just stayed that way, sticking out in every direction but managing to not look absurd. No one pulled off that hairstyle the way Danny did.

He gave me a one-armed hug. "Good to see you, too, Silvia!" he said in a way that made me feel legitimately welcomed. He gave an extra squeeze before letting me go. "I look forward to see what you've done with our baby."

I smiled. "You have a lot to be excited about it. I think you'll be glad you sent her to finishing school, Danny."

"Finishing school." He clapped my shoulder, nearly knocking me off my toes. "I like that."

Christopher wasn't a hugging kind of guy, but he energetically shook my hand and expressed his excitement over the film as well.

Danny interrupted my moment with Christopher by saying, "Did she tell you she's calling editing cuts *finishing school*? That's funny, isn't it?" He laughed; Christopher smiled. I laughed, though it was more from sleep-deprivation than because I felt genuinely funny.

"Well, we're looking forward to seeing your work." Christopher echoed Danny's earlier sentiment.

Dean heard the comment and hurried to interject. "I think you'll like what you see, gentlemen. I've worked tirelessly on this project. *Sliver of Midnight* has been my top priority for months." He smiled big for the director and producer. "But let's stop talking about it. Let's prove it to you." He swept his arm toward the theater entrance.

I blinked and shook my head. Had he really just done that? Had he really just cut me out of the film *I* had worked tirelessly on for months and that had been *my* top priority? Had he really taken full and complete credit for something he'd had nothing to do with?

Yes. Yes, he had.

But he wasn't going to get away with it. People always said that my ability to call people on their crap was my superpower.

It was time to get super.

Chapter Five

"This is my second and last encounter with you lunatics."
—Jo Stockton, played by Audrey Hepburn in Funny Face

Everyone else filed in, but I held back, crossed my arms over my chest, and stared at the man who'd spent the night passed out on the ugliest couch on the planet while someone else did his job.

He noted my stance and lifted his eyebrows. "You have something to say, Bradshaw?"

"You've worked tirelessly? *You?* And to call it your 'top priority' is a bit of a stretch, since the most work you've done on it is watch the end result of what others have done."

I almost said the end result of what *I* had done, but I wasn't going to be like Dean Thomas. I was not going to take all the glory when it didn't all belong to me. And I didn't care that his jaw worked or his bottom lip jutted out at me like a petulant toddler. I was mad, and the fact that I was tired meant that all filters were down.

My eye socket burned behind the glass eye. I hoped it wasn't going to start leaking blood like something out of a Stephen King story.

Dean's jaw continued to work as he stared at me. He moved his head slightly from side to side as if testing the different angles under which I could be viewed. He finally sucked in a deep breath through his nose and said, "I understand your irritation. But the fact remains that I am the editor. You are the assistant editor. My name will come before yours in the credits every single time until I die and you get promoted. And until that happens, the words will always be either *me* or *we* when we're discussing the work done on any project. *I* get credit because I've been here longest. I've helped build this studio into what it is today. It's my tenure and my right. Get used to it, or get a different job editing video production for some mom-and-pop marketing firm somewhere. Do we understand each other?"

"I understand you, but I don't think we understand each other just yet. I understand *your* irritation," I said, throwing his words back at him, "and I understand how this industry works. But I need you to understand how I work. I *worked*. I get that you will be receiving unearned credit on this film. But I had better get credit as well. I refuse to be left off. Especially when you couldn't think of one change you would have made in the film. If you can't even offer a single thoughtful critique, then you do not have the right to remove me from my intellectual property."

I had moved close enough to smell the stink of his night and morning on him, but backing down at this point would have defeated the purpose, even if the reek of him made me want to gag. I thought about my grandma, of having to face her and tell her I hadn't stood up for myself. I thought about Eliza Doolittle in *My Fair Lady* finally getting a backbone by the end. Playing nice had landed me in this position. It was time to find out what playing tough got me.

"Hey! You guys coming?" One of Danny's assistants came out to check on us.

Dean started to respond, but I spoke over him. "We'll be right there. We're just working on a little collaboration."

The assistant nodded and disappeared behind the double doors.

Just in case anyone was still in earshot, I leaned in and whispered, "I am never to be left off, or next time, I won't bother pulling you out of a bar at midnight and making sure you wake up on time for a review. And don't think that leaving Portal Pictures would mean I'd have to go work for some obscure marketing firm. I'm good at what I do, and I will not be undervalued."

I stepped back and took a cleansing breath that my yoga-going best friend would have praised me for. "Now that we *truly* understand each other, I think we'll be good friends, don't you? At the very least, we can respect each other."

I walked away from my boss, certain he'd never been put in his place by any woman in his life.

If I was being honest with myself, the conversation would never have happened except that lack of sleep had turned me into a wild thing.

Maybe being tired was the best thing to ever happen to me. I'd never been such a doormat in my entire life until I started working with Dean Thomas. No job was worth the loss of self I'd felt every day. I took a shaky breath of relief, deciding I'd never again cower because of that man. I would be standing up for myself from now on.

I entered the theater and sat behind and to the side of Christopher and Danny. I sat behind them so I could observe them during the film. And I sat to the right side so nothing was outside of my periphery. Sitting in the middle of a room meant half of it disappeared from my view. Sitting to the left meant the entire room disappeared. People from the unobserved side of the room might speak up and startle me because I'd forgotten they were there. Sitting where everyone and everything remained in my visual field made my life vastly easier.

Dean seated himself next to Danny, and when Danny joked that he'd been hoping for me to sit by him, Dean offered a tight smile and a casual glance at me from over his shoulder. He might have been prepared to make some snarky remark about my prickly and antisocial behavior, but the lights dimmed.

Sliver of Midnight filled the screen.

I think I stopped breathing.

Everything changed when a film went from the computer screen to the big screen. All the details that felt insignificant and ignorable, but that had taken me painful hours to fine-tune, made all the difference on the big screen.

What I'd done with Danny's movie made him forget to breathe, too. I could tell by the way his shoulders stopped moving and by the small smile of wonder and awe that stayed unchanging on his face. Christopher's reaction wasn't too far different.

They were captured from the first moment.

The film played out on-screen. The small audience re-acted with the ebb and flow of timing. They laughed when the wave peaked. They breathed in relief when the wave pulled away. Ben's voice whispered in my mind. *"A film that lives on in the memory of the audience is the one that breathes like a person. You take picture and sound like a human takes lungs and air, and you make them work together until they breathe."*

I hated that Ben wasn't with me, wasn't seeing what we'd made together living a life beyond us. I imagined he was just sitting on my blind side. I imagined he observed it all and approved it all.

Maybe it was the long hours and stressful work. Maybe it was the fact that my standing up to Dean Thomas meant he would have me in his crosshairs for the rest of his life. Or maybe it was because something beautiful filled the screen in a lovely ballet of movement and sound that touched my soul to the core.

Whatever it was, I cried. And when I wiped at the tears on my blind eye, I found it was weeping blood again.

Somehow it felt appropriate.

When the lights went up, no one spoke. The initial, rev-erential silence paid homage to something wonderful. Then came the applause. They praised Dean, taking turns clapping his back and laughing with the joy of those who knew they had something magical on their hands. I allowed them to praise Dean. It was only natural, since they believed he'd done the bulk of work, but I made sure to interject myself to guar-antee that the same praise found its way to my head as well.

I would not be passed over.

"She's a real find, isn't she?" Danny said, smiling at me.

"She's certainly something." Dean also smiled, but his red-rimmed eyes were never touched by that smile. I thought of the shooters and stabbers that he drew in his notebooks and decided to walk back to the editing studios.

While praise shifted to the musical director and sound editors, I remembered I still didn't have a ride at the end of the day. I wouldn't be able to walk home as easily as I would be able to walk back to the editing studios.

I'd totally lied to Ben about already having plans for dinner with Emma tonight, which meant I'd have to call her at some point anyway. Yes, I felt guilty for lying. But it was for his own good.

I called Emma.

She answered on the second ring. I loved that about her. Even though she was neck-deep in dealing with her job as an executive marketing officer and also planning her own wedding, she always took my calls.

"How busy are you?" I asked.

"Right now?" She paused. "I'd need an hour to get un-busy. What's up?"

"Could you come get me from work later?"

"Of course. What's going on? Why do you sound like you've been crying? Do you need me to come now? I'll cancel meetings. I can come now."

"No," I assured her. "Don't cancel meetings. I was up all night finishing a film. Which . . . leads me to my good news." I walked farther away from where Dean, Christopher, and Danny were talking. Just thinking about my good news flooded me with new energy.

I could almost see Emma honing all her attention to the phone at her ear. "Well? Spill it! You can't just announce good news and not share it!"

"The director and the producer loved it!" I squealed into the phone, trying to keep a cap on the noise so it didn't carry through to everyone eating from the craft services trays or congratulating themselves on a well-made product. "They loved it, Em. And I mean loved it as in they couldn't stop gushing. They hugged me and thanked me for shining it up so much. And Bronson's team worked miracles with the sound and musical score. The film is almost perfect!"

She squealed, too. That was the great thing about having a best friend: my feelings always had a mirror in her. "That's amazing! And they hugged you? Does that mean *Mr. Thomas* actually acknowledged you did all the editing work?"

She said *Mr. Thomas* with a definite tone of mockery, making me glad she wasn't on speakerphone. He was unhappy enough with me. He certainly didn't need to hear my friends making fun of him on the phone.

I searched for the right words. "Well . . . he didn't acknowledge I was even there at first, but—" I lowered my voice and glanced at the small crowd surrounding him. "We had a discussion, and I'll probably be fired as soon as he can figure out how to do it without making a scene, but for now, he knows better than to try to take credit entirely away from me. For now, he's sharing it."

"Sharing? Even though he did absolutely nothing?" She sounded like she was already plotting ways to hide his body.

"I know. It's not ideal, but it's better than it would've been if I hadn't stood my ground."

She sighed. "That was something you were always better at doing than I've ever been. Anyway, congratulations. I am so glad to hear they're recognizing your talent. You're amazing! I'll be over as soon as this meeting is done. We'll go to dinner to celebrate."

"Only if I buy."

I smiled to myself as we hung up. *See, Ben,* I thought, *I didn't totally lie to you.* I *was* going to dinner with Emma. My earlier statement to him was just predicting the future. I sighed. Justifications were not going to make an honest woman of me. I hated that Ben hadn't gotten to see the reactions of a respected producer and an award-winning director. He deserved to see how they felt about the work we had done together. He deserved to know that his talents were good enough for bigger studios, bigger movies.

I would tell him. Of course I would tell him. But how would it have been to have had him in the theater at my side watching those reactions together?

Dean didn't linger too much longer. Once the applause and praise had died and Danny and Christopher had left for another meeting, Dean said, "Time to get back to work." I got back in the golf cart in spite of my earlier decision to walk. Maybe now that he'd seen the film, he would feel better about me.

I expected something from him. A "good work" or "nice going," but the vacuum of space would have proven to be noisier than the brief ride with Dean Thomas. We parked and went our separate ways to our offices without so much as a glance.

Oh well.

I was asleep at my desk when Nathaniel buzzed me to let me know Emma waited at the guardhouse. Nathaniel knew that Emma was on the list of approved guests, but he lived a by-the-books kind of life, so he checked every single time. The taste of sleep in my mouth and the ache in my eye socket let me know I'd managed to get in a pretty decent nap. I gave Nathaniel permission to let Emma onto Portal Pictures property.

Taking a bleach wipe out of the plastic container to clean off my desk, I realized I had yet to throw away the pillow where Adam had taken his turn at napping. The studio was becoming a regular bed-and-breakfast—only without the comfortable beds or the awesome breakfast part. I stood, straightened up my rumpled clothing as much as possible, checked the time, and realized it was fairly late in the afternoon. I wondered if anyone had ever cleaned the kitchen.

A bright white tugged at the periphery of my vision. I turned my head and saw a vase of flowers sitting on the bookcase across from my desk. That hadn't been there before. Confused, I crossed the room and plucked the card from the plastic holder jutting out from the bouquet of white tulips. I slid my finger along the seal of the envelope and opened it up to read.

> *Dear Silvia,*
> *Thank you for making my film into something magical. I know I owe the credit all to*

you. It's too fresh and innovative to belong to Dean. The white tulip was Audrey Hepburn's favorite flower. Since you look like you could be her sister, I thought you might also like them. I've always considered myself her biggest fan. I am happy to say I am now your biggest fan as well. I hope we'll work together again soon.

With much gratitude,

Danny

"You look terrible," Emma said as she leaned against the door frame and surveyed me standing by the bookcase with the card still in hand.

I smiled weakly. "Thanks. I'm sure you meant that to be a compliment, right?"

"No, really, you look terrible," she said. "When was the last time you slept?"

"About two minutes ago." I pointed at my desk.

Her eyes went to the desk and then snapped back to me. "You're doing the cyclops squint." Emma took a few steps closer. "Seriously, desk sleep does not count. When was the last time you got real sleep?"

I dropped the smile. It wasn't working anyway. I tugged on my right eyelid to make it stay open. "Honestly, who knows? I've had so much to do with so little time to get it done. . . . But, see how it all worked out?" I waved the card at her. "They like my work. I've succeeded."

Emma took the card, her smile growing as her eyes scanned the cream-colored paper. She pulled me into a tight hug when she'd finished reading. "I am so proud of you! And how funny that he called you Audrey Hepburn. Did you tell him your eye's name is Audrey?"

"That's definitely not information for public consumption."

"Fair enough. Well, sister-of-Audrey, let's get you fed and in bed. Got your stuff?"

Going to dinner with Emma was always relaxing. She was the sort of friend who didn't require a lot of maintenance. Well, she *usually* didn't require a lot of maintenance. Emma, like everyone, required some attention every once in a while. We spent dinner talking about how her company was expanding into new locations and how her wedding plans were going.

For my half of the conversation, we talked about all of the editing I had to do, how Dean Thomas was the most worthless boss on the entire planet, and how I appreciated that everything still managed to work out okay with the film. I didn't mention anything about Ben's help with *why* everything turned out okay. He and I had pinky promised after all, and pinky promises were unbreakable. I didn't love not telling her, though. Keeping secrets from Emma tore at my soul. We'd told each other everything since the time we were both five years old and she showed up in my bedroom like some specter out of a ghost movie with her pale face and her nearly white hair gleaming in the moonlight.

Emma just happened to show up on the same day I'd been released from the hospital after my eye surgery. After the initial scare of her ghostly presence passed, she climbed into bed next to me, and we'd been best friends ever since.

Losing my eye had been a major ordeal. The entire world

shifted for me after that. It was like everything had been divided in half. I had to remember to turn my head to see the half that was missing. Looking both ways to cross the street required more work, more attention. I'd had a couple of close calls when Emma had needed to snatch me back just before my foot left the curb.

My mom used to tell my dad that she believed Emma saved my life the night she showed up, and even beyond the times Emma kept me from walking into traffic, Mom was totally right. But Emma and I knew that we'd saved each other. Emma had lost something, too, the night she showed up at my bedside. Her mother had walked out on the family. Both of us losing something that the other could not imagine made it impossible for us to feel sorry for ourselves, because we were too busy consoling the other.

"I'm proud of you for standing up for yourself. Finally." Emma mopped up the remains of her balsamic dressing with a remnant of bread and popped it into her mouth. "What?" she said when she caught me giving her the stink eye.

"You say that like I never stand up for myself."

She shrugged sheepishly. "While it is true that you have the backbone in our friendship, not me, it is also true that you don't use that backbone very often when that guy you work for is around."

I conceded the point. "It's just the nature of the business. Half the guys in Hollywood are still unaware that suffrage has happened."

She laughed while at the same time calling me out for the crazy exaggeration. "That is not true!"

"It's not true," I agreed. "It just feels true when I'm dealing with Dean."

"The Dean of Misery. We should get him a T-shirt with that on it." Emma effortlessly rolled into a different topic. "Lucas is out of town next weekend. Want to watch *Mansfield Park* at my place?"

I agreed to her plan. I loved Jane Austen—not like Emma loved it—but what wasn't to love? Jane had helped Emma and me ride the turbulent waves of romance. And when Emma called me an "obstinate, headstrong girl," she managed to make me feel capable and strong.

The waitress left the bill on the table closest to Emma. I took the black folder and popped my credit card in it. "Even the waitress thinks I look like a homeless person who can't afford dinner."

Emma tapped her fingers on her glass stem, obviously working to keep herself from snatching up the black folder and switching out the cards. She behaved herself and let me pay for dinner, as was our deal, but I could tell it bothered her. As CMO of one of the nation's hottest fitness chains, Emma made more money than I did. A lot more. This meant she worried about me financially. But my own independence mattered, and I was grateful she gave me the chance to stretch out in the luxury of my own autonomy.

"My mom called the other day," I said. "She told me to thank you for the day spa gift card."

"Oh good! I'm glad she got it."

"She wanted to see if we were going to visit her soon, so we could use it all together." I grinned at that. Mom loved when Emma and I shared major mother-daughter activities with her. "I know," I said with a sigh when Emma grimaced. "I don't have time right now, either."

Finding time to do road trips of that variety was harder and harder. Even weekend trips by plane were nearly impossible. Mom couldn't come to us because she was taking care of her parents in Washington, and their health had declined to the point that leaving them was not an option. My parents had moved a long time ago, promising they'd come back someday, but as the years dragged on, I began to think they were never coming home.

The only reason Mom hadn't come to drag me up there with them was that my grandma on my dad's side still lived locally, and I spent a lot of time with her. Forget the fact that I was a grown woman with my own apartment. They would have packed me up already if it hadn't been for Grandma Bradshaw.

The waitress returned with my credit card slip, which I signed before releasing a deep yawn.

Emma saw and frowned. "Where am I taking you, again?" she asked as we gathered the to-go boxes from the table.

"Do you remember my boss from Mid-Scene Films?"

"Ben? The blue-eyed and thick-haired hottie?"

I felt the flush in my face and hurried to turn away so she couldn't see the red-cheeked evidence. "He does have blue eyes, and his hair is thick, I guess. And who are you, and what have you done with my best friend? You never use the word 'hottie.'"

She ignored my reluctance to admit he had handsome features. "I've finally embraced my ability to appreciate the appearance of a beautiful man. Besides, my niece, April, uses it all the time. Her language has been rubbing off on me. But that is beside the point. Why is your car at the hottie's house?"

I groaned. "Don't call him that."

She poked me in the back. "Why? I know you're down an eye, but your left one still works, doesn't it? You can't tell me you haven't noticed. Answer the question: why is your car there?"

So I explained about Dean and how he'd been impossible and how Ben had shown up and helped me get Dean back to the studio.

"And now Hottie Ben has your car. That's convenient."

"Don't call him that. He's my boss. It makes it weird."

"He's not your boss any longer. Which makes it not weird."

This was the sort of conversation that came from calling my friend for a ride rather than calling for a hired driver. This was the payment required for such favors. "We're only friends."

"I'm just saying that sometimes friends make the best boyfriends." Emma, knowing when to quit pushing, wisely changed the subject. "So, what's the address? Where am I going?"

When I rattled off the address to Emma, she smiled wide as she entered the information into her car's GPS.

"What?"

"You just happen to know Hottie Ben's address by heart?"

Okay, so maybe she didn't know when to quit pushing. "We used to work together; that's not so strange."

"You don't think so? I work with dozens of people. And I don't know any of their addresses. Sure, I know the general direction in which they might live, I might even know the city name, but an exact address? Admit it. It's not a crime to just admit that you like him."

"I don't have a problem admitting I like him, but liking a guy doesn't automatically mean you want to date him."

"That's true. I've liked many people in my life, and I haven't wanted to date most of them. But that doesn't change the fact that Ben is a nice-looking man who is also a nice man, which, let's be honest, is an incredibly rare combination. You're the one who's always telling me that."

"You being engaged does not mean I need a relationship, too, but thanks for the concern," I said.

"This has nothing to do with me being engaged. It has everything to do with you bringing him up and you no longer being held hostage by the Mid-Scene Films contract." She flipped her blinker and made a tight turn.

Rather than comment further on a subject that made me feel awkward for reasons I didn't understand, I just let her drive. Soon we were parked in front of Ben's house.

"Is it really weird that I know his address by heart?" I asked as I stared at his house. It always made me think of gingerbread and Christmas. It was an older home in all the best ways and matched the man who lived in it.

"It's only weird if you don't do anything about it," she said.

When I didn't get out of the car immediately, Emma asked, "Do you want me to go with you to get the keys? Is Hottie Ben a creeper, and you forgot to tell me, and I'm suggesting you get cozy with someone likely to be featured on *America's Most Wanted*?"

I laughed. "No. Hottie Ben isn't a creeper. I'm just enjoying the warmth and vibe you radiate." The truth was, our conversation regarding Ben had hit repeat in my head. *It's only weird if you don't do anything about it.*

Her words wouldn't have held any effect on me if his absence at the film review hadn't been sorely felt. His absence in general was sorely felt. And now that his house loomed in front of me, only the dark wood of the door separating us, my stomach fluttered in apprehension.

Because I was almost considering the idea of asking him out.

Why not?

I didn't work for Mid-Scene Films any more.

No rules dictated by several sensitivity trainings stood in the way of getting to know Ben on a different level.

Nothing stood in my way except my own feet that seemed to have forgotten how to move and my own hands that refused to reach for the door handle.

Emma didn't rush me. Emma never did. I was the bossier one of the two of us. I rushed her on stuff all the time. But she seemed content to let me sit and stare at Ben's house while I debated with myself over my actual intentions.

"I'll call you later," I finally said. Putting it off any longer just made it that much later before I would get home, that much later before my head could hit a real pillow. I leaned in quick to give Emma a hug. Then I wrapped my fingers around the handle and pulled.

Here goes nothing.

Emma started her car as I walked up the sidewalk, but she didn't pull away from the curb until light from the open door shone out into the darkness.

She must have figured I was safe now that Ben had

answered the door, and, like a good friend, she wanted to give me some privacy. She must have sensed I planned on putting myself out there with him. Emma usually knew what I was doing before I did.

What she didn't know was that it wasn't Ben who answered the door.

It was the girl from the club—Alison, Ben's old film school girlfriend, who had apparently not given up on the idea of reconnecting.

Chapter Six

"I hate girls that giggle all the time."

—Sabrina Fairchild, played by Audrey Hepburn in Sabrina

I think I blinked and stared for a full minute. Well, probably not a full minute, but it certainly felt like one. Questions like "What in the world do you think you're doing here?" died on my lips. Because that would have been rude.

It also would have been more her right to demand an answer to that question, since I was the interloper to this party.

What I actually said was, "Hello. It's nice to see you again, Alison." Which wasn't technically true since I had just decided to ask out her boyfriend apparent. Though she wasn't spangly any longer in her jeans and tactically fitted T-shirt, her dark hair looked softer and shinier than before. She'd had a shower at some point in the last twenty-four hours.

Which was more than anyone could say for me.

"It's nice to see you, too," she said, though it was hard

to believe her when her eyes took in my rumpled, unwashed appearance. "Your name's Sara, isn't it?"

Thanks a lot, Dean, I thought.

She seemed confused by my presence, and being that we hadn't really been introduced the night before, it made sense why she got my name wrong.

Now that I saw her standing in Ben's doorway and looking so beautiful, I was confused by my presence as well. "No, actually my name is Silvia—Silvia Bradshaw. I'm here to see Ben. Is he home?"

Instead of answering my question, she said, "But didn't your boyfriend call you *Sara*?"

"Yes, well, he's not my boyfriend. And he was intoxicated, so he's hardly a credible source for information. I don't actually have a boyfriend." Why had I slipped that nugget of information in there? My relationship status had nothing to do with anything. I hated being tired. I was such a jerk when I was tired. "Is Ben here?"

Before she could answer, Ben's voice called from the back room. "I can't find it anywhere. It probably got lost in one of the moves." He came into view from the hallway, and our eyes met over Alison's shoulder.

"Silvia." He halted and blinked in surprise, though he shouldn't have been too shocked to see me. He did have my car, after all. His face split into a smile, and he lengthened his stride to reach the door, which he pulled open wider. "Come in! I'm sorry I didn't hear you knock or ring the bell. I was in the closet looking for some things Alison thought I might still have from college. Come in!"

Alison scooted to the side, finally allowing me access to the house, though she clearly took no pleasure in the action.

I couldn't blame her. She was the one having her date railroaded by a member of the unwashed masses. Again.

"I'd introduce you, but you two already met the other night, I guess." He took my hand, something that felt so natural and right, and yet also so strange, considering our current setting. He led me to the couch and gave me a nudge, indicating I should sit.

Alison's eyebrows furrowed slightly, a tiny crease appearing right above her nose as she watched Ben's hand release mine. Though she had dismissed me as insignificant the night before, my appearance at her would-be boyfriend's house and his immediate acceptance of my presence must have changed her opinion of me.

I was no longer a helpless old coworker with terrible hygiene habits. I'd become a person of interest.

"So," Ben said, sitting in the recliner directly across from me. "You had a busy day, right? Christopher and Danny . . . how did it go?"

With those words, I forgot all about the dark beauty queen in the room. Those words—*Christopher and Danny*—were like taking an elixir of energy. My spine straightened, my shoulders squared, my lips found the strength to smile.

Before I could answer Ben's question, Alison interjected, "Wait, you know Christopher and Danny?"

Just like that, I'd gone from a person of interest to a person of downright fascination. When those two names were put together, even people in the big studios knew who you meant. They were *the* up-and-coming duo.

It was Ben who answered. "Silvia is the assistant editor at Portal Pictures." He turned to me. "Tell me everything. I've been thinking about you all day."

"Portal Pictures?" Alison latched onto the information that she felt was the most important, but she missed the most important part of what Ben said, the part about how he'd been thinking of me all day. That part filled me with an irrational happiness that summoned what I was sure was a goofy smile on my face.

Alison was still talking. "That's a cool studio to be working for. Good for you." She eyed me with keen interest now, completely ignoring my greasy hair, the disheveled clothing, and the fact that my teeth had yet to see a toothbrush for what felt like a week. As she looked at me, I felt I understood her better.

Alison was still in that unfortunate position of being a climber. Well, not even a climber yet. She'd gone to film school and was still looking for an *in* to the business. Not that she could be judged harshly for that. We were all—to some degree or another—climbers and clawers. Climbing up and clawing in. The problem with Hollywood was that most, if not all, relationships were thought about in terms of how they could be manipulated for an advantage. I hated that about the industry.

Alison being a climber made me frown because it made me wonder: was she interested in Ben as *Ben*? Or was she interested in Ben as Mid-Scene Films?

Ben tapped my knee. "You're killing me, Smalls! We're talking about the review! How did the review go?"

Right. Focus on the review, not Alison. "Ben, you—it went so great!" I almost said *he'd* done so great, but Alison was right there. I'd give proper credit where credit was due at some other time when we were alone. "They loved it. They laughed. They cried in all the right places. They gushed when it was over. There was nothing but praise. It was . . ." I sighed. "It was almost magical."

I also didn't add that the *almost* was only because he hadn't been there. I had done good work on the edit, but Ben had filed away the sharp edges.

"Did they ask for any changes?" Ben asked, his face lit up with excitement, the kind I used to see all the time when we worked together. How had I not noticed how much that excitement had been missing from my life over the last four months?

"Yes. A few. They always ask for changes. But nothing major. It felt like every change they asked for was more because they wanted to be doing their jobs than actually wanting anything changed. They really liked it, Ben. They were so excited to have it ready."

"And Dean? How did that go down?"

"Dean was . . . Dean. You know how it is; he tried to take all the credit, but I had a talk with him, and I think he understands that cutting me out of my work is not going to be allowed."

"Wow! So good day, huh?" Alison interjected, apparently feeling left out of the conversation for long enough.

"Definitely a good day," I said, my eyes not leaving Ben's. "Thanks, Ben. I owe it all to you."

He nodded and only broke eye contact when Alison sat on the arm of the chair he occupied and put her hand on his shoulder. He glanced up, and the smile he gave her was shaky, less certain, undefinable.

I wanted it defined, however. I wanted to know why he seemed less confident when he looked at her than when he looked at me. Was it because he felt more comfortable with me because I meant something, or was it because I didn't mean anything? Why did my life suddenly feel like junior high?

"So, Sara—I mean . . ."

She appeared to be experiencing genuine frustration that she couldn't come up with my real name, now that I was someone worth knowing.

"It's Silvia," I said.

"Right." She flushed, but blazed ahead like it wasn't a big deal. "How long have you been with Portal Pictures?"

"For the last four months. And what about you?" I asked, not wanting to talk to her about my job, not wanting to be a relationship Alison could use for strategic maneuvering. "What do you do?"

She seemed surprised by the question and floundered for a moment before saying, "I studied film with Ben at USC, and I have been working to get my hands on some real movies ever since, but right now, I'm working at Gem Experience in their marketing department. I make commercials and provide content for their social media."

"Gem Experience?"

She pressed her lips together in a visual display of unease before nodding. "It's a clothing line for pets."

That took me off guard. Considering that Dean threatened to have me out on the street working for some little marketing department somewhere, Alison's reality sobered me. There was nothing wrong with what she did for a living. It was the kind of job a lot of people would love. But it was evident that Alison had been led down that same rabbit hole I'd gone down. Maybe it hadn't been because of Audrey Hepburn, but the same passion blazed in her eyes. She wanted to be in *the* business, and she seemed unhappy about her current circumstances. Her situation could have been mine if it weren't for a few lucky breaks early on in my career. I would have been unhappy anywhere else, too.

Ben brought the conversation back to my film. "Is the release date on schedule, then?"

"Yes. On schedule. The edits they want are so small, I can do it in an afternoon. At least, I could do it in an afternoon after I've had enough sleep to allow my brain to function at full capacity."

Ben jumped to his feet. "That's right! I'm so sorry, Sil. You must be exhausted after being up all night. You probably need to get home and get to bed. Let me get your keys."

"You have her keys?" Alison didn't say it with any hint of meanness in her voice, but she clearly wanted an answer because she followed him down the hall toward wherever he'd placed my keys.

I felt only slightly bad that I had ruined a Friday night date for Alison and Ben, and now I'd ruined a Saturday night date as well. I considered coming back Sunday just for the sake of consistency.

Okay, so maybe I didn't feel so bad after all.

And it wasn't because I didn't like Alison. I liked her just fine. I just liked Ben more.

But, I told myself, *she was here first.*

But, I argued, *I was here second, and two is a bigger number.*

A soft giggle bubbled up in me at the silly argument

inside my own head. Ben had never made any kind of move in my direction, and now he basically had a girlfriend. Did I really want to make things more awkward? The outcome of me behaving badly would be irritating his girlfriend and alienating his friendship. And since I'd only just decided to like him, I could shrug it off and pretend it never happened. Yes. That was what I would do.

The beauty of the battle being only in my head was that Ben never needed to know that any such battle was ever fought. We could go on as friends, business as usual.

Whispers came from the back rooms, but I didn't venture back to take part in the conversation or to even eavesdrop. I stayed on the sofa and let the hiss and hum of the conversation fuzz in my head as I sank deeper into the cushions.

I woke up to heated whispers—two teakettles hissing at one another. Even though my mind had come to consciousness, my eyes refused to open.

"I can't do that! Do you know that one in every one thousand six hundred and sixty-four deaths are because of drowsy driving?"

More whispers. Female this time.

Ben's answer was also a whisper, but I could pick through his words enough to determine what he said.

They were arguing over me because I'd fallen asleep. I felt incredibly stupid for falling asleep and then guilty that they were arguing about it, but I couldn't make my eyes open. Not for guilt, not for pride, not for anything.

"I don't think she's slept in days," Ben said, then their voices faded away as they migrated somewhere else.

Sometime later, something warm and soft settled gently around me. I snuggled deeper into it and slept on.

When I awoke again, it was to mostly silence. The lights had all been turned off, and only the hum of a fridge from the kitchen broke the silence. I jolted upright, my senses hyper-alert in the confusion of where I was. A thick, fuzzy blanket slipped down my shoulders and onto the floor.

I swung my legs off the couch and planted my bare feet on the carpet.

Where were my shoes?

Where was I?

I blinked in the dark several times to try to make shadowy shapes form into something recognizable. A coffee table sat between two recliners opposite the couch. A few more blinks and I was able to pull a memory from my mind. Ben. Ben had sat in the recliner closest to me. His college girlfriend had sat on the arm of the chair.

Embarrassment flooded me. I'd fallen asleep like some stray. I curled my toes into the plush carpet before realizing I didn't remember taking off my shoes. Someone else had done that for me. That same someone had removed my socks, too, making me wish I'd taken the time to get an updated pedicure. My nails were chipped and overgrown and probably horrible to look at.

Had Ben taken off my shoes, or had Alison done that?

An answer either way horrified me to think about.

What must Ben think? What kind of person passed out on random couches? Aside from Dean Thomas, I didn't know of anyone. My fingers fumbled over the floor by my feet until they finally tangled into a shoelace. Success!

My socks were stuffed into my shoes, and I tugged them over my feet before stuffing my foot into my left shoe without bothering to untie it first. My keys jingled as I pulled my other shoe closer. Ben must have left my keys for me to find. I swept up the keys and stood. I had to leave immediately.

I didn't leave immediately. Instead, I pulled out my phone and squinted as it came to life under my fingerprint ID and filled the room with light. The time read 4:27. I'd essentially spent the night at my old boss's house. It was the stuff scandals were made of.

I took a few steps toward the hall, thinking for a moment that maybe I should thank Ben for letting me crash on his couch and inform him I was leaving, but then I halted. Sleeping on his couch was one thing. Heading to his bedroom was another entirely.

Not wanting things to get more awkward than they already were, I retreated to the couch and stood for several seconds wondering if it would be more rude to leave without letting him know or to send a text that might wake him up. I certainly wasn't going to talk to him in person, and I absolutely wasn't staying until morning when he was awake again.

Besides, what if he had plans with Alison? They were obviously together, which was weird to think about. How could someone like Ben, who loved the ironic and interesting, and who belly laughed as much as I did, be friends with someone who only barely smiled as if she was the Mona Lisa? Honestly, did the woman not know how to give a real smile? Did she never laugh? I hated girls who never laughed.

In my heart, I knew I was being harsh, likely stemming from my newfound interest in Ben as something more than my friend. Some vague memory of Alison acting pleasant at the club nudged the back of my mind. Alison was a nice person, which meant I needed an appropriate exit strategy.

In the kitchen, I used my phone as a flashlight and rummaged through Ben's incredibly tidy drawers to find some scratch paper and a pen. The drawer closest to the fridge had a stack of sticky pads and a tray with pens and pencils in it. I pulled the top sheet from a sticky pad and used the Darth Vader pen to scrawl a quick message thanking Ben for allowing me to crash on his couch. I stuck the note on his fridge next to a picture of him and Mickey Mouse and . . . *me?*

Ben had a picture of *me* on his fridge?

It was from the Mid-Scene Films company party a couple of years ago when we all went to Disneyland. I made Ben and two of our other coworkers, Jan and Mary, get Mickey Mouse ears with me and pose for a picture. Jan and Mary had been on one side of the mouse. Ben and I had been on the other.

As far as I could remember, we only had one picture taken, but Jan and Mary weren't in this picture. Did Ben have them Photoshopped out? I looked closer and realized he'd just cropped the photo when he printed it.

But he'd left me in.

Not that he really could have cropped me out. We were standing close together, our arms over each other's shoulders. He would have had to cut off his own limb to remove me from the picture. So if he'd wanted a photo of him with Mickey, he really had no choice but to leave me in it, too. But . . . to have it on his fridge?

I stared for several moments at this thing I couldn't make sense of and realized it was time to leave. If Ben woke up and found me mesmerized by his large appliances, we'd both have some explaining to do.

I was too exhausted for explanations.

I left the sticky note next to the picture. I wanted Ben to know I had seen it, because it was definitely a conversation we needed to have. Pictures on fridges were signs of intimacy. The only people who had my face taking up space on their fridges were my parents, my grandma, and Emma.

I tiptoed to the front door and pulled it open as quietly as possible. I thumbed the lock so he wouldn't get murdered in his sleep after I left and wondered what the odds were of being murdered in your bed. Ben would likely have the answer, but I decided not to ask him. Some things were better left unknown.

I regretted leaving almost as soon as the door skimmed over the carpet and clicked shut. What if it didn't mean anything that my face was on his fridge? What if he didn't think a conversation was necessary?

What if he liked this girl who never laughed, and my leaving too soon took me out of the equation? Because, though I had decided to stay away from him and let Alison win, I'd changed my mind. Him putting me on his fridge changed things for me because it meant he was thinking about me too.

I frowned as I worked my way down his sidewalk between two tidy rows of daylilies to my car. A sleepy fog still occupied too much space in my head for me to question or fret for long.

I could not allow myself to speculate on anything, good or bad, and I definitely would not give the girl who didn't laugh a second thought. She could no longer be part of the equation between Ben and me. *Ben has me on his fridge.* I slid behind the wheel of my car and thought about the weirdness of such a thing. Another giggle bubbled up and led to full-on laughter. Whereas Alison didn't really laugh, I probably laughed too much.

I really needed to get some quality sleep.

Chapter Seven

*"You don't have to be friendly to work
together. Acquainted will do."*

—Jo Stockton, *played by Audrey Hepburn in* Funny Face

I went straight home and crashed hard for nine hours. I didn't wake for Emma's four texts, Ben's three texts, or my grandma's one phone call and voice message.

The doorbell finally won in reviving me. The UPS driver rang the doorbell to deliver a package from my parents. I used a knife to cut through the packing tape and discovered a new snorkel mask and a note from my mom informing me that she'd seen this in one of the seaside shops in Washington and thought I might like a new one. Mom bought me little things all the time as her way of staying in contact with me. I sent her a quick email letting her know how much I loved the mask and promising to send pictures when it made its maiden voyage. Then I texted Emma, assuring her of my safety, ignored Ben, because I wasn't sure how to tackle that mountain, and called Grandma, because no one ignored Grandma.

"I need help unpacking," she declared when she picked up the phone.

"You wouldn't if you hadn't moved," I said and popped the last bite of butter-slathered toast in my mouth.

"Don't get sassy. Just come help." She pretty much hung up on me after that.

And she called *me* sassy?

I considered putting off the shower for a while longer, since I was going to help unpack boxes and move furniture, but the way I kept running into people made me rethink shower avoidance. I could barely stand to be around myself. I showered, shaved my legs, brushed my teeth, and even took the time to do a side braid just so it would look like I'd put some effort into my appearance. By the time I arrived at Grandma's new address, I could have passed as a human.

Grandma reintroduced me to the meaning of hard labor. While we worked, I told her about the film, about Dean, and about my options now that Dean pretty much hated me for standing up for myself, even though I'd saved his job and he owed me.

"Hollywood is filled with liars and thieves. It's absolutely no place for a lady. I think you should find a different line of work."

Such were the wise words of my grandmother on the subject of Dean Thomas. She'd apparently been talking to Old Ben Kenobi about hives of scum and villainy. Her advice might have been helpful had it not been for the fact that I was holding a forty-pound, framed-and-matted painting of Paris against the wall above her couch. We'd, or rather *I'd*, moved the picture seven times already, and no amount of time spent in Emma's gym had prepared me for the task. My arms shook with the exertion.

"Can we focus on finding a home for your art before we criticize my job, Grandma?" I asked.

"Don't pull your Sassy Silvia out on me, young lady. I'm not your mother."

"Thank heavens," I said, irritated to be scolded like a teenager when I was into my third decade of life.

Gut instinct said she'd tacked on the "young lady" part to her nickname for me to reinforce the fact that a lady like me didn't belong in villainous Hollywood. I stretched my neck to look over my left shoulder, barely catching a glimpse of her cotton-swab white hair. "You're the one who worked in Hollywood for most of your life," I reminded her. "Are you trying to tell me you lost lady points from the whole ordeal?"

She ignored the question and kept up the lecture. "If your mother knew about your boss trying to take credit for your work, and you putting up with his treatment of you, she'd chain you up in a room full of Virginia Woolf writings until you came back to feminism with a protest sign declaring your apology."

"Exactly. Which is why I didn't tell her about it; I told you. Honestly, Grandma, out of everybody in my life, I really expected you to have my back." I blew away a strand of hair that had fallen loose from my braid.

"I do have your back," she insisted. "Opening your eyes

to the truth of what you've gotten yourself into is the best way I can support you."

"You mean prying my eyes open with a crowbar." I thought the words muttered under my breath were too low to be heard, but Grandma harrumphed from behind me.

"You're sassing again."

"Do you like the painting here?" I asked, changing the subject, since my arms weren't likely to hold up for too much longer. She didn't respond. I grunted. "I can't see if you're nodding or shaking your head. You're in my blind spot."

She made a noise of irritation. "I don't like it there at all. It diminishes the couches."

I lowered the painting, carefully stepped down from my perch on the back of the couch I'd been using as a makeshift ladder, and bit my tongue to keep from asking how long she'd known she didn't want the painting above the couch. My arms were jiggly bags of unhappy muscle. I could actually feel them frowning at me. "So where do you think you *will* like it?"

She pursed her lips and plucked at the necklace dangling down her front. Several silver jangly bracelets slid down to her elbow as she twirled the long chain of her necklace in a slow circle while she contemplated where she wanted her picture. "The entry hall over the table," she said finally.

She hadn't liked it there at the very beginning of this whole decorate-Grandma's-new-retirement-villa scheme, but I didn't mention it. She had to know she was killing me, and she probably found some dark, twisted humor in the act. I turned to face her directly, and smiled despite myself.

Grandma's hair had gone gray when she was still in her thirties. By the time she'd hit sixty, it had gone white. She kept it cropped short and used styling gel to spike it on top, which I'd loved as a little girl because the sharp ends were pokey and fun to pat. Grandma wasn't one of those double-chinned, housecoat-wearing grandmas. She was a hipster-jeans-and-sassy-T-shirt-wearing grandma. Today, she was wearing the jeans she bought the last time we'd gone to the mall for pedicures—the jeans with stylishly placed rips and tears—and her shirt sported the Lakers logo. Grandma loved the NBA.

I went to work getting the picture hung. Once done, I put an arm around her as we stepped back to admire my handiwork, along with the handiwork of the artist. "You know where I liked it best, Grandma?" I asked.

"Where's that?"

"In your actual house."

"We've been through all that." She wriggled out from under my arm and scooted away from me as if, by being in my physical proximity, she might catch the disease of common sense and change her mind about the move.

"Going through it and making sense of it are not the same thing," I reminded her. "You are not a decrepit geriatric in need of frequent diaper changes by pinch-faced nurses. You're in better physical and mental condition than most forty-year-olds I know. Assisted living is for people who need assistance."

"I do need assistance," she said as she ripped the tape off a box.

"You do not need someone to puree your food so you can eat. You might need someone to schedule your hair appointments, but that's it. I could totally use an assistant like that, too, but you don't see me moving into a last-resting-place-before-the-final-resting-place joint. This villa is a tenth of the size of your home. Their community pool is half the size of the personal pool at your house."

She sighed and looked away. "A house that big echoes loneliness with every step inside its halls."

I stared at her, but she refused to meet my gaze. Grandma never mentioned feeling any kind of loneliness. Not once in my whole life. "But I visit you all the time. I practically live there with you." My high-pitched protests came with the intense desire to defend myself. No one could ever compare me to one of those crummy grandkids who didn't care about their grandparents. Grandma was my life and breath. She was the reason I hadn't run away to Peru when I was a teenager and clashing with Mom. Well, her and Emma, though I'd planned on taking Emma with me if and when I ever did run away.

Grandma went back to unpacking the boxes containing her movie collection.

"You're lonely?" I asked when she started pulling old DVDs out of the box and placing them on her shelves in an order that must have made sense to her but made no sense to me.

She moved the now-empty box to the floor and opened up the one underneath it without responding. When she exclaimed, "My Audrey Hepburn collection!" I knew she'd slammed the door closed on the lonely conversation forever.

Grandma felt lonely.

And she wouldn't talk to me about it.

"You know they have an Audrey Hepburn society here at Ocean View? I plan on joining as soon as I get settled."

Things were worse than I thought. She was not only lonely and moving into an assisted-living complex called Ocean View when there was no ocean view from any window in the entire complex, but she planned to join clubs at the assisted-living home? "Next you're going to ask me to order you some Vicks VapoRub. Grandma, what is going on with you?"

She whirled on me with demon fire in her eyes. "Don't you dare compare Audrey Hepburn to Vicks VapoRub!"

I actually fell back in surprise at her ferocity, but I kept my verbal ground even after losing my physical ground. "Oh, come on, you spent the last hour telling me how Hollywood is nothing but lies with beautiful set dressing, and how I should run—not walk—to any other form of employment, but now you want to join a society fanning themselves over an icon from that same Hollywood? Yeah. Okay. That makes sense."

It wasn't that I didn't get it. I totally did. Audrey was the reason I existed in my current state. Without her, I would have been someone totally different. Today, with my career going well, I didn't actually mind.

"Audrey's different," Grandma said reverentially. "She was never like the rest of them." And then she smiled for the first time that day. "She was like you, actually. Dark hair, dark eyes, big heart, hidden insecurities—"

"I am not insecure." I interrupted only because my insecurities didn't like being poked. Grandma had told me all this before. She had known Audrey personally from a movie set where Grandma had worked as a makeup artist at a time when Audrey was winding down in her career. Audrey had cupped my grandmother's chin in her hand and said, "You are lovely." My grandma described it as similar to the moment in *My Fair Lady* when the queen of Transylvania declares Eliza

Doolittle as charming. No one before or since had ever said anything to my grandma that meant as much.

The fact that Grandma compared me to Audrey was always a compliment to me. But today, I didn't feel like hearing it, not when Grandma was moving into a retirement community. Not when she was hinting at being lonely and making plans to join a club that sounded like something someone made up to keep the almost-deceased busy until they were no longer in need of trivial entertainment.

"If you want to be part of an Audrey Hepburn society, why don't you volunteer to work with needy children?" I asked.

"You don't understand my purposes. I'm looking for social interactions as well as social good."

"And volunteering isn't social?" I was being petty because I didn't like her moving into this place with a bunch of other old people. It made her mortality a little too real for me.

"Volunteering is a different kind of social. Oh! Be careful with that!"

I glanced at the box I'd selected from the stack. "Why?"

She tugged the box from my arms as if, by questioning her motives, I had declared my intentions to put explosives in the box and ignite them immediately. "It's my movie collection."

"I thought we already put your movies away." I lifted the lid and peeked inside as she pulled the box back in an act of genuine distrust. My mouth fell open when I saw the contents. "Okay, I knew you had old movie cans, but you have actual movies in them? We're talking reel-to-reel movies?"

She nodded.

I stared at the box with a new interest. "Seriously? How cool is that? And you never told me? Reel-to-reels are awesome." I glanced up at her, legitimately intrigued at the idea of this relic from my chosen profession. "Do you have a projector that can play them?"

She harrumphed and set the box on the couch, then she carefully removed each canister and set them on a shelf near the fireplace. "I'm an old woman moving into a retirement home. Of course I have a projector that can play these. I'll bet everyone in this complex has a projector that can play these."

I frowned at her putting such incredible antiques so close to the fireplace. Was she serious? Shouldn't they be kept in a fireproof room somewhere? "Maybe we should move these to your bedroom—"

When she faced me with a dramatic roll of her eyes, I grinned. I loved it when my wrinkly, old grandmother rolled her eyes at me. She harrumphed again when she saw my smile. "I've had these since before you were born. I think I know how to care for them properly."

I decided not to argue the point. "What movies do you have?"

She shrugged and flipped through the cans in a casual way that made me cringe. Did she not realize the value of such antiques if the movies inside were high-profile films?

"*Mary Poppins*, *To Kill a Mockingbird*, *Vertigo*, *Charade*, some Abbott and Costello, *Tammy and the Bachelor*—you know . . . movies."

I stared at her. "Seriously? How did I not know that you had these? What's happening between us? First, you move into a retirement home when you're in better physical condition than I am. Then, you tell me you have cool stuff that you've never shown me before. Next, you'll probably tell me you know who D. B. Cooper was." I was only half-joking.

She bent down to settle the last of the cans onto the shelf before straightening and fixing me with her eagle-eye. That eye was the bane of my childhood. It knew everything about me, guessing my darkest secrets and misdeeds. "How do you even know about D. B. Cooper at your age?"

"One of the first films I ever edited was about D. B. Cooper." I sighed, remembering the hatchet job I'd done simply because I was new and inexperienced and working with the single worst budget ever.

"I don't remember that movie," she said.

I moved to get another box and see if she had any other cool things she'd failed to tell me about. "That's because I never let anyone see it. I was too embarrassed. The only thing worse than a film editor not getting work is a film editor having to put their name on work done badly."

"I bet you're exaggerating." She stretched her five-foot-two frame. I wasn't a tall woman by anyone's standards, but next to my grandma, I looked like a giant. "Well then," she said, "we've had a long day of working. I think we could use a break."

A break to my grandmother usually involved lots of bad-for-you foods and a movie. This was usually appreciated, but after the grueling schedule I'd endured, I really needed to get back home and actually pay attention to my apartment and all the things inside it that had been neglected while I finished *Sliver of Midnight*.

I smiled at her. "I love the idea. You know I do. But I really can't today. We're unpacking, remember?"

She waved my words away. "I have the rest of my life to unpack. Let's watch a movie. We can get back to it when the movie's over."

"I'm not making excuses. You know I love hanging out with you, but I do have to get home sometime before the neighbors call the board of health on me."

"If you had a date, that might be an acceptable reason to bail on an old woman. The cleaning-your-house excuse is just offensive."

A date. As if I had time for dates. What I said instead was, "You make it sound like I never go out. I go out all the time."

"Going out is not the same as dating. Going out is something you can do with people you don't even like. Dating requires emotional connections. The last time you had an emotional connection—that I can remember—was with that Sam kid."

I sighed and pulled her into a hug. "It's so cute you think that Sam and I could be anything long-term." I unlinked our arms and patted her head. "Sam and I were a three-date situation."

I picked up a box of books and headed for some empty shelves. With all the boxes I'd lugged around, plus all the art I'd hung, I could skip the gym for a month.

She let out a puff of exasperation as she followed me. "Do you ever have dates that move past the five-date situation?"

I stopped, rested the box on a shelf, and unpacked with renewed zeal.

I didn't answer.

She shook her little head at me. "And that's why you need a movie day. Romance movies."

"Maybe," I conceded. "But not today. I can't get past the five-date situation if I never make it to the one-date situation. And no one will want to date me if my house smells like garbage that is three weeks past putting out." I kept to myself the fact that my apartment smelled that way only because the garbage really was three weeks past putting out.

"Well, I'm watching a movie." She fished her phone from her pocket, swiped her finger over the screen, and her TV flickered on. A few moments later, the screen was full of flowers and credits, and her surround sound blared music only classic Hollywood knew how to produce.

"What? No reel-to-reel?"

She looked aghast. "You don't play antiques. The film is much too delicate. You of all people should know it's blasphemy to even suggest it." She abandoned the TV and went to the kitchen.

I finished unpacking the books onto her shelf. "I thought you were watching a movie," I called out to her.

"You know it's a long introduction," she called back.

I did know. I knew the moment the music started that she'd put on *My Fair Lady*. The introduction took so long that it was easy to forget you were watching a movie and not just listening to a soundtrack until the movie's dialogue finally kicked in. By then, I'd unpacked four more boxes, and Grandma had exited the kitchen with a smorgasbord of cheeses and flatbreads and cucumber sandwiches—her favorite.

I allowed myself to pause and take some of the food off the tray with a stern, "I really have to leave after I'm done with the boxes in this room."

She waved me off as she focused on the screen playing

out a movie she probably had memorized. "I'm only listening to you if you happen to be telling me you have a date with a prospective new grandson-in-law."

Since the conversation had become cyclical, and neither one of us would back down, I opened another box. A date. When was the last time I'd been on an actual date? The closest I had to any such thing was hijacking Ben's dates over the last two nights. I blinked. "Date?" I blinked again. "Oh, no! Ben!" I jumped to my feet and tugged my phone from my back pocket.

I'd forgotten all about the fact that we'd left Ben's car at the club.

Chapter Eight

"You can't celebrate a crime; that's immoral, eh?"

—Nicole Bonnet, played by Audrey Hepburn
in How to Steal a Million

I told myself I was justified for forgetting the fact that Ben had no vehicle. I'd been pretty out of things last night and even this morning when I'd left Ben's house. But when I woke up this morning, that responsibility should have been my first priority, especially since Ben had left his car at the club in order to come to the studio to help me. Was his car even still there? Was he stranded at home because I'd gone to pick up my car and then ditched in the middle of the night without thinking he'd need a ride to go get his car?

"I'm an idiot," I said out loud as the door to Grandma's back porch shut behind me. I scrolled through my list of contacts until I found his number and hit the call button. The least I could do was offer him a ride to his car.

When he answered the phone, however, my mind went blank.

Thoughts of that picture on his fridge crowded out my words.

"Hello?" Ben said. "Hello? Silvia?"

"Ben!" The word exited my mouth like a bark, but I felt proud I'd managed to get that far. "Hi . . . Ben. I was wondering if you had your car yet. I don't want to leave you stranded any longer than I already have. And sorry it took me so long to get to you about this. You probably already have it taken care of. I crashed pretty hard when I got home."

"You crashed pretty hard when you were at my house, too," he said, though the laughter in his voice indicated he didn't mean anything negative in the comment. "But actually, I've been home all day. Laundry. I'd forgotten my car wasn't in the garage."

"Oh, good!" I said. "I mean, not good that it isn't taken care of, but good that I can still help, since you helped me, and it's my fault your car is currently stranded. I thought maybe we could go get it, and then I could make it up to you with dinner." The words rushed from me like they couldn't exit my mouth fast enough.

Yesterday, I was able to talk to him without feeling tongue-twisted or stomach-knotted. Funny how the discovery of a person's importance in your life changed the way you communicated with them. Learning I was important enough to him to warrant fridge space changed everything for me.

"Dinner. Dinner sounds great . . . except . . ."

He paused long enough to make the hesitation feel like he might have died on the other end of the line. When he finally spoke again, he said, "I kind of have a date tonight."

"Oh." That was not at all what I had expected to hear.

After seeing the picture on his fridge, I had expected our next conversation to be something like planning for our future. I must have been really delirious when I left his house if I'd allowed my imagination to get so carried away. I plopped down on one of my grandma's patio chairs and stared at the koi pond that fringed her back patio. This was definitely a time where feeling stupid was an accurate response. The good news was that Ben had no idea what had been running through my mind and therefore spared me from feeling stupid publicly. It was bad enough I had to feel it privately.

"Right. I bet Alison wouldn't like it if I crashed yet another evening," I said, keeping my voice light and unconcerned.

He didn't deny the date was with Alison. I hadn't realized how much I hoped he would deny it until he didn't.

"But I still need a ride to get my car, if you don't mind," he said after the awkward pause became almost too unbearable. "I really did forget I didn't have it, which would have been less than ideal when it came time for me to leave tonight."

"Of course!" I said. I might not have wanted to facilitate his date with Alison, but I did owe him a solid five-star favor. "I'll be right over."

Discussing my dating life with my grandma had made me realize how much I missed having a dating life. I missed having a significant other who was obligated to go to social events with me, and who would be there when I needed a cuddle, and who would reassure me about all the things going on in my life.

Maybe that was what Grandma meant when she'd said her house felt lonely. Grandpa had died a long time ago.

Maybe here, she was hoping to find the sort of companion-ship that came from living in close proximity to someone else.

I sighed with the ache of realizing I was missing that same thing in my own life. Maybe it was because Ben smelled good, or because he had a picture of us on his fridge that made us look like a couple, or because he'd bailed me out in a way that earned him definite white-knight-on-a-valiant-steed points, but when I thought about missing that special someone in my life, the only face that came to mind to fill the emptiness was Ben's.

And he had a date with his old college girlfriend.

Grandma must have sneaked out onto her back patio, be-cause when I turned to go back into her retirement villa, she stood sentry at the door. "Who were you talking to that could possibly make you sigh like that?" She crossed her arms over her chest, the many bracelets on her wrists clicking together as they settled into place.

"I don't know what you're talking about." If she didn't have to talk to me about being lonely, I didn't have to talk to her about it either.

"That was the sigh of your mother telling you that film school was a waste of your life, the sigh of your father telling you he would not buy you a pony, the sigh of the time Emma went to New York with her dad and your parents said you couldn't go with her. In fact, that might be the biggest sigh I've ever heard you give."

My resolution to not talk to her lacked resolve, because I slumped back in her outdoor armchair and covered my eyes with my phone. "You know that moment when you finally see potential in a relationship, where you think that it could really go places, and that all those places were places you actually wanted to go? I had that moment today."

"That doesn't sound so bad," she said.

"Unfortunately, I also had the moment when the other part of the relationship equation is taking someone else to all those places. Gah! I'm stupid."

I felt her come closer and knew that if I let her, she'd be sitting next to me, settling her arms over me, and offering to hire a hitman for my competition.

Every girl needed a grandma like mine.

Instead of giving in to my self-pity, I stood and gave her a quick hug, stealing some of her energy to fortify myself against the upcoming task. After all, I had told Ben to expect me right away. Making him late for his evening with Alison would be more petty than hiring a hitman. Stepping into Grandma's premade embrace and squeezing her tight was all I had available to me for comfort. "Anyway, I gotta go. Really. I owe someone a favor, and the time to pay the piper has come. Don't worry about me or my sighing habits. I'm fine."

She pulled back so I could see her raised eyebrows of doubt. "Are you?" she asked.

No. "Yes," I said, because really, *no* was the wrong answer, too. It's not like I could feel any keen sense of loss over Ben when it only just barely occurred to me to care about him in a romantic way.

The right to feel badly did not belong to me.

I told myself that the whole way to Ben's house. When he answered the door before I even knocked, and smiled at me like I was the best thing to happen to his day, I realized I was a liar. I had every right to feel as bad as I wanted, because that smile was valuable.

"Look what I can do," Ben said before pulling me in by the shoulders and wrapping his arms around me.

Astonished, it took me long enough to react that Ben had to say, "It's called a hug, Silvia. It works best when you hug back. I thought you'd be proud of me remembering how without any practicing."

I laughed because it made the entire thing so much less uncomfortable. "I'm sorry about your car," I said, since all other comments and questions came with too much real conversation. I didn't have it in me for real conversation.

He shrugged. "As long as the tires weren't stolen while it sat in the parking lot, we're good, right?"

"Right."

I let him into the passenger side before getting in, starting the car, and pulling away from the curb.

"So, tell me more about the screening," he said when it became apparent I'd become a mute.

Of course! We *did* have things to talk about. Glorious, wonderful things! We had what we'd always had.

Movies.

"Seriously, Ben, you've never seen people so pleased with a first cut in your life. And I can't take all the credit for how great it was. The director did everything right. The actors delivered their lines like they were born for them, and the score was sublime. With your help to give it a polish, it was a perfect storm. I was just lucky enough to be the one to report the weather."

"Perfect storms are pretty great," he agreed. "But they lose some of their power if the weather reporter has pictures of Egypt on-screen when the storms are happening in the Bahamas."

He was right, of course. I *had* done my job well. I needed to enjoy that fact. I'd never felt insecure about myself until Dean came into my life. That man would have been the ruin of me if I hadn't finally stood up for myself.

"We should celebrate the great edit caper sometime." I took my eye off the road long enough to flash a wicked grin in his direction. "Have a toast to a perfect crime."

He went quiet, and I realized he must have been thinking about the fact that I'd sort of asked him out earlier. Since I was now chauffeuring him to his car so he could pick up his college girlfriend for their date, hinting at any kind of get-together probably made him uncomfortable. "As friends and partners in crime," I added. Ben had been my friend first, and if he was unavailable any other way, I was still glad to have the friendship part. Me getting carried away in romantic notions was absolutely not his fault. Really, what did a picture on a fridge actually mean?

It meant we were friends and that we'd had fun in Disneyland together once. No big deal.

His voice took on a much lighter tone than it had before. "A celebration sounds like a great idea. Sometime soon. Let's get together soon, okay?"

I agreed and wished I could see his expression. It had been more convenient when he'd been in the back seat of my car and I could see him in the rearview mirror. With him sitting in the passenger seat, and my right eye being nonexistent, it was difficult to turn my head far enough to get more than a glance at him without taking my attention away from the road. If I looked at him fully, we might end up as one of Ben's mortality statistics.

We discussed the movie, a few of the changes I was thinking of making, Dean's work habits, and even some of the possibilities that might have driven Dean to become the man he was.

"It's probably the classic case of social drinking getting out of control," Ben suggested. "A lot of people in our line of work end up with issues. It happens all the time when you work a job that practically requires that form of social networking."

"I don't think that's it," I said. "I think he's hiding out in the bottle to escape personal stuff. Every time he talks about his family or home life, his left cheek twitches and he can never make eye contact. And he never talks about his personal life on purpose. He only does it when someone asks a direct question, or if he's talking to himself about something and has forgotten you're there."

"You're the expert," Ben said.

But I wasn't the expert at all. It was just a guess. Whatever was going on in his personal life that would spiral him to a place where he had no control over himself no matter how high the stakes, no matter how much he needed his sobriety to stay on top of his game, had to be pretty bad.

I sucked in a deep breath and let it out slowly. "I almost feel sorry for him, drinking himself stupid and mean all the time. Top ten reasons why I don't drink—too easy to lose your head. I get why someone would want to numb themselves from reality when life gets too horrible, but better to feel everything than to feel nothing and end up with nothing."

"I know I've told you this before, and I will likely tell you again, but I love that you can hold a person accountable for the things they do and yet still feel compassion for them."

I shook my head. "I don't always. It's easier to see all sides when it's other people. When I'm in the middle of it, my side feels like the only side."

"Like when you refused to believe that Koya was trying to get me fired because she said you and I were too good of friends to not have something going on in the background."

I tsked. "That's different. Everyone knew she was lying. You weren't going to get fired just because one crazy person started making up rumors." I added a laugh, but it sputtered in my throat. She'd mentioned how Ben and I always sat together at meetings, how every project we worked on was a full collaboration between us, but that we left out other members of the staff . . . like her. Suddenly, Koya's stupid assumptions seemed less stupid. Had she seen what I hadn't? Had she ascertained my feelings before I processed them myself?

"Rumors . . ." Ben tapped his fingers on his knee. Even without being able to see, I recognized the low thump from years of working with Ben. He always tapped a pattern of five beats, the first three beats fast and the second two after a brief hesitation. "I heard something interesting about rumors once," he said, as if starting another conversation entirely.

Good. Another conversation would keep me from wondering about how little I knew my own self. If someone as vapid as Koya could see through me enough to know that some part of me preferred Ben to any other person, what did that mean about my own self-awareness? "Oh, yeah?" I said.

"Yeah. Someone once said that every rumor hints at truth."

I felt the blood drain from my face fast enough to leave

me light-headed. Did Ben know what had been running through my mind? Was I that transparent to everyone but me?

When I didn't respond, Ben kept talking. "Well, Mid-Scene is definitely less interesting without you. Or Koya for that matter. She was fired just after you quit."

"Really?" Better. It was better for us to talk about something else, something that didn't make me feel so exposed.

"Yeah. Turns out she was dating Jason." Ben laughed.

"Jason? The squirrely guy from effects?"

"The very same."

I laughed, too. "Well, there's your hint of truth."

We talked about other ways life at Mid-Scene Films had changed since I left the company. The conversation wasn't anything special or amazing, but it was comfortable.

I tried once to bring up the topic that filled my thoughts, but all words regarding my face smiling from his fridge or my sudden awareness of him clogged up my throat and suffocated me until I swallowed them back down again.

Instead, I allowed the conversation to remain casual and comfortable.

At least until the distracting behavior of Ben texting someone on his phone began. I might not have even noticed, since his phone was out of my sight line, except for the buzzing vibration every time a message came back in, and the slight tick noise his phone made when he hit send. He was in the middle of a full-on conversation.

A lot of people turned to their phones for entertainment even in social situations where splitting attention would be considered rude, but Ben was not one of those people. Ben groused about people who refused to be present enough to stick it out through a single conversation without turning to a device for something better. Ben even called people our age the "Something Better Generation." He often shook his head in disgust because no one committed to anything due to the time they spent looking for something better—better outfit, better car, better job, better vacation, better girlfriend or boyfriend, better spouse. "Loyalty," Ben often said, "doesn't happen in a world where the new generation of iPhone is never longer than three months away."

Ben wasn't wrong in that. In a world where people were used to trading up, how was anything supposed to stick?

Now, here he was on his phone, trading up on our conversation for whatever better conversation existed on the other end of those text messages.

I finally stopped talking, not wanting to compete with the digital relationship he considered more important than the real one, and felt grateful he had a date. He didn't seem to notice the silence settling between us but continued on his phone like I was a hired driver and not a friend of more than three years.

He looked up after grumbling at his screen and spoke after a six-minute lag in our conversation. "Let's not get my car just yet."

"What about your date? Is she meeting you later? Do you want me to drop you off somewhere else?" The words probably sounded snippy. I certainly felt snippy, since he'd obviously been talking to Alison or he wouldn't have been able to give me new instructions.

At least, I felt snippy until his hand touched my shoulder like a jolt of electricity. I know he was just trying to get my attention because he was on my blind side, but when I had been thinking of him on a date with someone else, his touch wasn't exactly appreciated.

"My plans just got cancelled. You know how I said our celebration should be soon? Maybe let's make it really soon, as in tonight soon. How about it? Want to go celebrate our great editing caper—is that what you called it?—tonight?"

I frowned at my windshield and tried to make sense of his offer. "What happened to your date?" I shouldn't have asked, but I had to know because this new way of thinking about Ben in terms of something more than a friend was driving me to madness. If his date just had the flu, but they were planning on going out tomorrow night or next weekend, then that meant Ben and I were still living in the friend zone. If she cancelled because she'd decided to run away with the owner of a local food truck, then Ben and I had a new set of possibilities in front of us. "Won't Alison decide to stick the business end of her high-heeled shoe in my heart if I do another hostile takeover of one of your dates?"

"Alison doesn't actually wear heels very often, so I doubt she'd use them in a homicide situation. Did you already make plans for tonight?" He said all of this instead of answering my question.

"I don't have plans." Friend zone it must still be.

"Great! Then let's get celebrating. Where should we go?"

I shrugged and turned toward Santa Monica, because even though I'd shrugged, I'd already decided I wanted ice cream.

It took me several minutes longer to admit that my desired big celebratory plans consisted of frozen dairy. But I finally fessed up by way of suggesting, "How does Three Twins ice cream sound to you?"

He stopped whatever he'd been about to say as a message buzzed on his phone. He hesitated long enough for me to wonder if Alison had texted again and he was trying to figure out how to tell me to turn my car around because *our* plans were now cancelled.

"We could get it and then eat on the beach," he said. "But if you give me any crap over getting a waffle cone instead of a bowl, I will never buy you ice cream again."

This sounded like the Ben I'd always known: the teasing, silly, funny Ben. Friend Ben.

Right.

I knew how to act with Friend Ben. I had to erase the idea of there being any other kind of Ben in my life right out of my head. Making the mistake of believing there might be some other kind of Ben would basically kill the chances of keeping Friend Ben.

I parked on Main Street in front of the Cameron Building that housed the ice cream parlor. I turned the car off and got out, waiting for Ben to get out so I could hit the lock button.

"I haven't been to Three Twins in a long time," he said once we'd both made it to the front. He held the door open for me, and I stepped into the ice cream parlor with Ben right behind me.

I breathed in deep. "I love that smell."

Ben grinned. "Yep. Nothing better than the scent of sugary, creamy calories to make a day brighter."

I ordered the lemon cookie. Ben ordered the mint confetti in a waffle cone. We took our orders outside and walked until we came to a through street that would lead us to Venice Beach. The place was crowded, but what else could be expected

on a Sunday evening? We had to weave around the street per-
formers and skateboarders to get to the sand teeming with kids
gripping bucket handles and shovels or running in and out of
waves and parents taking pictures. There were joggers, skim-
boarders, body surfers, and couples taking leisurely walks.

Like Ben and me.

Only we weren't a real couple. We were just friends. A
lump settled in my stomach at the thought.

As we walked slowly along the sand, Ben lifted his spoon.
"A toast!" he said. "To the worst fraudsters in all America."

I tapped my spoon to his, and we both ate a bite of our
ice cream.

"What makes us the worst fraudsters?" I asked around a
mouthful of lemony happiness. "We got away with the crime.
Doesn't that make us the best?"

"It's not about getting away with it. It's the absurdity of
our crime," Ben confirmed.

"And we're absurd why?"

He gestured with his spoon as if he were a conductor
at an orchestra. "The lack of actual criminal intent. Calling
what we did criminal would be like calling a girl who delivered freshly baked cookies to her neighbor a criminal. Unless
those cookies are laced with cyanide, the criminal intent just
isn't there." He leveled his ice-blue eyes at me and gave me his
best infuriating smirk.

"If we'd been caught, the studios—both of them—would
definitely see criminal intent. We'd both be in a lot of trouble."

"Trouble." He said this with kind of an accent, in a way
that let me know he was quoting a movie, only I couldn't

place which one. The gesture seemed familiar, but the one word was so vague, it was hard to place.

"All right. I give up. What is that from?"

He put his hand to his chest as if mortally wounded. "You don't know? You? The girl who prides herself on knowing lines from movies even if she's only seen them once?"

"You gave me a single word. It's not much to go on." I pointed my spoon at him.

"I gave you a sentence. It's just that there's only one word in that sentence."

I rolled my eye at him. "Your snide-ways look is really annoying." But then I stopped in my tracks, inadvertently kicking sand into my shoes. I definitely should have taken them off once we left the front walk. *Wait Until Dark!*" I said triumphantly, the movie finally coming to me.

Ben stopped walking, too. "Correct! And honestly, I'm surprised you got that one."

"Only because *Wait Until Dark* was one of the most controversial movies for me from film school, no matter how much everyone else loved it."

"You're going to harp about the first and last five minutes of the show, aren't you? They don't even really count." He leaned against one of the graffitied walls to get out of the way of a lady walking her dog, even though dogs weren't allowed on the actual beach.

"As an editor, how can you say that? The first and last five minutes count the most. The first five minutes dictate how you'll feel about the movie while you're watching it. The last five minutes dictate how you'll feel about it after the lights come up." I took a big bite of my lemon cookie ice cream, hoping to chase away how disgruntled that particular film left me feeling.

"Lots of husbands were less than ideal back then. So, at the time, the audience likely didn't think anything of it, and they went home feeling fine."

"Are you kidding? That ending killed my soul."

Ben lounged against the wall with his back against a painting of a woman's hair flowing in the wind. He casually nibbled at his waffle cone and watched me as if I was about to put on a performance.

"Sam in that movie had to be the world's worst husband ever," I said. "He's a creep to Susy in the beginning, and he's a creep to her in the end." I started walking again so my rant had extra energy. Ben pushed off the wall to follow me.

"How does him refusing to enable her make him a creep?"

I whirled on Ben so fast he had to take a step back to avoid getting slapped with my ice cream bowl. "Seriously? Are you seriously asking me that?" I shook my head. "Do I even know you? It makes him a creep because his wife is blind! At the beginning, fine, he's trying to help her understand that she can do things even though she's blind. As a half-blind woman, I can appreciate that. But at the end? Ben! He had to break down the door and step over two dead bodies to get to his blind wife. When he sees her, she's covered in blood and there's glass and all kinds of stuff all over the floor—stuff she wouldn't be able to see because she's blind—and instead of being a good husband and checking to see if any of that blood was hers, he stops the little girl from running to her and says the stupidest thing ever." I lowered my voice to mimic the gruff voice of Efrem Zimbalist Jr. "No. Let her come to us.

You can do it, Susy. You can walk over the debris you can't see to reach me to prove your independence and self-sufficiency. You need to prove to me that you're a strong woman, even though you're blind and single-handedly stopped a drug deal from going down and managed to outsmart three criminals, one of whom was trying to murder you. No, Susy, you walk to me to prove you're strong, because what you've done already isn't enough." I growled in irritation. "She should've walked to him and punched him."

Ben busted up laughing. "Tell me how you really feel. Seriously, Silvia, I think you're holding back."

I bumped him with my shoulder and allowed myself to smile over getting so worked up. "Shut up."

"Terence Young was a good director. Audiences were terrified by that movie. It was totally before its time. The scenes done all in the dark were brilliant. The audience was invested because they had to fill in the darkness with their own imaginations. I liked that movie."

"I'm not saying I didn't like the middle," I said defensively. He gave me his snide-ways look.

"I'm not. I did like it. Everything but the beginning and end. It's an easy fix. Just cut the film where the scenes were stupid and tape them together without her husband's callous cruelty in them. Or you could keep them in and have her husband be stabbed by Alan Arkin's character, and then have Mike survive his stab wound, and then Mike and Susy could run off together and live happily ever after, because even though Mike had a criminal past, he was still the only one who appreciated Susy for the strength she displayed under pressure. Metaphorically speaking, Mike and Susy were the

ones who could see in that film. It was the rest of the characters who were blind."

Ben grinned at me. "An astute observation on vision from
a half-blind woman."

I smiled, too. "I guess it's a bit of a sensitive subject for
me."

"Clearly."

I felt pretty certain there was a pun hidden in that word.

"Anyway, I'm not saying I hate the movie. Audrey's performance in that film was really great, and you're right, the
scenes in the dark allow the audience to use their imaginations
and was a really brave direction for the director to take. The
treatment of Susy just seemed pretty caveman to me—she was
a wife and a woman and a person with a disability."

Ben listened with a half-smile on his face. "That was the
mind-set back then. I like movies like that because they show
us how far we've come. But we've only come so far because
of people like Audrey Hepburn. But you already know that."

"Why should I know that?"

He gave me a long look of disbelief. "Because she was a
huge advocate for growth and change. Because you work in
Hollywood. Because everyone knows that."

I shrugged. "Audrey and I have an interesting relationship.
I don't pry into her life, and I hope she doesn't pry into mine."

Ben had finished his ice cream during my rant. My half-
eaten ice cream melting in the bottom of my bowl showed I'd
been doing a lot of the talking. "Sorry for the rant," I said.

"Don't be. Feisty you is my favorite you."

"I don't think Dean likes feisty me."

"Dean doesn't even like himself right now, or he would show up to the things that matter in his own life."

"Yeah, well, I think he's the sort of guy who could have played the Sam character in *Wait Until Dark*. I don't think he's used to women standing up to him." When Ben gave me a questioning look, I explained how it had become necessary for me to confront Dean outside the reviewing theater.

Ben listened with rapt attention, almost tripping on the uneven sand as I unfolded the story right to the end. "So I'm probably fired," I finished.

"For what? For not letting him steal all the credit for your intellectual property?" Ben shook his head. "Nah. If he tried that, the lawsuit would be all yours. It would be easy to prove the edit is your work. Every person has a style, a brand that they put on their own work. I've seen Dean's work, and his style is so far removed from yours that no one would ever be convinced that it belongs to him. Even the bits I added aren't enough to mark the work as mine. This one was all you. If he tries to fire you, you would have evidence that the action was wrongful."

"I don't think he'll try," I said after a moment. "Not really. I mean, yeah, I joke about it, but he's not always a jerk. I've seen him be decent to people."

"Decent to you?" Ben asked.

"Not yet, but maybe in the future. We'll see what happens."

Ben let out a low chuckle. "There you go. Giving people the benefit of the doubt."

The sky faded from blue to pink as the sun sank into the

sea. I finally finished my ice cream and threw away the cup and spoon.

Ben threw away his napkin as well and wiped his hands together with a dramatic flair. "That was a lot of sugar. And since we both know our chances are one in one thousand, two hundred and eighty-two of dying of diabetes, we should probably get real food for dinner."

"We *both* know that statistic?"

"Don't disappoint me by telling me you didn't know."

We ended up getting gyros at Malaka Brothers, and neither of us commented either way on whether or not it was healthy for us. The food was good, and the company was better. Sometimes that was all that mattered.

And I laughed a lot. I'd forgotten the silliness that came with Ben, the light and easy way we had when we were together. And worse, while I was with him, I forgot we were hanging out in the friend zone. I forgot he was with me only because his previous date had fallen through.

I forgot that I wasn't supposed to imagine anything but Friend Ben for myself.

Which is why, when we reached my car and his phone buzzed with a call coming in and he frowned and said, "Hang on a second. I've gotta get this," and he walked a short ways away to give himself privacy, but I still heard the words, "Hey Alison," I suddenly remembered, and the remembering slit a tiny hole in my heart.

Chapter Nine

*"There can't be any feeling between the
likes of me and the likes of you."*

—Eliza Doolittle, played by Audrey Hepburn in My Fair Lady

I tried not to eavesdrop with an intensity I'd never known before because I was afraid I'd hear a salutation like "I love you" or something similar. It felt wrong to not like Alison. After all, she obviously cared about Ben, which was great for him, and she hadn't been mean to me or done anything that was in any way offensive that I had seen. Okay, so she did dismiss me at the dance club, but she could hardly be blamed for that, since I'd looked like a walking hazmat threat.

"Sorry about that." Ben's voice from behind me startled me out of my wandering thoughts.

I worked at a smile. "No problem. You ready to get your car?"

He frowned. "You okay?"

Dang it! I really wished my face wasn't a window into my thoughts. "Totally okay."

"Totally?"

"Exactly." I nodded my head and said this with a finality that pretty well closed the conversation on my well-being.

We got into the car, and I pulled out onto the road, abandoning Santa Monica for West Hollywood, where Ben's car still sat at Burnout. At least we hoped it still sat there. For all we knew, it had been ransacked or hot-wired and was now sitting at the bottom of a ravine somewhere.

The tone of the drive didn't match the tone of the walk or of dinner. The fun of the evening had been dampened by the gloom of that phone call.

I should have eavesdropped. If he'd ended the call with "I love you," then I'd know, right?

But maybe not. Lots of people didn't end calls with sappy farewells, even if they felt actual love for each other. Though I had the feeling Ben was the sort of guy who would call attention to the sappy. He loved logic and often had to bring me back to it when we'd gotten into deep discussions about things I felt passionately about, but he was also silly and fun in the goofiest way possible. I imagined him to be the sort of guy who would give in to the emotion because it was the logical step to take for someone who felt those emotions.

I breathed a sigh of relief when I turned into the lot at Burnout and saw Ben's car still in the parking lot. Unfortunately, his car wasn't alone.

It had the unwelcome company of a tow-truck driver backing up to the front end of Ben's car.

"No," Ben whispered. "No," he said again, louder. He barely waited for me to come to a complete stop before he practically leapt from his seat in his panic to keep the tow-truck driver away from his car.

Through my windshield, I saw Ben waving his arms and heard him calling out to get the driver's attention.

I turned my car off and hurried to join Ben.

The driver saw Ben and me, visibly sighed, and put his truck in park, though he didn't turn it off. He opened his door and swung his legs to the step as he lumbered down. He approached Ben and me with a look that said our presence was a huge inconvenience.

"I'm going to assume this is your car here?" the driver asked.

"Yes, sir," Ben said.

"You can't park here."

"Funny," Ben said, "because I'm certain that the sign at the entrance to this lot said *parking* on it." Ben flashed an amiable smile that was not returned. When Ben realized the driver didn't feel like participating in jokes, he tried appealing to his better nature. "We never meant the car to be here so long, but we left it because we had a friend leaving the club who needed help getting home. You wouldn't have wanted him on the road intoxicated, would you?"

"Nope, I wouldn't. But the report we got was that this car has been parked here for over thirty-six hours. It doesn't take thirty-six hours to sober up. Sorry, but we're under contract to tow the car. You can pick it up at the impound lot."

Alarmed at this news, I stepped into the conversation. "I really am sorry the car has been here so long. It's my fault we didn't come back for it immediately. I know you've come here all the way from wherever your garage is, and I will happily pay your costs, but towing and impounding really isn't necessary."

He seemed to think over what I'd said before sighing deeply as if I'd caused a great disturbance in his personal life force and finally nodding. "Fine. But there's going to be a fee."

"Absolutely." I nodded, too, just to make sure he knew we were in agreement. I pulled my credit card from my wallet and handed it to him.

"It's my car," Ben protested, fumbling for his wallet. "Why should you pay for it?"

"Because it's my fault you had to leave it here. Let me make this right." I pressed my card toward the tow-truck driver, who seemed confused as to which card to accept until he met my eye.

He took my card and shrugged at Ben. "Sorry, dude. The lady looks more dangerous than you do." He stomped back to the cab of his truck, where he likely had a card reader and the paperwork. Even from where we stood, his muttering about his dad not raising any dummies and that only an idiot argues with women could be heard clearly.

"What did you do to convince him you were dangerous? Cry your blood tears at him while I wasn't looking?" Ben stuffed his card back in his wallet and scowled.

I laughed. "I just gave him a look that let him know I meant business. It's an important look for a woman to master if she's going to work in Hollywood."

"Has working in the industry been so bad?" Ben asked, genuinely interested in my answer, though the crease in his brow indicated he didn't like thinking about what that answer might be.

I shrugged and leaned against my car to wait for the tow-truck driver to come back. "Maybe it's different for actresses. I don't really deal with the casting couch so much as the cold shoulder. Old-school guys like Dean believe if women are going to be involved in production, they belong in wardrobe and makeup or on the secretarial and administrative assistant side of things."

"I'm sorry," he said and leaned against the car alongside me so the length of his body barely brushed against mine as he breathed.

"It's getting better. *Stuff's getting better. Stuff's getting better every day.*" I grinned at him, glad he was on my left so I could actually see him. "Name the film."

He thought about it for a long time—long enough that the tow-truck driver came back with my card and paperwork to be signed. I glanced over the paperwork, noting that the price he charged me was considerably less than I expected, but considerably more than what the work he actually did was worth. The receipt was going to the *Sliver of Midnight* budget for reimbursement. I signed my name in two places, and the driver readjusted his stance in a challenge.

"Well?" he said.

I raised my eyebrows. "Well?"

"I need to see you drive that car off. I'm not an idiot. For all I know it's broken down, and you plan on leaving it here for days longer."

I passed my hand over my eyes and then scrubbed it down my face. This meant any kind of goodbye with Ben would include an audience of the NASCAR hat–wearing variety.

"It's probably for the best since you need to get home and

get some sleep," Ben said to me. He paused like he might say something else, but he only smiled and gave a salute to both me and the tow-truck driver.

He strode purposefully to his car and got in, turning over the engine and giving the tow-truck driver a smirk when the engine revved to life.

"He thinks he's funny, doesn't he?" the driver asked.

"Usually."

Ben waited until I was safely in my car with it started up again before he put his car in gear. Then he waited for me to leave the parking lot first. I turned right and watched out of my rearview mirror as he turned left.

I drove home and thought about my grandmother, holed up in her new villa and watching *My Fair Lady*. The idea of joining her dangled in front of me, but my itchy glass eye reminded me that a good night's rest that didn't involve crashing on someone else's couch first didn't sound all that bad.

Once home, with the door locked, I was back in yoga pants and the T-shirt from my first movie premiere. I brushed my teeth, removed my glass eye, washed it off, and placed it in the music box Emma had bought for me when she'd been in New York several years prior. The box played "Moon River." Emma put a note with it that said, "Everyone says you have Audrey Hepburn's eyes. I figured if you store one of them here at night, it would be like giving it back. xoxo, Emma."

Emma's gift came from the fact that she'd spent more than one sleepless night searching the bathroom, living room, tent, or wherever else I happened to be when I removed my eye and dropped it.

I flipped back my covers and slid inside, prepared to sleep

just as hard as I had the night—well, *morning*—before. Just as my eyelids closed, a text chimed on my phone. I didn't move from the fetal position I'd curled myself into and debated whether or not to reach for my phone to see who would possibly need me when my whole body was in shutdown mode.

The phone won. It usually did, because curiosity was a weakness I couldn't seem to shake.

The text was from Ben, which made my heart do a happy flip. *"The Postman!"*

Ben wasn't much of a digital communicator. Getting a text from him was pretty rare, which was how I'd lost touch with him after moving to Portal Pictures in the first place. Getting a text now, when he was all that filled my head, made me feel so much more than I had a right to. I pulled my thoughts back into alignment, gave an appreciative laugh at his finally figuring out my movie quote, and answered, "Did you know or cheat by looking it up?"

While I waited for him to respond, I rolled over on my back and contemplated what a text from him at that moment meant. Hearing from him now, so soon after seeing him, made me feel like he cared.

But of course Ben cared. He'd helped me move upward in my career because he knew it mattered to me to achieve my goals and dreams, because he knew that Mid-Scene Films was only a tiny stepping-stone along a complicated path.

His understanding of my drive and ambition made him the very best of friends.

How had I not seen him and this possibility with him sooner? The minute I left Mid-Scene Films, I should have been on the phone asking him out.

"I confess," Ben finally wrote back. "I looked it up. Is it bad to admit I haven't seen that one?"

"So many movies . . ." I wrote.

"So little time," Ben responded. We bantered a little while longer before he told me to go to bed and said good night. Even after the conversation ended, I blinked at the screen for the better part of twenty minutes, rereading the messages, looking for . . . what? A sign that I should pry us out of the friend zone? That it was time to act on the stirrings fluttering in my belly? With a roll of my eye, I put the phone down and allowed sleep to take me away.

The next day, Dean showed up at the office before I did, which was something unusual all by itself. But he also had Adam keeping vigil at my office. Adam derailed my intention to stow my purse in my file drawer by insisting that Dean needed to speak with me immediately.

"For what?" I asked. My heartbeat quickened. Had he found out about Ben in the editing room? Did he know?

"He didn't say. But he looks like someone just told him his cat died."

"Dean? With a cat? If Dean had a cat and someone told him it had died, he'd likely pull a few bills from his wallet and thank the person for the favor while asking them to keep it quiet." Knowing my assessment of Dean wasn't exactly fair, I sighed the heavy sigh of steam-rolled hope. "You really don't know what it's about?"

"I'd tell you if I did."

I nodded. Adam probably would tell me. The collateral respect of spending a night in the trenches together formed an unexpected friendship. Even if Adam had slept through half of it, he'd still been there. I left my purse on my desk and followed Adam to Dean's office.

When I knocked on his open door, he glanced up and said to Adam, who stood right behind me, "Did you tell her what I wanted her for?"

I shot a scowl at Adam, who had said he'd tell me if he knew. Clearly, he had known and chosen not to tell me. So much for respect formed in the trenches. He shrugged and gave a smile that might have been an apology, but probably wasn't, as he closed the door to give us some privacy. I squared my shoulders and moved slightly to keep my line of sight clear in the room. So what if Dean knew about Ben? I regretted nothing about my actions regarding *Sliver of Midnight*. I did what had to be done when faced with hard choices.

"Good morning, Dean."

He bristled at my use of his name. He'd become spoiled during my time of deference and apparently hadn't believed that my newfound confidence would last. Even though he still intimidated me, and even though my confidence was all for show, I would not cower again to this man. Talking to Ben reminded me that the days of the casting couch and passed-over women creatives wouldn't, *couldn't*, get better if I gave my permission for everything to continue.

Dean no longer had my permission to walk all over my work.

For all the time I'd spent complaining about Dean Thomas not showing up, I didn't know how I felt about him not continuing the trend if he was going to insist on impromptu meetings first thing in the morning. He was clean-shaven, and his eyes had the desperate but lucid look of a man recently coming off an addiction. Dean muttered a quick, "Have a seat. We have things to talk about."

I sat. No reason to be uncomfortable. Then I waited. Whatever he needed to say would be said when he wanted it said.

"*Sliver of Midnight* is already creating buzz. Just out of the gate and already flying." His dark brow furrowed over his nose as he contemplated what his own words meant. "We only have those few changes to make, and it'll be screen ready. I was wondering what your timeline was regarding this film. We've put all our focus here and need to get going on other films that have been neglected. I let you get your feet wet with this project, but now we need to get serious and get to work."

He let me get my feet wet? The man had dumped me in an ocean and held me under the surface in an attempt to drown me while he stayed in the boat, drinking martinis. "With all due respect, Dean, I am always serious, and I come ready to work every day. That's why *Sliver of Midnight* is all but screen ready."

He cleared his throat, stretched his neck, and adjusted a small stack of papers on his desk. "Right. So, what I need from you is to finish up the film as soon as possible, but I've also uploaded a few scripts to your box. I'd like you to read through them today. We'll be doing them both simultaneously, so work will be double time for us."

"Us?"

He gave one short nod. "Yes. Us. I will be more hands-on going forward."

He still hadn't complimented me or commended me for the work I'd done on *Sliver of Midnight*. I shouldn't have been surprised, but I kept waiting for . . . *something*. Some acknowledgment.

When the silence stretched on without any further comment from Dean, I straightened in my chair and leaned forward. "All right, then. I guess since that's all . . ." Dean still didn't say anything. I stood, taking his silence as my cue to leave.

Before I reached the door, he mumbled. "Danny knows I didn't do much with the last film. He asked me about it when we were alone after the screening. He said I needed to get sober . . . like he knows anything about it."

I stopped. Was I supposed to respond in some way? Was he even talking to me? Or talking to himself?

"Everyone liked working with you," Dean continued.

He had to have been talking to me because I felt certain no one would have ever said they liked working with him. Maybe in the past, he hadn't been so sullen and broody, but lately . . .

"I liked working with them, too," I said, turning to face him.

He met my eye, and though he hadn't been drinking, there was definite unhappiness behind those dark eyes. It made me want to ask what was going on in his life. It made me want to know all the reasons why he had abandoned a career he used to love enough to do well. I didn't ask, and he didn't offer any personal information.

"I'll be to all the meetings with the sound engineers and directors going forward," he said. "My mark will be apparent on any work with my name."

"That sounds like a good idea," I said. I'd almost added the deferential title "sir" but caught myself at the last minute.

"You're not the only one here capable of taping a good movie together."

I stiffened, going from feeling sorry for him to being offended by him in an eyeblink. Taping? Did he think the work an editor did had no real artistic significance? "Why did you hire me, Dean?"

He blinked, obviously not expecting the question. He shrugged. "Because you're qualified. Get to work. Those scripts need to be read. We can talk later." He nodded toward the door, an evident dismissal.

I left, closing his door behind me so I could take a deep breath without him seeing or hearing me. I put my hand on my stomach. What did I feel? Dizzy? Sick? The conversation was strange. His even being in the office so early was strange. It made me wonder exactly what Danny had said to him to make him so evidently agitated. Dean calling me qualified might be the closest he'd ever come to paying me a legitimate compliment.

I raised my eyebrows at Adam. "What was that?"

Adam ran his hand under his nose and shrugged. "Danny really liked your work," he said. "That was pretty much all I could hear through the door. He called you one of the top up-and-coming talents of the film editing world. Told Dean you had a distinctive style. He called your sense of timing *genius.*"

I forgave Adam for his earlier lie of omission. This new information proved too valuable to let a little annoyance get in the way. "Did he really?"

Adam nodded. "At least one of us is having good luck with our chosen careers. The season is almost over for *Gray Skies.* The part I'd originally wanted went to a half-baked actor. But new parts come in all the time, you know. I've seen the scripts. Every one of them has a part where a new character is introduced that I could slide into." He shook his head. "Dean is never going to get me an audition."

"Have you reminded him?" I was glad I wasn't waiting on an audition opportunity for anything. Postproduction had its glitches and inconsistencies, but it was insanely better than trying to schmooze your way into actual acting.

"He said there would be a shot in a few weeks."

I shrugged. "There's your answer then. A few more weeks isn't so long to wait, is it?"

"It's the same thing he told me a few weeks ago." He jiggled his shoulders and turned his back to me.

I headed to my desk. I had scripts to read and a film to finalize.

I texted Ben to tell him the good news.

He texted back a movie quote. "You've been officially labeled a disturber of the peace."

"*Fellowship of the Rings,*" I texted back. "And why am I a disturber of the peace?"

"It's not a bad thing. Anyone who excels at what they do is bound to create buzz—the noise of success. I'm proud of you."

"Thanks," I texted. "I appreciate you."

Ben didn't text back immediately. I reminded myself that it was okay, that we were just friends and he didn't owe me anything as far as consistent communication went. I thought about the call he took from Alison. What if she was the sort of girl who read her boyfriend's texts from other girls. What would she think of my conversations with Ben? I ignored the radio silence from Ben and got back to work.

During the week, I finished the edit on *Sliver of Midnight* and received a personal letter from Danny letting me know how spectacular he thought I was. He even used the word *spectacular*.

The film would be going out to test audiences in the next week. Dean came in every day but never again beat me into the office. He made a point of entering the editing studio as soon as he showed up so we could discuss tactical decisions he'd made during the night, even though he'd told me something entirely different the day before. I wondered if he traded his time at the nightclubs to time rethinking each and every frame of the movie.

Ben finally texted me again, nothing personal, just a movie quote. "Anyone who ever gave you confidence, you owe them a lot."

I gave myself a full day of thinking about it to come up with the movie, but finally gave up and Googled it. The quote came from Holly Golightly in *Breakfast at Tiffany's*— the book, not the movie, which is why I hadn't recognized it. I wasn't sure what Ben meant by it. Did he mean me? Did he mean him? When I texted him back the answer, I asked him why the Audrey Hepburn reference, though I did not ask what he meant by the quote itself.

His response came immediately. "I heard you had an 'eye' for those sorts of quotes. Anyway . . . can I ask you an important question?"

Had I told him I named my eye Audrey? Possibly. When you spend a few years working directly with someone every single day, things are bound to come up in casual conversation.

"Why are you smiling?" Adam asked.

I was in the studio kitchenette making myself a cup of herbal tea. "Just reading a text from a friend—from the guy who helped us get Dean home from the bar, in fact."

"Oh, cool. He seemed like a nice guy. His girlfriend is stunning."

Right. I'd forgotten Adam would have met Alison as well. "She's not his girlfriend," I said.

He popped a pod into the coffee maker. "She looked like it when I saw them together at the movies the other night."

I stiffened as if someone had filled my veins with concrete. "The other night?"

"Over the weekend," he confirmed. "Turns out he and I both live close to that new complex with the VIP theater. I've seen him there before. I just didn't know who he was."

Why did those words "together at the movies" cause a physiological reaction in me?

I'd meant to respond to Ben's request to ask me a question with something clever or smart or at least with another movie quote that might stump him, but the news of Alison still being an active player in his life took the wind out of my sails. I swiped the page of texts off my screen. I didn't want to encroach on another woman's territory, and if we kept playing texting games, the chances of becoming emotionally tangled in him were colossal. A little distance would be good, if only so I didn't get the wrong idea about our friendship again. I was glad to still be friends with Ben, but with all the work I had to do, I could text him later.

Chapter Ten

"Ahh . . . Do I detect a look of disapproval in your eye?
Tough beans, buddy, 'cause that's the way it's going to be."

—Holly Golightly, played by Audrey Hepburn
in Breakfast at Tiffany's

The problem with later was that later didn't come because with two movies, countless commercials, and the extra help the TV series *Gray Skies* demanded from me, I found myself overwhelmed with grueling work. Ben texted again asking how things were going. I shared the excitement and buzz that *Sliver of Midnight* was generating and thanked him over and over for his help, but I didn't allow us to engage in the banter that felt dangerously close to flirting. Instead, I asked how Alison was doing with her career. He responded that she had some good prospects coming up and that she actually wanted to meet up with me sometime and ask for advice. The conversation was enough to assure me that he really was still seeing her, which meant I had to forget how good he smelled.

I had a career. Ben had a girlfriend.

It was just that traces of his scent filtered to me from the weirdest places. And I made the unfortunate discovery that trying to not think about someone meant you had to think about them quite a lot to continually remind yourself not to think about them.

Over the next two months, *Sliver of Midnight* became a phenomenon, and every compliment that came my way made me twinge with guilt that no one would ever know that someone else spent an entire night of his life working on it as well.

Because the test audiences loved *Sliver of Midnight*, and because a lot of what they loved were things Ben had taught me, even if they weren't things he did directly, it meant that I thought about Ben all the time. The press junket went off so well, it almost felt scripted. The press had nothing but glowing reviews and contagious excitement, and all the buzz would be worth a lot in advertising as the trailers hit theaters. The first reviews coming in from the press directed a message to the Academy to prepare to give all the awards to this one flawless film.

The film I had been a part of creating had been declared flawless. So why wasn't I happier?

It was while at my grandma's villa when my obsession finally found a voice.

"Who is he?" she asked.

"Who is who?" I didn't look up from my laptop where I was scrolling through toothpaste options. She'd been tired a lot lately, so we'd switched our plans from going out to the farmer's market to staying inside, watching a movie, and doing her grocery shopping online together. For an extra ten dollars, we could even get the groceries delivered.

She snapped my laptop screen closed and forced me to

look at her. "Who is the reason for you sighing like an asthmatic?"

I lifted my screen and shook my head. "There's no sighing here. We're deciding between the ultra-white and the gingivitis fighter, though I don't know if you should trust a toothpaste tube with muscles."

"You know what I mean." Her usually spiky white hair laid flat over her round head. She'd been so tired she hadn't wanted to bother with her hair or her makeup. When I tried to pry information about her health out of her, she waved me off with a *psh* noise and said, "A woman of my age has a right to be tired every now and again!"

My phone buzzed. Grandma snatched it up before I could. "Is the person texting you the one making you sigh?"

Her question sucked another sigh from me. How did she know stuff? Did they teach emotional-information extraction at Grandma School or something? I didn't bother trying to take my phone back, not wanting to wrestle an old woman, especially when she would read my texts whether or not I granted her permission.

The truth was that Ben had been texting all day to say he'd heard the latest review of the movie, and he wanted to tell me how proud I'd made him. He also wanted to set up a meeting between Alison and me.

"How about tomorrow? Would you be able to meet tomorrow?" was his texted request on the screen, along with my response of, "I'm helping my grandma tomorrow night."

Grandma read the messages and then turned to me with her getting-into-trouble smile. She started typing on my phone.

I made a grab for it, but she evaded my reach and kept

typing. "Grandma!" I wailed as she stabbed her finger onto the screen with a finality that proved whatever she'd written had been sent.

I narrowed my eye at her. "Why do I have the feeling that I really regret teaching you how to text?"

She shrugged and handed me back my phone. I read her message: "But I'd be happy to have some company. We're doing charity work. Want to come?"

"Grandma!" No matter how much angst I put into my scolding, the woman refused to look guilty. "Why would you do that?"

"To find out who we were dealing with. A man not willing to do charity work is a man not worth sighing over."

The phone buzzed in my hand with Ben's response.

If anything, the noise made me glare even harder and her grin even wider.

"Don't you want to know what his answer is?" she asked.

"No! He wants to bring his girlfriend over so we can talk shop. You've just invited both of them to join us tomorrow."

Her smile dropped. "Guess I should've scrolled up on that conversation."

"You think?"

"Don't get mad. At least I'm admitting my error."

Unwilling to let my current grumbly mood go, I read the rest of Ben's message. "Charity sounds awesome. I'm sure Alison would agree, especially since she's so excited to meet the woman responsible for the movie that's Hollywood's new favorite thing. What do you want us to do? Where should we meet?"

"Well," I said to Grandma with another sigh and genuinely feeling as asthmatic as she'd accused me of being, "at least now you have many hands to make light work for your charity tomorrow." I read her the message and then waited for her to tell me how to respond. Like it or not, Ben was bringing his girlfriend to hang out with me. I would have brewed up a monster illness to excuse my absence from the whole mess, except that it was for charity, and Grandma had been acting so strange lately that the last thing I wanted was to leave her alone to work on a project she'd depended on me for help.

She shifted as if she wished she could brew up her own monster illness to excuse herself from my presence. "Um . . ." she began. "It's not exactly *work*. It's more of a charity *ball*. A masquerade ball, to be exact. I've already got your costume, so you won't have to worry about that part."

"A ball? A masquerade ball?" Grandma hated it when I repeated her like some kind of puppet, but the words had to be repeated to make sure I understood them properly.

She nodded, her apology evident in the slump of her shoulders and her sad eyes. "After we talked a while back, I thought about Audrey and what I could do to be more like the woman I admired. So I joined the Audrey Hepburn Society."

"You joined a fan club?" I tried to keep the worry out of my voice, but her announcement made me want to call my mom for advice on how to handle all the odd things going on with Grandma: the move, how exhausted she got when we did activities together, and now joining a fan club?

"No!" Some of the spark and fire returned to her eyes. "I joined the *Society*. It's not the same thing at all. I made a donation to UNICEF, and if the donation is large enough, you get to be a member of the Audrey Hepburn Society."

I narrowed my eyes at her. Grandma easily qualified as

a wild card. No one ever knew what she planned to do next. "How much of a donation?"

She smiled, showing off the white of her flawless dentures. "Let's just say I'm a Guardian now. So are you. I would've joined the inner circle with my donation, but I decided to split it and do half in your name. Merry Christmas."

"It's not Christmas."

"Oh. Well, then . . . happy birthday."

"It's not my birthday." I tried to put us back on track. "I am gathering by your incredibly evasive answers that you spent a lot of money with this endeavor."

"Of course not."

I breathed a sigh of relief.

"I *invested* a lot of money."

Did a sigh of relief come with a refund? "Grandma! Can you afford to be doing stuff like that? Please don't tell me you just blew your entire retirement."

"What? Afraid for your inheritance?"

"Don't get sassy!" I repeated the phrase I'd heard from her since I was a child. "You know I don't care about an inheritance. I care about your future. Your quality of life. Grandma, you mean everything to me. If something happened to you, I would never recover."

She put her soft, wrinkled hand on my cheek. "I'm fine, Silvia. I have enough to live quite extravagantly for at least a decade now that I've sold my house and moved into a space that's more reasonable."

"What if you live longer than a decade?" A sense of panic welled up in me. What if she *didn't* last longer than another decade? The idea of losing her so soon filled my heart with stone.

"Well, if that's the case, I'll simply live slightly less extravagantly. All right?" She cupped my chin and forced me to meet her gaze. "All right?"

"All right."

"Good. And don't go telling your parents about any of this. They won't understand. They'll think I've lost it and declare me incompetent and put a stop to my plans of extravagance before I can even start them."

"We wouldn't want that," I said. She seemed so confident and rational. Maybe I wouldn't call my mom after all.

"Of course not. Especially since I've already bought us a table to the masquerade ball."

Right. The ball. The one she had inadvertently invited Ben and his girlfriend to attend. In my worry over her, her possible bankruptcy, and worse, her possible nonexistence in my life, I'd forgotten the problem at hand. "So, let me get this straight. You bought a table? To a ball? And you don't already have the spots filled for that table?"

"We are attending a charity ball, after all. Every penny will go to charity. I bought a whole table because being charitable means giving more than you need to. And while the table *wasn't* full, if your friend brings a date and you bring a date, it will be. It's a masquerade. You'll all need costumes. Well, you won't. As I said, I have one for you already."

"How many people can sit at this table?"

"Ten."

I frowned. "So who else is coming?

Was that a blush crawling up her neckline? "I have friends. I'd better have friends, or who's going to help carry my casket when I die? I need at least six."

"Grandma!" My frown deepened. When had her humor become so dark? I, for one, didn't find it at all funny.

She must have found it hilarious, because she laughed. But then she sobered. "I'm sorry about butting into the situation with your boy there. I won't do it again."

I absolutely did not believe that promise as far as long-term actions were concerned, but at least she was likely to behave for the short term. "It's okay. You didn't know. But now I have to respond to him. Do you really have room for his spare?" I asked.

"Only if you're bringing a date, too. He can't come with a plus-one if you're coming alone."

I considered my options before answering. "I'll find a date. I might as well get this meeting over with sooner rather than later, since he's determined she and I meet up sometime. If we're all wearing masks, maybe it'll be easier."

She shot me a look of sympathy and apologized again. I waved her off and smiled. The whole conversation reminded me that she might not be around in another decade. That sobering thought made the current moment more meaningful and the issue with Ben less horrible.

I texted Ben with the information regarding the ball, the need for costumes, and that, yes, Alison was also invited. His responses were all generally excited—excited to see me, excited to do something so fun, excited for my movie that was doing so well, excited Alison would finally get to meet with me.

Excited.

I was not excited.

Because I had to find a date, and the only man I wanted to go to a ball with was the one who was going with someone else.

Chapter Eleven

*"At midnight, I'll turn into a pumpkin
and drive away in my glass slipper."*

—Princess Ann, played by Audrey Hepburn *in* Roman Holiday

Morning came, and I still didn't have a date. Every person who could possibly work as a date for my current situation was either in another relationship or would get the wrong idea and think I wanted a relationship. The one person I would have called for a situation like this was Ben. He was already going. And he was bringing a date.

Grandma insisted I had to have a date, too, but why? Bringing a guy wouldn't get me a guy, so if that was her plan, she was wrong. Besides, I didn't want just any guy. I wanted one who fit with me. It seemed far better to take my time and continue to be picky than end up in a situation that was not ideal.

To fulfill Grandma's stipulation and satisfy my own sense of self, I decided she would be my date. I didn't want a fake date, and I couldn't imagine anyone I'd rather go with.

Ben called that afternoon in a panic. He called, not texted, which only proved how desperate he really was. "I don't know what to do about a costume. I don't have anything that would be appropriate," he said before I'd even finished saying hello. "I scoured the internet about masquerade balls, and nothing I have will work." Ben, who normally acted so casual about everything, was practically shouting into the phone.

"Just wear a suit and go to the costume emporium in East Hollywood and buy a mask that covers half your face. I doubt they cost more than ten dollars," I said, checking my watch. Grandma had requested I arrive at her house early so she could dress me. She apparently wanted to make up for never having had a Barbie as a child. I was already running late.

"That's just it," Ben said. "I don't own a suit."

"Yes, you do," I argued. "Every guy owns a suit. How do you go to premieres if you don't have a suit?"

"You know where I work. Our movie premieres involve balloons and hot dogs, not caviar and paparazzi."

"Oh." I thought about it for a moment before realizing that my grandmother would have something. She'd worked in movies for a lot of years and had become fluent in all kinds of disciplines. Her specialty was makeup, but she understood hair and wardrobe as well. And she'd loved costume parties back when Grandpa was alive. Certainly she'd have something that would work for Ben. And it gave me an excuse to see him alone for a few minutes. Before I offered any solution, I asked, "Is Alison having a similar problem?

"Alison? No. She was born and bred for this sort of thing. She probably has a dozen choices. I can come either as Captain America or Darth Vader."

"I think I have a solution," I finally said. "Meet me, and I'll get you set up."

I texted him my grandma's address and then rushed off to her house. I called her on the way to let her know of Ben's emergency.

"What are his measurements?" she asked.

That unexpected twist in the conversation surprised me. Even more unexpected to me was the fact that I knew Ben's measurements. We'd done company shirts with the Mid-Scene logo on them, and Ben decided he wanted to also order a pair of jogging pants with the same logo sewn into the front pocket.

I still remembered the numbers.

And I never remembered numbers.

But, as Emma had pointed out to me before, I also remembered his address and his phone number and all sorts of other strange Ben-details that I didn't have the first clue about for anyone else.

Ben showed up at Grandma's door only a few steps after me. He wore the very same company T-shirt and jogging pants that had reminded me how I knew the guy's measurements.

When she swept open the door and saw us both standing on the porch, her eyebrows lifted. She sized him up, which could have been bad since my grandmother had no filter, but she didn't say anything aside from, "How nice! You're both here!"

She ushered us into the house and closed the door behind us. After introductions were over, she tossed Ben a wink. "You're lucky I unpacked the costume box the other day. I have just the right costume to fit you."

From the look on his face, Ben didn't count this as good luck. When I'd told him I could help him, he apparently didn't realize that the help would come from my geriatric grandmother.

"Before I get your costumes—Silvia, show Ben where the guest bathroom is so he knows where he can get ready. You can use my room."

"You know," he whispered as I led him down the hall, "when you asked me to help with volunteer work, I thought we might be serving in a soup kitchen, not sipping soup at a ball." Ben had the look of a man clearly wishing he'd made other plans for the day. "I looked up this particular event, too. It's really expensive, so I want to pay for our tickets."

I snorted at that. "What? And have my grandma put you on her hit list? That's a really bad idea. She's determined she's doing this. Plus she bought these tickets a while ago and was glad to have done it, whether they went to use or not."

"Okay, fine, but you said you could help me, and 'costume box at Grandma's house' doesn't sound any better than my Captain America cosplay. I don't know how I feel about going to this thing dressed in some mothball-covered housecoat that came straight out of last century's least-attractive decade."

"Which decade was that?" I asked. I looked over my shoulder to make sure Grandma couldn't hear.

"The undisputed seventies." He gave me a look that said if I dared to dispute him, our friendship would be over. Since I agreed, our friendship remained intact. "Do you know that the chances of dying from mothball poisoning is one in one hundred and thirty?" he asked.

I stopped in the hall to give him the stink eye. "There is no way that's true. You made that up."

"No, I didn't. The odds of dying in an accidental toxic poisoning really are one in one hundred and thirty. I am sure mothballs play into that somewhere."

I grunted at him and headed back down the hall. "How am I supposed to take you seriously if you always skew the statistics?"

"That's what statistics are: skewed numbers that suit the needs of the person quoting them."

"We don't even know that mothballs are poisonous or toxic."

"They are to the moths, which gives me enough proof on which to base an opinion. But all of this is beside the point—the point is that we need clothing that makes sense to wear to a charity ball."

I directed him to the left. "You don't need to worry about that. My grandmother's costumes aren't anything like other grandmother's costumes. She spent a lot of money buying replicas so that our Halloween costumes were fun and realistic and nice. People always gave me two or three extra pieces of candy when I went trick-or-treating in a costume supplied by Grandma. It was like winning a prize at every house. Anyway, trust me; if my grandmother says she has costumes that will work for this, she does. And since this whole ball is her deal, if she puts you in princess footie pajamas and calls it your costume, you will wear it and smile while you do it."

He shot me a look of alarm that gave me a twinge of happiness. Of course Grandma would get him a decent costume. I only mentioned the footie pajamas because he was bringing a date that wasn't—and couldn't be—me. I took revenge where I could get it, and I refused to feel evil about it.

Well, maybe only a little evil.

I opened the door to the guest room, the one I decorated to suit my tastes since, out of everyone in Grandma's social circle, it seemed most likely I would be the one spending time sleeping over. "The hall bathroom is adjoining."

He poked his head into the room before pulling back and looking at me. "Are you sure about this?"

"Whatever she brings will be great. Or would you rather tap out of this one, call Alison to cancel, and tell my grandma 'no, thanks'? Because you don't have to go, Ben. We were planning on it being just her and me in the beginning anyway."

He squared his shoulders and lifted his chin. "No. I just . . . no. Of course, I'm not backing out. I just don't want to embarrass you."

Sincerity. His eyes delivered a message of nothing but sincerity. Was he really worried about looking bad in front of me? We'd worked too long together and seen too much of each other in real life to feel embarrassed.

"Text me if you get too weirded out. But I promise, she knows what she's doing. We'll be fine." I left him standing in the doorway, a perplexed look in his eyes that I couldn't seem to interpret.

Grandma met me in the hall and swished me into her room. She held two suit bags on cedar hangers. "He's very handsome, isn't he?"

"Yes. He is." Why deny what she could clearly see for herself? She could probably see it even better than I could, since she had the advantage of not being half-blind.

"Those blue eyes. Startling, aren't they?"

"Yes. They are."

"Here's your costume. I'll come back and help you with it in a moment." She laid one suit bag on the bed, but she kept the other draped over her arm. "Let me just take this to your boyfriend."

"He's not my—"

She waved me off and left. My phone buzzed in my pocket. I pulled it out and read a text that had come from Ben.

"Did you know there is a one in one hundred thousand chance that you'll die at a dance party?"

"This sounds like you trying to bail on this activity," I wrote back.

"Not at all. Just wanted to make sure you know what we're getting into."

I laughed and unzipped the bag on the bed and pulled out a long, sleeveless, black evening gown. A necklace of four strands of pearls clasped together by a diamond pendant hung at the neck. Long black evening gloves had been carefully folded over the hanger, but as I held the dress up to my frame, the gloves slipped to the floor.

So, Audrey, I thought. *We meet again.* She seemed to be everywhere I turned lately. She showed up in my conversations with the director, in his card to me, in my conversations with Grandma, the donation given in my name, and now in this costume Grandma expected me to wear. Why? Wasn't it enough I named my eye after my cancer compatriot? Why was she suddenly everywhere?

It made me nervous, uncomfortable in that way that fears from childhood usually were. Of course, fearing that her name was a harbinger of some phantasm of disease was ridiculous, I knew that. But the visceral shiver of my nerves didn't care about logic.

If I dressed like her, would the cancer come back?

"Stop being stupid, Silvia," I said out loud.

"Don't call my favorite granddaughter names!" Grandma returned, her pragmatic realism interrupting my irrational internal struggle.

I startled out of my dark thoughts and almost dropped the dress. "Don't you have any other costume for me?" I asked, barely preventing the dress from hitting the floor.

"Of course I do, but do you really want to make an old woman sad when she's the one who bought your tickets to the ball in the first place?"

"Ouch. I know I said I needed a vacation, but a guilt trip was not what I had in mind." Without further argument, I went to her personal bathroom, dress in tow.

While I was stepping into the dress, Grandma tucked a pair of heels just inside the door. She would be disappointed, because I had no intention of switching out my black ballet flats for heels.

After zipping up the dress and clasping the necklace at my throat, I turned and studied my image in the mirror. It could have been Audrey Hepburn's ghost staring back at me.

"I'm sorry about the cancer," I said to the mirror and then shook myself. Gah! That was not Audrey in the mirror. It was me. Just me.

I opened the bathroom door and stepped into the bedroom so Grandma could see what she'd done to me.

She put a hand to her chest and fell back a step. "Oh!"

she exclaimed. "You look . . ." She didn't finish. She didn't say
"You look just like her" or declare Audrey could have been
my sister. Instead, she walked over to me, cupped my chin in
her soft hand, and said, "You are lovely."

I suddenly understood why the comment meant so much
to my grandmother when Audrey had said those words to
her. Something about the words "You are lovely" filled a person with more than just compliments on an appearance. It
was commentary on a heart, on a soul, on a person. Love,
light, and goodness were all the things that made up the word
lovely.

She blinked several times to clear the shine from her eyes
and clapped her hands together. "Well, let's get your makeup
done."

Since Grandma had worked for her entire lifetime as a
makeup artist in Hollywood, I was in good hands. It didn't
matter what kind of makeup job became necessary, Grandma
knew how to make it happen. Needed to look bruised and
beaten? Done. Needed to look like your cheek had been
ripped off by something with claws? Done. Needed to look
like the best actress to have ever appeared in Hollywood?

"Done," Grandma declared and whirled me around on
her spinning stool to see the finished product in the mirror.

She'd done my hair, too, and though hair wasn't her
specialty, no one would've known she hadn't been the actual
hairstylist on set for *Breakfast at Tiffany's*. Grandma was just
that good. "It's . . ."

"Perfect," she finished.

I stood and hugged her, and then stepped into my black
ballet flats.

"What? No. You need to wear the heels." Grandma actually looked distraught.

"Grandma, you've seen how I walk, which means you know why I don't wear heels. Have you ever seen a woman wearing heels who wobbles and walks on the side of her foot? I'm that times ten. So it'll be a hard pass on the public disgrace of this baby giraffe."

"The heels look nice," Grandma insisted.

"So do the flats."

She gave up the fight with a harrumph and a declaration that she needed to get ready, too. I had my mouth open to ask if she needed help when her doorbell rang. I changed my question to, "Are you expecting someone?"

A goofy smile filled her face. "That'll be Walt. Will you let him in and make sure he's comfortable?"

"Sure?" I hadn't meant for the word to come out as a question. "Who's Walt?"

"He's my date."

What did she say? "Date?" I repeated out loud.

"Yes. Date. We've been seeing each other for a while now. A few months. He lives in the villa next to mine."

All the things that hadn't made sense clicked into place. There was a boyfriend—one she liked well enough to move closer to. "You didn't tell me?"

She pointed at her bedroom door. "When were you going to tell me about the beautiful boy in the guest bathroom?"

"That's different. He has a girlfriend."

The doorbell rang again. She gave me a pointed look.

"Fine. I'm going. But we *will* be talking about this." Even

Grandma had a date. How lame did that make me that I didn't?

I met Ben in the hall. He was in a coat and tails with a cape fastened by a silver sword at his throat. His black-and-silver face mask covered only his eyes. I stared at his mouth. My stomach flipped. Had anything ever looked so fine on any man?

"Did you know the doorbell's ringing?" He wasn't really looking at me, pointing instead in the direction of the doorway, and when he turned to face me, he exhaled a breath that almost sounded like a whimper. "Wow. Just wow."

"I was thinking the same thing about you." I did a half turn, needing to look away from him for a moment to keep myself from staring too hard. I turned back once I felt I had enough control. "Do you think it's too much?"

"I think I've never seen anything more perfect in my life." His intense gaze locked me into place and seared through me. Though neither of us moved, it felt like the distance between us was closing in micro-shifts.

"Ben," I started to say.

Whatever might have come after was anyone's guess, since we were interrupted by the doorbell ringing a third time. Apparently, Walt didn't like to be kept waiting.

I opened the door to find I had to crane my neck back to look up to see the shiny-headed bald man named Walt—my grandmother's boyfriend. He also wore a black tuxedo like Ben, only without tails. His jacket had silver piping that swirled through the oversized cuffs of his sleeves, and his mask made him look like a pirate king. I had to give the guy credit. It was a costume Grandma would approve of.

I barely knew what to say to him and felt a little shell-shocked over the fact that he was actually dating my grandmother. It made sense, but it also hurt my feelings at the same time.

Walt's smile immediately put me at ease. He shook hands with both Ben and me, then walked around the living room, commenting on all the family pictures, art, and book titles. He asked me a zillion and thirteen questions about myself, my job, my family, Ben, Ben's job, Ben's family. He was enormously entertaining.

By the time Grandma showed up, Walt had pretty well wrung us dry of information—nearly enough to steal our identities later if things didn't work out between him and Grandma. But he gave information, too. He was a retired engineer, had three kids, four grandkids, and a rabbit named Bunny Foo Foo that he liked to take for walks so she could get her exercise.

Ben laughed at the Foo Foo part. I laughed imagining a rabbit on a leash.

"Why, don't you look beautiful, Ms. Bradshaw?" Walt said, bending low over her hand.

He wasn't lying. Grandma wore a beaded, black-and-white, formfitting gown, and, for an old lady, her form was still respectable.

His black gloves made the way he took her white-gloved hand appear to be the most elegant thing I'd ever seen. And after the rigorous question-and-answer scenario we'd been through, I found I quite liked the tall, bald man.

Grandma giggled and even blushed, which was adorable. So much so that I couldn't even be mad at her for keeping this part of her life private until now. She informed us that the other members of our dinner party would be meeting us at the ball, settled her black-and-white mask on her face, handed me a mask with cutouts shaped vaguely like cat eyes, and asked if we were ready to go.

Ben and I looked at each other as if waiting for the other to say something. When it became apparent he wasn't going to speak first, I spoke for him. "Ben still has to pick up his date, so he'll be meeting us over there as well. If you don't mind, I can drive with you two, but if you don't want a third wheel, I can take my own car. It's no problem."

Ben narrowed his eyes at me as I spoke. Grandma did, too. Walt took a step back in an obvious show of wanting to be excluded from whatever dialogue brewed under the surface.

Ben pulled his gaze from mine and finally said, "Alison is driving herself to the ball. If you two would prefer some privacy, I'd be happy to bring Silvia."

Grandma didn't let the conversation go that easily. "You said you were going to get a date!" she said to me.

"I thought I did. I figured you could be my date. How was I supposed to know you had one already?" I smiled at Walt so he knew I approved and didn't feel like he was being slammed in any way. My grandpa had been gone a long time—long enough that the only position this new man usurped was mine. And even though a part of me felt waspish over it, I tried to see things from Grandma's point of view. She'd been alone for a lot of years; she had to crave companionship. If I craved it and wanted it, why shouldn't she?

Grandma sniffed her disdain at my datelessness, but she must have decided now was not the time to get into it. She turned her attention to Ben. "We're a little old—not a lot, mind you—and our eyes aren't as good at night. Would you mind driving all of us?"

Ben, of course, agreed. I wasn't sure if this irritated me or if I felt relieved from not having to make small talk on the way. Regardless, we made our way out to Ben's car so we could drive together to what my grandmother referred to as a volunteer opportunity.

I'd never gone to a volunteer opportunity in a gown before.

At the car, I moved to take my place in the back seat with Grandma. The idea of her sitting next to Walt, snuggling like a couple of teenagers, gave me anxiety, but the idea of sitting in front with Ben gave me even more anxiety. As I moved toward the door, Ben gave me a strange look and motioned his head towards the front, where he'd opened the door and stood waiting for me to get in.

Grandma had her eyebrows raised above her mask and her lips pursed in that wry look she gave instead of a verbal reprimand. Walt chuckled at Grandma's sass. He obviously thought it was cute to see her getting bossy.

I cleared my throat and stepped up to the door Ben held open for me.

"Miss Hepburn." Ben inclined his head in deference.

He removed his mask to drive, and I kept mine in my lap. The car ride was accompanied by the animated back seat chatter of Grandma and Walt talking about a play they'd both seen together. Grandma was going to plays?

"So," Ben interrupted the back seat banter. "This is atypical of the usual volunteer work, isn't it? Going to a ball, I mean."

"Sometimes volunteering means cleaning out messes or

organizing supplies," Grandma answered. "And sometimes it means showing up to fundraising events so people see you there. Fundraising events are like raising your hand in agreement. The more people who raise their hands, the more people will want to join them. We are to be counted today so people know we can be counted *on* for tomorrow."

"Fair enough," Ben said, and the conversation continued with Ben feeling comfortable enough to join in. He missed some very easy spots where he could have told my grandma and her boyfriend apparent the statistical chances of dying at a dance party, probably figuring that people as old as Walt and Grandma didn't need mortality reminders. I wanted to ask why Alison decided to drive separately, but how did a person start that conversation without causing a commotion?

As I walked behind my grandmother and her date along the red carpet to the hotel entrance, people stopped and stared. Then whispered. Then asked if they could have their picture taken with me.

Grandma and Walt went on ahead, unaware that I'd been detained.

"You look just like her."

"What a striking resemblance."

"Where did you get such a perfect replica costume?"

These were the most common phrases uttered by the people crowding around me. It was almost like I'd become the event photo op. Ben stood to the side and kept watch. He knew I had difficulty with people claustrophobia and was watching for the signs. It hurt my heart that he knew such personal things about me when we couldn't *be* personal.

As the crowd closed in, my heart rate spiked and my

breathing became ragged as I tried to smile for the many flashes of light blinding my eye and the many different scents of perfume engulfed me as women I didn't know hugged me and thanked me. My confusion over all the attention didn't help matters any.

Once we were able to disentangle ourselves from the front-door crowds, we entered the event ballroom. Items for the silent auction lined the walls in elegant displays. Life-sized pictures of Audrey were strategically placed around the room, standing tall as if keeping watch over the proceedings of the event.

We made our way to the table reserved in Grandma's name just as the emcee stepped up to the microphone. Alison hadn't arrived yet.

"What took you so long?" Grandma whispered to me. "I thought you'd decided not to come in after all."

"People kept wanting to get pictures with me," I whispered back.

She smiled. "Who could blame them? Where's your mask?"

I glanced around as if it would magically appear on my plate. "I must have left it in the car."

She patted my hand. "It's not like you need it," she whispered, and then turned her attention up front.

It was a good ten minutes into the emcee's opening announcements before my heartbeat regulated itself and my breathing became steady and normal. The incident confirmed to me that stardom would not suit me at all. All those people pressing in, wanting to take a piece of you away with them—it would frighten any introvert.

As the thought crossed my mind, the emcee's words

finally broke through my personal thoughts. "Audrey's incredibly reserved nature made it very hard for her to be the center of attention, and so it makes sense that she spent her final years putting the spotlight on others, taking care of the needs of people who had no voice of their own yet."

A UNICEF video began with children singing in a language I didn't understand. The voice-over of Audrey Hepburn came on at the same time images of children in third-world countries being cared for by Audrey flashed across the screen. "I think I've been terribly privileged," she said. "And it's logical that somebody who's privileged should do something for those who are not."

I felt suspended in my seat at the sound of her voice. I'd seen her movies, but I'd never heard her voice when she was just being herself. With every word she spoke, I felt myself changing, convinced of the plight of the world's children, convinced I had a role in helping those children. Audrey said she felt she didn't have much to give, but that everyone had something they could do or offer. The call to action rose up in my soul, vibrated through my heart, and left me contemplative when she ended with, "There cannot be enough voices. If I can be one more and speak up for one child, it's worthwhile."

The short video reached deeply into me, so that when the emcee returned to the mic, I paid full attention, wanting to know more about the charity and my part in it. Grandma's decision to make donations and buy a table to this dinner no longer seemed silly, and suddenly, though I was sure she spent a lot, her donation didn't seem like nearly enough, because none of it came from me. I didn't even notice when Ben's date slipped into her seat, and I startled when I reached for my water glass and saw Alison sitting beside Ben. Her rich blue mask glittered, and the feathers along the top curled over her forehead. The gown she wore was similar to the one in the club, but instead of being short and meant for dancing, this one was long and meant for fine dining. She looked very pretty.

Awards were given throughout the whole meal and dessert, leaving little time for small talk. Which was fine with me, since Grandma and Walt only had eyes for each other, and I didn't know *how* to talk to Alison and Ben. People were applauded, heroic stories were told, and then we were invited to enjoy the dance, indulge in the chocolate bar, and bid generously in the silent auction. Grandma and Walt beelined it to the dance floor to show off the moves of a couple who grew up in the heyday of great dancing.

Alison tugged Ben's hand and whispered something to him, likely asking him to dance. Not sure what else to do with myself, I went to the displays. Or more specifically, I went to the life-size portraits of Audrey that stood between the displays. Black, carved wood framed each portrait in classic elegance. I stopped in front of one that could have been a mirror. The Audrey in the picture stood about as tall as I did. She wore the same sort of dress, had her hair done in the same way, wore a similar necklace. Even her makeup was perfectly identical in a way that only a master makeup artist could have managed. A cold chill shivered through me at the memory of lying in that hospital bed alone in the dark, terrified of the cancer monster lurking in the shadows.

That monster got part of me when they took my eye.

They got her, too—all of her. Why did it frighten me? Why did learning about Audrey make me uncomfortable? Why did I always feel such a loss when I thought of her as a person and not as a character in a movie? Surely a grown woman could see enough reason to know that what happened to Audrey and what happened to me had no link at all aside from bad luck and timing.

Surely.

But my logic did nothing to quiet my fear.

I imagined, while gazing at the portrait, all the wasted years where the knowledge of Audrey could have been mine. For the first time in my life, I was sorry I'd held Audrey at arm's length. From everything I'd heard about her tonight, I realized that Audrey Hepburn's life could have been my own personal blueprint for how to be a fully-realized woman—as a career woman, a friend, a mother—someday—and, an advocate—all the things I wanted to be. But I'd avoided getting to know Audrey, and now I felt guilty at the neglect—of her and of me.

Ben's fingers wrapped around mine, tugging my attention away from the portrait where I'd seen more of myself than I'd ever seen before. "I know you hate it, but . . . care to dance?"

I startled at his touch and at his request.

"What about Alison?"

"She found the managing editor of Sony by the auction tables. They're dancing now."

"Oh. Sure."

We joined the other couples on the dance floor, where Ben revealed his ability to actually dance, not just the turn-slowly-in-a-circle dance that had encompassed all my real-life experiences of dancing with men. "So," he said, leading me in a way that made both of us look capable. "How have you been?"

How have I been? That was certainly a question with too many answers. Instead of opening all the miniature Pandora's boxes, I said, "I don't hate it, you know."

"What?"

"Dancing. I don't hate it. I actually really enjoy dancing, just not in a nightclub with all those bodies pressing in. I think it's because I live in a half-dark world. I never know what's coming at me from that darkness. And my depth perception isn't great, so I'm afraid of flinging an arm too far one way or another and accidentally hitting someone in the face."

"But this is okay?"

So okay. What I said was, "This is you being my eyes, my guide, through the dance. I'm not likely to stumble over something I didn't see or have anything come from my blind side to surprise me, because you're watching for both of us. Traditional dancing is this half-blind woman's best friend."

"You're good at it," he observed.

"I took several ballroom dance classes in college. They counted as fitness credits. You're good at it, too."

"High school ballroom dance team." He extended his arm and twirled me under it. I might have been out of practice, but I managed the maneuver without too much difficulty.

Dressed in a gown that made me feel empowered and beautiful, and dancing in the arms of a man who looked like he'd walked straight out of any of my favorite romantic classics, I felt an inner sigh of satisfaction swelling inside me. This was what happy endings were made of. I gave my head a shake to pull me back to reality. Ben wasn't my Prince Charming. There could be no happy ending when you were dancing with someone else's date. Only a terrible human forgot details like that. "So your date . . ." I said.

"Alison." He said it almost as if he meant to correct me.

"Yes. Alison. You said she wanted to talk with me?"

He guided us to the side in a move meant to allow another couple to pass. Though they were on my right, I felt the air change as they passed and felt grateful I was in the arms of a capable lead. If they had run into me, I likely would have left the floor and stayed off it.

"She's been dying to talk to you ever since the press junket. Since you've worked on a movie that is the rage and talk of our industry, she's hoping you might be able to help her get her name out there and recognized. She does good work. You know—if there are any positions open at Portal for underling work . . . She's happy to take anything and work her way up."

"So you'd like me to give her an endorsement? And employment if I can?" I didn't ask why he wasn't getting her a job at Mid-Scene. The company no-dating-coworkers policy was reason enough.

"Yes. If you're willing. I can show you her work. You'd be impressed."

I nodded. "Sure. I'll take a look at her work if you want me to."

Ben pulled back so I could see his face. "I'd think you'd do it because *you* want to. Another woman in the field is good for the whole industry, right?"

His response surprised me, as if he was doing this thing for Alison as a favor to me. "Right. Sure."

We danced the rest of the song in silence.

"You okay?" he asked as we moved back to the table.

"Of course." Total lie. I hated how much I liked how Ben looked, how much I liked how he danced, how much I liked *him*.

Alison was already back at the table and looking rosy. Her conversation with the editor from Sony must have gone well. She jumped up and gave me a hug when she saw me like we were long-lost sisters, parted at birth.

Ben and I both sat, and I spent a great deal of time fielding questions, talking shop, and shooting glances at Ben, who seemed to hang onto my every word. I almost felt grateful when Ben asked Alison to dance because it was weird that they were here together but acting as intimately acquainted as two strangers in a checkout line.

Rather than watch them dance, I went back to the Audrey Hepburn pictures. I thought of *My Fair Lady* and the song about how she could've danced all night. No matter how hard I tried not to, my head turned to look at Ben dancing with Alison. I could have danced all night, indeed.

Except Ben's dance card was full.

Chapter Twelve

"Because I don't love him, and he doesn't love me."
—Reggie Lampert, played by Audrey Hepburn in Charade

They danced two more dances, but as I watched, Ben kept Alison at a distance farther than he'd kept me while we'd been dancing. Shouldn't he have held her closer? They laughed a little, but it seemed like Alison did most of the talking, and he only seemed to be half-listening, like his attention was somewhere else. The crease in his forehead appeared several times while they danced. The crease was Ben's biggest tell for confusion. Why would he be confused? Was it something she said?

I sat back at the table and hated myself for staring at them. Toward the end of their last dance, Ben's eyes fell on me and stayed on me. When the song ended, he pulled away from his date and moved in the direction of the table, even though Alison tugged on his hand and smiled as if to say, "Done already?"

He apparently was, because he didn't hesitate in claiming the chair between me and one of Grandma's friends from her new assisted-living villa, which meant Alison had no choice except to sit next to me on the other side—my blind side.

"Ben tells me you're willing to have lunch with me and view my work sometime," she said.

I had to turn my whole body to face her so I could actually see her. "Sure. We can do that sometime."

Sometime, however, was not good enough. Alison seized the elusive and noncommittal *sometime* and was determined to pin me down for an exact date. I finally tugged my phone from my handbag, checked my calendar, and gave her a few dates to choose from. I shot a scowl in Ben's direction, but with me turned away from him so completely, who knew if he saw or not, or what his response was if he did see.

Once Alison had my promise to meet her for lunch and an actual time and meeting place picked out, she turned her attentions entirely to Ben, directing the conversation to things they did in college, professors they had, crazy antics they got into trouble over. She mentioned things I knew Ben had mortality statistics on, but he never once said, "Your chances of dying from . . ."

For my part, I stayed silent. The conversation didn't have anything to do with me and was awkward, considering that I sat between them but couldn't see her at all. It was my own fault. I'd sat in a chair different from the one I'd occupied during dinner.

Grandma and Walt finished dancing and finally found their way back to the table. Ben turned his attention to Walt. They both had an apparent love of baseball, and Walt boasted

owning a whole collection of signed balls from various famous ballplayers. He suggested that Ben come over to see his
collection. Ben happily accepted the invitation.

Walt. Grandma's boyfriend. I shook my head. Grandma's
boyfriend? Would that ever seem normal to say?

Alison engaged me in conversation again, since Ben was
occupied with Walt, which meant I was stuck with small talk
regarding movies and directors, and where Alison grew up,
and how her sister always stole her clothes. Small talk was
hard for me because I always felt like I had to dilute my per-
sonality to participate. If I became overly passionate about a
topic—as I usually did—people usually took offense or decided I was a little too forceful and opinionated.

At the end of the evening, the emcee announced the close
of the auctions and thanked the guests for their generosity.
It was time to leave. I passed the portrait of Audrey on my
way out and sent a silent apology for holding myself at arm's
length for so long. I would do better. I would be one more
voice to bring attention to a good cause. If nothing else came
from the evening, my commitment to helping had been so-
lidified into something useful.

Alison hugged me good night. She hugged Ben longer. I
knew because I counted the seconds. Her hug with me was
only a one-one thousand. Her hug with Ben was a count of
nine-one-thousand, long enough to be awkward. At least she
didn't kiss him.

Grandma and Walt kept the ride home blessedly noisy,
commenting on costuming, on the charity itself, on the food,
and on Ben and me, and how we looked perfect on the dance
floor.

"Some people are made to dance together," Walt said. "Fred Astaire and, well, . . . everybody. That man could make a monkey look like a graceful dancer."

"That's what you did for me tonight," Grandma said. I was turned in my seat so I could see both of them and Ben, depending on who was talking. Being turned in my seat allowed me to see my grandma bestow Walt with a look of such approval and admiration, it made me smile. Their chatter filled me with gratitude; inconvenient silence would have meant I'd have to try to figure out how to feel about tonight.

As it was, I couldn't seem to stop fiddling with the mask I'd left in the car and only just managed to keep from sitting on when I got back in for the return trip to Grandma's house. When Ben shot a look to my hands that were rolling the mask over and over, I opened my purse and put the mask inside. Since we were close to my grandmother's house, I pulled out my keys.

The problem with pulling out my keys was that now I had something new to fidget with. When Ben shot another look at my hands, I cupped the keys between my gloved hands and held them clasped together until Ben pulled into a parking place in front of Grandma's villa.

We all tumbled out of Ben's car, and Grandma and Walt said they were going to take a walk through the gardens over by the pond on the property. Ben walked me to my car.

"You hardly said anything all night," he observed.

I cleared my throat and stretched my fingers in the black gloves I still wore. "There wasn't much to say, I guess." My hands suddenly felt hot, claustrophobic in the gloves the same way I felt claustrophobic in crowds. I began picking at the fabric to try to strip it off.

Ben noticed and took my hand, pulling on the individual fingers as I'd been doing until he was able to peel the glove away. He gently settled my hand back at my side and went to work on the other one. He moved slowly, his fingers hot through the satin. I watched as the material slid away, revealing my hand and then my fingers. I didn't dare look up because I couldn't trust myself to not grab him by the collar and kiss him until he pulled away.

And he would pull away, because he was dating someone else, which made this small intimacy of him removing my gloves too much, too far.

"Thanks for coming," I said, my eyes fixed on my own hand—the one still in his. "I'm glad the tickets didn't go unused." I withdrew my hand from his and straightened. "You don't have to worry about Alison. We've got the meeting all set up. It's taken care of." I had to mention Alison, if only to remind myself that she was in the picture. To remind myself that kissing Ben and wanting to kiss him were off-limits. I firmly believed that dating other people's guys would bring the worst kind of karma.

I gave him a quick hug and opened my car door.

He tapped on my window. "Silvia. Where are you going?"

"Tired!" I called. "Gotta go home." *To forget that he's beautiful. To forget that he's funny, to forget how safe he makes me feel.* To forget everything before I ditched my resolve and encroached on territory that wasn't mine. I pulled out of the parking space before he could say anything else and drove away.

When I got home, I reached for my phone; I needed to call Grandma and apologize for leaving without saying good-bye. But my phone was gone. So was my clutch. Not with my black gloves. Not on the seat next to me. Not in my car any-where. I thought about all the possibilities and all the places I was sure I had it. Ben's car. I had it for certain in Ben's car. Which meant it was probably still there.

I groaned.

I almost turned back but stopped. The last time I'd been in Ben's house I'd fallen asleep on his couch. And there was that picture. How would it make me feel to see he'd taken it down? Because he *had* to have taken it down. No way would any self-respecting guy keep a picture of one woman on his fridge while he was seriously tangled up emotionally with an-other.

With another groan, I shoved open my car door and headed inside my apartment. I slammed the door behind me and leaned against it. Beautiful Ben. Hottie Ben. Tangled. I replayed the night—a mental fast-forward—and then re-played certain parts in slow motion.

The way he looked at me. The way he danced with me. The way he oriented himself to me no matter where we were in the room together.

The way he looked at Alison. The way he danced with Alison. The way he hugged her back when she said goodbye to him, like the embrace was a thing to be endured.

The way he stripped those gloves off my hands and brushed his thumb over my bare fingers. My eyes fluttered closed at that memory.

And popped back open again. "He doesn't love her," I said to the empty room.

I replayed everything again, faster this time. He definitely didn't love her. So why was he dating her? Why stay where you don't want to be? Especially since I felt certain that, whether he knew it or not, where he wanted to be was with me.

I considered going out and confronting him with this information right then and there. If nothing else came from the visit, I could at least get my clutch and my phone back. But I was too vulnerable, too emotionally needy, too not ready.

I'd do it in the morning. I dressed in my pajamas, cursing the lack of a phone. How was I supposed to text Emma for support or Grandma for advice if my phone was riding around in Ben Armstrong's car?

Hopefully, the conversation could happen without advice or support.

Because in the morning, I was going to tell Ben he was with the wrong woman.

Chapter Thirteen

"I might as well be reaching for the moon."

—Sabrina Fairchild, played by Audrey Hepburn in Sabrina

When Ben answered the door the next day, his face went white like he'd seen a ghost, and then flushed as the blood that had drained from his face flooded back with force. "It's a surprise to see you here. I thought you couldn't wait to get away from me," he said.

"I left my phone in your car." His initial reaction to me was so hostile, I could only think to explain my presence in the easiest form possible.

Understanding dawned on his face. "That's why you ignored me. I thought you'd . . . Well, that makes more sense than your radio silence. Not that radio silence was too far off the mark. You seem to do that to me a lot." He shoved the door open wider to allow me access and stalked back into his living room.

I followed him in. "What do you mean, I do that to you a lot?" Ben's angry behavior derailed my intentions entirely.

"No texts, no calls, no cookies to say thanks for helping on your film. I thought for sure I'd get some sort of contact when the press went wild after the junket, but nothing. But even before that, after you left Mid-Scene, you didn't keep in touch."

"What are you talking about? I answered every time you texted or wrote."

"Exactly my point. When *I* wrote you. When you got the job at Portal Pictures, you never kept in contact with me, even though I tried to stay in touch with you, your answers were brief, and you never initiated contact. The only time we've spent together at all is when you were in a mess and needed help, and I happened to walk in at the right time. You say we're friends, but we aren't even good enough friends for you to have called me that night when you were having trouble with your boss. If my showing up hadn't happened organically, it sure wouldn't have happened by design. After that, I thought maybe you'd stay in touch, but you didn't. No texts, no calls, no communication. Last night only happened because I've been bugging you, and your grandma got ahold of your phone."

Ouch. How did he know it was Grandma who had extended the invitation? Heat flooded my veins and pumped furiously through my thumping heart to my extremities. "That is entirely unfair!" I stabbed my pointer finger at him. "You have a girlfriend. I was being respectful of proper co-worker boundaries."

He raked his hands through his hair as if the motion kept

him from strangling me. "We *aren't* coworkers. We're barely coconspirators, and considering how you fled from me last night like I have the plague, that's all we are. I got the message."

Ben had been mad at me before. We'd worked together too closely to not irritate each other every now and again. But this level of anger was new, and upsetting, considering how I thought the conversation with Ben would go today.

"I need a glass. Water." It should have been weird to be so forward in his house. Especially since there was a comfortable feeling there—one of safety, of acceptance, of just being who you were. Especially when, at the moment, I was a woman in the beginnings of an anxiety attack—something that had only ever happened when I was trapped in a crowd. I didn't wait for him, but instead fled to the kitchen to seek out a glass. I went to the cupboards nearest the sink, opened them, and found plates and bowls.

When I closed it, Ben reached an arm over my shoulder, opened the cupboard just to the side of me, and pulled out a glass. In order to reach it, he had to press into my side, basically pinning me against the counter.

Instead of sending me into a further spiral of panic, the cocoon of his body had an oddly comforting effect where I felt sheltered, not imprisoned. He placed the glass in my hand, put his hands on my shoulders, and slowly spun me to face him.

He had lost his previous angst, but his mystified expression in his ice-blue eyes meant he still wanted answers—likely all the answers: the ones about why I hadn't called him in months, and the ones of why I was acting like the resident crazy cat-lady.

It was hard to think of answers with him close enough that I could feel the heat of his body against my bare arms.

"Silvia?"

He said it with the right tones, the ones Emma always used when she was joking around. I couldn't help it; I responded automatically. "Yes, Mickey?"

Ben busted up, leaning his head down on my shoulder while his body shook with laughter. "How am I supposed to respond to that?" he asked.

I shrugged, grateful for how quickly his presence calmed me, grateful for how quickly we moved from the tense scene at the door to this playfulness. "You could always ask me how I call my lover boy."

Ben laughed harder. "I have said your name a million times, and you never once did the *Dirty Dancing* routine with me."

"It's the tone. You've got to say it just the right way."

He stepped back as if only just aware he'd moved into my personal space. "If I use the right tone, will you always answer like that?"

I shrugged again, my fingers playing over the pattern on the glass. "Usually. I always do for Emma."

He shook his head. "If only I'd known. To think I've missed years of this game."

Feeling hyperaware of him and the situation, I glanced at the glass and the patterns my fingers were tracing. I laughed. "Kylo Ren?"

"What? Kylo's cool."

"He needs counseling. Spoiler alert: he killed his father."

I remembered that I wasn't there to comment on his glassware. My purpose in his house was to tell him Alison wasn't right for him, to maybe put myself out there as being the one for him. I was still a little shaky on that part of the plan.

"Thank you for the glass." I stepped past him to the fridge, where I filled the glass with both ice and water and chugged it until the glass was empty. A Doctor Who TARDIS magnet held the picture with me in it firmly in place. So, despite the fact that he was furious with me when he answered the door, he hadn't been irritated enough with me to take down the picture. And he hadn't taken it down for Alison's sake, either. Or maybe the picture didn't mean that much to him, and he hadn't really considered the ramifications of putting the picture in a location where he would have to see it every day.

Not that any of my meandering thoughts actually mattered. Ben watched and said nothing, not even when I refilled the glass.

"What's wrong?" he asked after I had downed the second glass as well. "You're being way too weird for a casual phone-pick-up."

I looked at the picture. I couldn't do this here, not while staring at the picture of us with our arms over each other's shoulders. I retreated to the living room.

He followed me. When I reached the couch, I didn't sit. Too much energy coursed through me to allow such static actions. I turned to face him. And then the words I'd wanted to say tumbled out, badly. "You don't love her."

His eyebrows shot up, and his mouth fell open. "I don't love who?"

"Alison."

He stood there a moment, processing, the way Ben did with everything, before he said, "Really? And you think you have some kind of finger on my emotional pulse, enough that you can tell me how I feel?"

"Yes." I lifted my chin. "You've never once, in any of the times I've seen you together, thrown out a mortality statistic."

Ben raked his fingers through his hair again and scratched at the back of his head, a move of obvious frustration. "And that means I don't love her?"

"It means you can't be yourself around her. Does she know that you can rattle off obscure statistics? Does she know that you know what the chances are of dying in a bowling accident?"

His jaw worked. He was still mad at me, and likely getting angrier because this blunt conversation was obviously none of my business. But we had to have it now, while we still could, while he was my friend and not her fiancé or worse, her husband. His answer came out low, like a growl at the back of his throat. "No. She doesn't know."

"See!" Nothing could have kept the gloat out of my voice.

But Ben immediately shot a hole through the inflating part of my ego. "But that's because *I* don't know the chances of dying in a bowling accident."

"Oh." For a moment, he had me stumped. "But you're thinking about it now, aren't you? The next time we're together, you'll probably have an answer. And that's my whole point. Has Alison ever heard a mortality stat?"

He didn't answer, which, to me, *was* an answer.

"You can't be yourself fully when you're with her, Ben. As your friend, I had to say something. I don't want to see you unhappy."

He sucked in a ragged breath and turned his back on me. He stalked back to the kitchen, where, from the sounds of it, he got his own glass of water.

I considered everything else we'd discussed since I barged in on his morning. I felt bad for not initiating texts or communications. Thinking back, it occurred to me that since I'd left Portal Pictures, he'd also made comments on my social media updates and had forwarded me a few jokes and online videos that were funny or poignant. He'd reached out to me on occasion, not a lot, not enough for him to act like he'd been dialing my number every hour every day for this whole time. But he had reached out. I just hadn't reached back. Why? Why hadn't I reached back?

In the beginning, it was genuinely being busy.

After that, it was out of respect to the girlfriend.

But lately, the girlfriend barrier hadn't mattered as much as me not wanting to be *just* friends.

It had been easier for me to cut him off altogether than drag my emotions all over the place, acting the part of "just a friend." Once I realized how involved my heart had become, I couldn't go backwards.

When I found out he'd been dating his old girlfriend from film school, it was easier to just step away. I always told Emma she forgave too easily and that was why she'd ended up in so many terrible relationships before she met Lucas. Emma always warned me that my ability to withdraw, to send a guy packing with little provocation, was my greatest flaw and why I never had relationships—bad or otherwise—which was both unfair and untrue. Mostly true, but not *all* true. But now. What did I do with Ben, now?

I stood in the middle of his living room for several moments before realizing he wasn't coming back. I made my way to the kitchen.

With the fridge door open, Ben stood, bathed in the glow from the light. He had one hand on the door and the other on the side of the fridge, as though using it to prop himself up. The picture of us that had been on the fridge now lay on the counter.

He'd tugged it off.

I wasn't stupid, slow maybe, and a smidge tunnel-visioned when it came to my own life, but not stupid. My face on the fridge *did* mean something. Ben taking me off meant something more. I instinctively knew it wasn't a bad-something-more, but an *encouraging*-something-more. We'd both managed to get under each other's skin.

"You go radio silent, too, sometimes," I said softly.

He didn't let go of the fridge as he shrugged. "Self-defense."

I nodded. "I think that goes for both of us."

We both stood there, not saying anything as he used the fridge to cool down his entire house.

"Are you okay?" I finally asked, not sure what else to say.

"Just hungry. I haven't had time to think about what to do for lunch, yet. And I skipped breakfast."

"Oh."

He continued looking at the contents of his intensely tidy

and organized refrigerator. But the glazed-over eyes proved he saw none of it. The rapid rise and fall of his chest betrayed the swift patterns of breathing. Ben was not okay.

I gently placed my hand on his, uncertain if touching him would calm him or provoke him. "I haven't eaten either," I said, choosing to stick to the mundane instead of talking about the elephant in the room—the picture, the feelings, the intentions. "Let's go get some lunch."

He didn't respond in any way to my touch, but he hadn't pulled away either. He held perfectly still, aside from his breathing.

"We have a lot to talk about," I continued. "We might as well eat."

He did pull his hand away then and used it to rub his chin before he closed the refrigerator. He walked to the other side of his kitchen and out into the hallway. "Let me get my jacket."

"I'll drive," I called to him. He seemed too emotional to drive. The idea almost made me laugh. Ben was never emotional. This emotional thing was definitely something new.

And terrifying.

And exciting.

I glanced at the picture of us that no longer took up residence on his fridge.

And terrifying.

Chapter Fourteen

*"You're mad. Utterly mad. I suppose you
want to kiss me good night?"*

—Nicole Bonnet, played by Audrey Hepburn
in How to Steal a Million

Once Ben had his jacket on and his house all locked up,
and we were in the car with no destination in mind, I asked
Ben what he felt like eating. His lack of response meant it was
up to me. I drove to Guisados, since it wasn't too far from
where Ben lived and because tacos had a knack of making the
world better.

Ben didn't ask where we were going once my driving took
on some purpose, so if he didn't like where we went, it was all
on him. But as we got out of the car and entered the restaurant, Ben didn't complain.

I ordered the tamales and an horchata, and Ben ordered
the sampler plate at the suggestion of the guy working the
counter. Ben had apparently never been to Guisados. How
anyone could live in LA and not have been to Guisados blew
my mind. I tried to pay, but Ben beat me to it with a smirk

and a, "You must not look like the more dangerous of the two of us today," as the guy at the counter took his credit card instead of mine.

I didn't bother telling him that I could be dangerous if he kept pushing, but the truth was I didn't feel dangerous; I felt vulnerable. A quick glance at the full tables inside sent us outside to wait for our food. We found a table and seated ourselves.

The drive over hadn't been as uncomfortable as it could have been, considering Ben's silence. But then I'd had something to do—paying attention to the road and trying to figure out where we were going. Now that we were seated with no food yet to keep us occupied, I wasn't sure what to do.

So, I dove headfirst. "Adam said he saw you on a date with Alison. He told me you were together. Being that I had personally disrupted your attempts to date her on three separate occasions, it was easy to believe that you really were together. I didn't want to give her the wrong idea by my continual interference. I'm sorry if that came across as abandonment to you. That was never my intention."

He didn't meet my eye while I explained, but instead stared into the street before saying, "Fair enough."

Our order arrived just then. I cursed the prompt service; we had talking to do.

The food did what food always did when two people found themselves together in the most awkward way possible—it served both as a focal point and a distraction.

After Ben proved he really had been starving by downing three of the six tacos on his sampler plate without much of a pause or a breath, he stopped eating long enough to exclaim that he'd never had a better tortilla in his life. Then he dove back into the sampler plate.

We finished eating at about the same time, and there was nothing else to do but face the elephant sitting with us.

Ben frowned into the street. "That's fair about you thinking all that about Alison. We were dating for a while because I promised her I'd give that a chance. When I realized it wasn't going to happen for me emotionally, I told her, and now we're just friends. So, you're both right and wrong. I do love her—she's a friend, and I care about what happens to her—but I am not in love with her. And the difference between those kinds of love is pretty substantial. The whole thing with Alison is complicated."

"Why then did you want me to meet with her so much? Why the whole date with her last night?"

"She wasn't my date last night, she was my . . . plus-one? That sounds like *date*, too, doesn't it? Anyway, she wanted to go because you'd been gracious and invited her specifically. She practically worships you now and wants to be your best friend. I wanted you to meet with her because you're always complaining that there aren't enough women in our business. It made sense for me to try to do something proactive to help change that. Since Mid-Scene already turned her down, I hoped you could help find a place for her."

"Right. That makes sense. And, yeah, I agree. Being proactive to change the business is the only way the business will change. Thanks for seeing that."

Sometimes, I really was the half-blind girl. Why hadn't *I* seen that? At least I had agreed to meet with Alison. At least

I had acted the part of a grown-up and not shut her down in mean-girl jealousy.

With Guisados becoming even busier, and people giving us the stink eye when they noted our empty trays and our stubborn occupation of a perfectly good table, I stood, not really feeling like defending my squatter's rights. "We'll receive a stern talking-to if we don't vacate the table," I explained, noting that a few different couples were talking quietly and casting glances in our direction—likely drawing straws for who had to ask us to leave.

We got back in the car, but Ben didn't give me any destination, so I turned in the direction of his house.

"So Alison didn't work out?" I asked, wanting to know how it all went down before we talked about anything more.

"No. Not exactly. She was willing to keep at it, but it wasn't working for me."

Alison couldn't be blamed for her persistence. She'd dated him before. She knew he was dependable and smart, caring and compassionate, funny and weird. She knew all there was to love about him, and what girl in her right mind would ever be willing to throw that away when she knew what she had?

The more I thought about her, the more I respected her.

And didn't respect myself. I knew all there was to love about him, and I'd still felt willing to throw it all away because I was . . . what? Too busy? Too apathetic? She deserved to win more than I did because she'd cared enough and dared enough to try. I had let him go without so much as a shrug or a farewell wave. No wonder he was mad at me. "Didn't you guys date a long time back in film school?"

"About two years. Most of our junior year and all of our senior year."

"That's a long time. I'm sorry things didn't work out. Why didn't things work out?" My lips felt cold, a sign that the blood in my system was all racing around in my midsection and ignoring my extremities.

His tone changed. He'd been reserved since we'd left his house—probably so he could process. But now his tone had shifted from reserved to amused, though I didn't understand what he found amusing about a question regarding a breakup.

Instead of answering me, he said, "Here's your phone." He pulled it from his jacket pocket.

"Right." I reached for where it seemed most logical for his hand to be. "Did you say you left me a message last night?" My fingers grazed over the smooth case of my phone as Ben pulled it away again. Then I heard the familiar tones of a message being deleted. "What? Ben! You can't delete my messages!"

"I can when they're from me. Trust me. A conversation will be better than that message."

That message. Whatever it had been, my not responding to it had been enough to incite Ben's anger.

We were silent a moment before he asked, "What wrong idea were you talking about earlier?"

"I'm not sure what you mean," I said, irritated that he'd deleted my message and hating how congested traffic was becoming and the fact that the road required so much of my attention when my attention wanted to be on the man in the passenger seat of my car.

"You said you didn't want to give Alison the wrong idea

by your continual interference. What would have been a wrong idea?"

I tried to answer, sputtered, and fell silent. Because the wrong idea was actually the right idea. I didn't want Alison to think I was falling for a claim she'd already staked.

When the silence from my nonanswer stretched so long that I almost considered telling a joke or playing the movie-quote game to fill the silence, Ben spoke up. "It was nice to see her again and see who she's become. It's interesting, isn't it?"

"Interesting?" Did my voice sound too high?

"You think you know someone and then some time without them goes by and you see them again, and you realize that they are exactly what you always believed them to be, or you discover you didn't know them all that well after all."

"Which was Alison? Was she what you thought? Or someone you didn't really know?" I shouldn't have asked, because it wasn't my business. They'd broken up again, and what did the why of it matter to me?

"I was talking about you just now, not Alison."

"What?" I took my eye off the road to look at him. Ben wasn't looking at me though. His eyes were on the road. His hand went to my shoulder as he shouted, "Silvia! Brakes!"

I looked back in time to see that traffic had come to a dead stop, and I slammed my brakes to avoid the business end of the bumper on the truck in front of us. The truck would have been fine; my car would have crumpled like a soda can.

"How about," he said, instead of addressing the part of

our conversation where he said he was talking about me, "you pull over so we can talk."

His request seemed so reasonable, and his hand warm on my shoulder knocked me so far off-balance, that I pulled over without any further consideration, at least not until I finally made it to the curb, where it occurred to me to be insulted by his insistence. "Is this because I make you nervous driving with my one eye? We've already discussed this. I'm perfectly legal. And in spite of what just happened, I'm still safe. You just surprised me. I've never been in an accident, which is more than we can say for you."

"That accident wasn't my fault," Ben insisted. "That was the work of an old woman who let her purse-puppy have free roaming rights of the front seat of her car while driving."

"Sounds like an excuse to me," I said.

With the car stopped and in park, I was finally able to turn my whole head and see him fully. He looked different than he had when we'd left his house. He seemed lighter, more good-humored.

I narrowed my eyes at him. "Your emotions are kind of killing me. Are you happy, furious—what? You're all over the place today. I want to talk to you about important things, but not while you're furious. And because I'm clearly a little clueless—but so are you, so don't judge—I need you to spell it out for me."

"I think I'm not furious," he whispered.

"That's good, I guess."

His hand still hadn't left my shoulder. He rolled the end of my side braid gently between his fingers. My breath quickened. Was this what I thought it was? The day had been so full of stress and emotions, I didn't trust myself to accurately interpret anything.

His eyes were hyperfocused on where his fingers met the end of my braid that rested on my shoulder—the same shoulder where his hand had seemed to become a permanent fixture. He tilted his head slightly as those fingers grazed over my collarbone, drawing fire across my skin.

He finally looked up, as if checking to make sure I was fine with this kind of contact.

I gave a small nod to tell him that it was, and, just like when *Sliver of Midnight* filled the screen in the miniature theater of Portal Pictures' property, I forgot to breathe.

"I am also not happy," he said. "I'm nervous and hopeful because I find myself in a unique position to be entirely honest, and that's actually a little terrifying."

"Honest?" It was hard to speak when you weren't breathing properly. "About?"

"I . . ." He widened his eyes and gave a low laugh. "Okay, maybe I was wrong. Maybe I can't do this."

It was instinct, probably powered by fear of him backing up instead of moving forward, but I reached out and took his other hand, wanting to encourage whatever was about to come next. "Aren't you the guy who says anyone can do anything?" I said.

He glanced around at where we'd parked on the side of the road and furrowed his brow over those ice-blue eyes. "Fine, throw my own trite, positive affirmations at me. This isn't exactly the right place either, but here goes. Stop me when it gets awkward."

He waited for a pause and then said, "No? Not awkward

enough yet? Okay, then, I kinda thought we were already all the way to awkward, but my mistake. Here goes. I hated it when you left the company to go to Portal Pictures."

"But you—"

"I know. I know I helped you get the job, but have you ever wondered why?"

"You were helping with my career," I said.

"That's the cover story—the one that makes me look like a nice guy. The real story is that I was so sick and tired of working shoulder to shoulder with you every single day and never being able to—"

His fingers brushed against my collarbone again, sweeping up to my jawline until they stretched out to the nape of my neck. "To reach you," he whispered. "All that time working together and knowing I'd get one or both of us fired if I ever reached out. You telling me I didn't love Alison is why I feel hopeful, not furious. If you were so adamant about my feelings there, maybe you were wanting me to place those feelings somewhere else, with someone else."

His fingers gliding along the back of my neck reduced me to a shiver. "This conversation would have been easier if you hadn't answered the door this morning acting like I was there to tell you I ran over your dog," I said, my voice thick and soft and not sounding like me at all.

"I was angry because you acted so excited to leave me all those months ago, and because you didn't look back. You never contacted me, never called, never texted, never liked my Instagram posts. And there were some really funny posts you missed out on. And last night, you were with me, in sync, and totally present, and then you were running away."

"That's not fair," I whispered. "It's not like you wrote all the time. You are as lousy at communication as I am. And last night, I thought you were on a date. I don't trespass in relationships. It's a good moral code."

"Which makes sense, given the circumstances. I'm sorry I failed to communicate that properly."

"Failed to communicate? You never once corrected me when I called her your date."

He didn't deny it but nodded in agreement. "Yeah, fine, I'm bad at communication. I get it. Anyway, Walt already chewed me out over that."

"Walt?"

"Your grandma's boyfriend. He told me if I didn't get out of the security of my training wheels, I was going to watch the girl ride her own bike away . . . or something like that. It was a bike analogy. It made sense last night. Anyway, the point was that he noticed I was keeping myself from taking a chance with you by being honest with how I felt. He said he understood wanting to protect myself—he used another analogy that I don't think I should ever repeat—and told me to expose myself."

I bit my lip to keep from laughing. "Glad you didn't expose yourself last night. That would have been awkward."

"Right. Ha ha. You laugh, but Walt's a wise guy—as in smart, not sarcastic. So I was gearing up to be honest, and then you left, and then I was hurt, rejected, frustrated, furious. And that's the guy who opened the door this morning. Sorry about that."

"Apology accepted. I'm sorry, too, Ben. You're right. My priorities were messed up. I should've called and written, stayed in contact. There were just so many important things that had to be done all at once, and it was overwhelming." How did my voice keep working with all this energy building between us?

"I had just hoped that even with all your terribly important, overwhelming stuff that I was important to you as well." His eyes filled with a vulnerability and desperate need I'd never seen in him before.

"You are. That's why I'm here."

"Finally." He smiled, a mesmerized look of awestruck wonder. It felt like a mirror of my emotions. We were in my car on the side of the road, and it didn't matter that it wasn't in a place where the set dressers had carefully prepared flower petals and candles, or where the sound director had prepared romantic music to herald the moment, because we were both here and feeling the same thing, breathing in the same hope.

The tension between us crackled with energy. We were so much closer than we'd ever been, and yet the space between us felt like universes.

He'd said that in those three years of working together, he hadn't been able to reach out to me and hated it. Now there were no lines that couldn't be crossed, so I reached out to him. My fingers folded into his shirt as I pulled him forward.

He tilted his head and leaned in.

His breath washed over my lips, a teaser for what was to come.

I closed my eyes, suddenly totally alive, completely aware, drinking in this moment that belonged to us and us alone.

The rap at the window made us both jump. His chin bumped my cheek, hard. I grabbed at my face and whirled to see who dared interrupt what probably would have been the most epic kiss ever.

A parking enforcement officer in his black jacket zipped up to his neck over his uniform stood just outside my window. "You can't park here!" he called loud enough to be heard through the glass.

I narrowed my eyes and briefly considered running him over.

It had been a long time since I'd been on a date, and a lot longer still since any of those dates produced any kind of physical attraction enough to warrant kissing.

I rolled down my window and made sure the officer felt the full measure of my glare. "We weren't parking. We were just—"

"Yeah, I saw," the man said. His name tag identified him as Officer Stern, which probably dictated the direction his life had taken that brought him to this exact moment where he ruined my moment. "This is a bus zone. You're not in a bus." His flat-eyed stare told me he was not a man to give emotional compassion or support.

At least he didn't have his ticket pad out.

"Thanks, officer," Ben called from the passenger seat. "We really appreciate you pointing that out." He sounded friendly and not bothered by the rude interruption.

I put the car in drive and said to the officer, "We were just leaving."

"Well, you weren't, but you are now," Officer Stern said. Yep. His name had to be why he'd chosen to walk down this path of humorless, emotionless harassment of random innocent citizens.

As I pulled out, a bus pulled in.

So maybe Officer Stern wasn't entirely wrong to make us move. The bus pulled in at a speed that would have made it hard to brake if my car had still been in the way.

"Close call," Ben said.

He could say that again. On so many levels.

Chapter Fifteen

*"I'm afraid you put yourself in the wrong place.
I have no desire to be kissed, by you or anyone else."*

—Jo Stockton, played by Audrey Hepburn in Funny Face

We'd endured an awkward minute of silence while I maneuvered through traffic before Ben spoke. "You're mad."

"Well, yes." Was my emotion so unusual considering the situation? "He ruined what could have been a perfectly good moment."

"Could have been? You don't think that was a good moment?"

Why was I still driving? I couldn't see his expression when I had to focus on the road. We should have switched places while we were pulled over. "You do?"

"Yes. I learned something very important." He sounded completely content.

Frustrated with Officer Stern and now Ben, too, I said, "And that was?"

"I learned you are not opposed to exploring romantic

options with a nerdy guy like me. That was pretty valuable information to obtain."

I laughed, the sound nervous and almost ridiculous. "Okay. I guess knowing what kind of ground you're standing on is valuable information. But I still hate the meter maid."

"Yeah, well, he's not making it to my Christmas-card list either, but he did save us from being smashed by a bus. So, there's that."

There was also the promise that a really amazing kiss was coming my way—and soon, if I had anything to say about it. I drove back to his house and might have broken a speed limit or two in the process. When we pulled up to the curb, a truck was already parked in front. A couple of guys lounged against the truck, ignoring me until they realized my car contained a passenger who was of interest to them.

They didn't even wait for me to get the car turned off before they were tugging the passenger side door open and pulling Ben out as he tried to disentangle himself from the seat belt.

"Dude! You said you'd help Mom with the new piano. The company can't bring the new one in until the old one is out. You're the one with the moving equipment, and then you just disappear for half the day. Where've you been?"

I stepped out of the car. Ben shot me a look of apology, not that he needed to. I didn't hold him accountable for the epic-kiss delay; I gave the stink eye to the two men.

"My brothers," Ben said to me as a way of introduction. "Guys, this is Silvia."

Three years is a long time to work with someone every day, so I knew a lot about Ben's family and growing-up years.

I already knew all about his brothers—the arm wrestling, tackling, broken furniture, rough-and-tumble childhood.

What I hadn't expected was that they'd heard of me, too, because they both pursed their lips and nodded their heads. One of them repeated my name with a slow and deliberate drawl. "Silvia . . . How nice to finally meet you."

"That's inconvenient," Ben muttered. He likely didn't mean for me to hear, but the loss of an eye meant I paid better attention to my other senses. Was it inconvenient that our time was interrupted, or inconvenient that his brothers had already heard about me and seemed to be unlikely to stay silent about what they knew?

The idea of them dishing out the information they had appealed to me on all kinds of levels. I waved and smiled. Ben came from a family of three boys. Ben was the youngest. I pointed at his two older brothers. "Jeffrey and Jimmy?" I said aloud, trying to figure out which one was which.

They both straightened. "Hey," the tallest one said. "You've told her about us? I'm touched." He crossed in front of the car and held his hand out to me. "I'm Jeffrey. The other clown is Jimmy. It really is nice to meet you, and I'm sorry if we're cutting plans short, but Mom will disinherit all of us if Benji doesn't show up."

"Yeah," Jimmy said. "She's one of those equal-opportunity moms. If one of us in trouble, all of us get to be in trouble."

Ben sighed heavily. "Unfortunately for me, those two were always in trouble."

His brothers didn't deny the fact.

Ben shot me another apologetic look as he rounded the car to where I stood. He gave a snide-ways look to Jeffrey, who understood its meaning and immediately returned to the driver's side of the truck. "I am sorry, but I did already promise to help today. I didn't plan on . . ."

"On me changing plans?" I asked.

"Yes. That."

"We do have to finish talking about things. Work things and everything else." I felt the flush in my cheeks as soon as the words were out of my mouth.

"Tonight too soon?" he asked.

Not soon enough, I thought, but what I said was, "Tonight is good." A Saturday night date plan. How long had it been since I'd had a Saturday night plan that didn't include work in some variety or another?

Ben looked like he might initiate a more physical farewell—a hug or a handshake or something—but he just inclined his head and said, "Tonight, then."

Knowing Ben wasn't a public-display-of-affection sort of man, I didn't push for a farewell embrace. We had time for that later. "Goodbye, gentlemen," I said to his brothers after offering a wave.

"Goodbye, Silvia." They drawled out my name in a singsong way. Yep, those guys knew some things about me. I looked forward to spending time with them and finding out what.

"Goodbye, Ben." Just saying his name made me happy.

I didn't remember the drive home at all because all of my thoughts were on the incredible lighthearted happiness that filled me. And maybe nothing would come from this new adventure. Maybe Ben and I would discover we weren't compatible, or that we didn't really care about each other in any way that could make it long-term.

But we'd spent three years splicing and taping, talking and laughing. We'd even had a few heated arguments, since Ben had a fire to him when he thought he was right about something, and since I hated to make concessions because they made me feel like I was giving up. We'd been together through hunger and fatigue, long hours and intense deadlines. All that time assured me that whatever this was with Ben, it could be something different from the relationships of my past, something special, something like what Emma had with Lucas.

Not that I was mentally picking out wedding dresses or baby names or anything, but the idea of Ben seemed to stretch into something long-term and permanent.

A text came in when I got home.

"Sorry about the interruption. I honestly forgot about them, which likely makes me a not-very-good brother or son. What's your favorite food so I can make plans for dinner tonight?"

"Anything but sushi." I actually stuck my tongue out as I wrote the word and made a gagging noise to my phone as if Ben could hear it.

"Really? I don't remember any relationship with you and sushi. Maybe I wasn't paying proper attention."

I thought back to my time of working with Ben and wrote, "It's because all company parties were catered with Italian food. The topic never came up."

"Fair enough. Tonight? Six?"

"Sounds great," I texted.

I snuggled down on my couch, crossing my legs underneath me, and scrolled up on my text screen. Ben had said I hadn't responded to his message last night. I wondered what sort of message would instigate such fury over me not answering. He'd deleted it, so I'd never know.

But we had a chance to start over here with honest communication. I hesitated with my finger hovering over the screen. "Just do it," I said out loud to myself before I wrote, "Ben?"

"Yes, Silvia?"

"Remember, a long time ago, when you asked me if I was happy?"

"Yes."

"I am now. See you soon."

The words might have been cheesy, but they were true. Happiness felt like it had seeped into my whole being, even with the extreme tension of the day.

His simple return text—"Not soon enough"—echoed my earlier thoughts and made me sigh. A real sigh, like the kind countless actresses did in all those romance movies I had pretty much memorized. Ben cared about me. I felt complete satisfaction.

Chapter Sixteen

"Can one kiss do all of this?"

—Jo Stockton, played by Audrey Hepburn in Funny Face

I had a date with Ben Armstrong! Tonight, *Friend Ben* would become *something-more Ben*, which meant I would be engaged by intelligent conversation and understanding. And, I hoped, there would be moments of no conversation at all. If the feel of his fingers at the nape of my neck could hyper-charge every nerve ending in my body, I wanted to see what a full-on kiss could do.

While I was waiting for Ben to pick me up, my mom called. I let it go to voice mail, silently promising I would call her in the morning. Emma called. Also to voice mail. Grandma called. I answered that one. Because no one ignored Grandma.

She needed help volunteering somewhere. Real volun-teering this time, the kind that required grungy clothes and physical labor. I only half-listened because my doorbell rang at pretty much the same time. Ben was early.

I wedged the phone between my ear and shoulder as I walked to the door to let Ben inside.

"No, Grandma, I'm still listening." Not true at all, because Ben and I were suddenly face-to-face. I pointed to the phone, and he smiled, and only then did I realize Ben must have gone home after moving his mom's piano and changed clothes. His typical attire was Converse shoes, jeans, and a T-shirt with a bad pun or superhero logo on the front. On occasion, he wore a blazer over his T-shirt so that he looked caught between nerd and hipster. The whole style thing fit him.

Tonight, he wore dress shoes, dark slacks, and a short sleeved, button-down shirt that he left untucked in a way that made him look casual and dressy at the same time. While it wasn't the tuxedo of the previous night, this look also fit him.

I glanced down to my own clothes. My black ballet flats and red chiffon shirt over a gray tank top dressed up the jeans enough that I figured there was no need to change. "No, Grandma. I think that sounds like a great charity. Children are important." She *was* talking about children, wasn't she? I couldn't honestly remember. "I'd love to help. Right." While she filled in the details, I shot Ben a look of apology. His slight shrug showed he wasn't worried about the delay. "Okay. Sure. I'll be there."

Once the call with Grandma ended, Ben took my hand and pressed his lips to my knuckles, his breath warm on fingers I hadn't known were cold until he touched them.

I'd seen every Jane Austen adaptation ever made, and

none of them ever came close to explaining how completely, shiveringly sexy a kiss to the hand could actually be.

Getting in the car, the drive to the restaurant, and getting out again made me self-conscious in ways that made no sense. This was Ben! Ben, the guy who'd seen me take out my eye on several occasions. Ben, who'd seen me throw a tantrum during a tricky commercial edit, and who had laughed at me when I threw a coffee mug at the project manager's closed door when I was still pretty new to Mid-Scene Films. Ben, who'd had chair races with me in the halls during work hours, and who'd ended up in the instacare when he fell out of his chair and I'd rolled over his arm.

Ben.

My friend, Ben.

How did we go from all of that to awkward?

"Here we are!" He spread his arms out to the restaurant in front of us.

My tunnel vision of figuring us out had allowed me to ignore our location up until that moment when we were on the sidewalk and looking up at the words Mori Sushi on the building. I laughed. Well, that was one way to kill the awkward. Make a dinner joke.

"Well played," I said.

"I knew you'd like this. Everyone says it's the best in LA." He took my hand and led me towards the door rather than back to the car where we could go to our real destination that didn't include sushi. His determination to get to the door allowed a different thought to form in my mind. Ben was one hundred percent serious.

"Oh." That one word summed up all my confusion. Just

oh. With Ben so eager to please, standing next to me and seeming to believe he'd done something wonderful, I had no choice; I went with it.

As far as I knew, there were no allergies preventing me from eating sushi. No. Not allergies. Just taste buds.

We were seated after our reservations were confirmed. I cleared my throat and shifted uncomfortably. Maybe this really was a joke and he was waiting for me to say something. But a reservation? That might be taking the joke too far. Maybe this was a test to see if I was open-minded enough to try the one thing I said I didn't want? Or maybe he just forgot that sushi was on my list of non-consumables? Except the list only had one item on it and had been texted to him on that exact same day . . . which made it really, *really* hard to forget . . .

I glanced over the menu and felt a spike of anxiety. It was probably unlikely that the tako salad on the menu was actually a taco salad, especially since octopus was listed among the ingredients.

Ben had the sad misfortune of being as transparent as I was when it came to facial expressions. I was sure I looked bewildered as my eye scanned the menu, but Ben didn't notice my obvious discomfort since he was too preoccupied by his own.

Okay, so he didn't choose this place because he was a closet sushi fan.

The waiter came to take our orders. I closed my menu, realizing it didn't do me any good since none of the listed items were familiar to me, even if some of the ingredients were recognizable. Ben soldiered on, scanning it like a man on the *Titanic* might have scanned the decks for a stray life-boat.

"Are you ready to order?" the waiter asked.

"Maybe give us a moment," I said, since Ben had not yet decided to throw up the white flag and admit the menu's victory.

Ben glanced up to see my closed menu and the retreating waiter's back. "At least one of us knows what they want." His head ducked down as he went in for another round with the menu. After several moments of him intermittently scowling and muttering, he excused himself to go wash his hands.

While he was gone, the waiter returned with two glasses of water, saw me alone at the table, and left again, probably wondering why people made reservations to eat at a specific time when they obviously intended on delaying that time for as long as possible.

I sipped at my water, tapped at my menu, and wondered where my date could have gone. After another three minutes, my phone buzzed from within my purse.

I had a "no texting at the table" rule because it was rude, but since there was no one around for me to offend, I tugged my phone out and swiped open the messages. It was from Ben. I glanced around to see if he was watching me from somewhere, but if he was, he'd managed to hide himself pretty well.

The text read, "I'm an idiot!"

While I was trying to decipher what this message actually meant, another one showed up. "Get your things, and meet me outside."

"You're outside?" I texted.

"Yes. Come out and meet me. But bring all your stuff. Don't leave anything at the table."

"Should I bring the waters the waiter left for us as well?"

Ben didn't reply to my sarcastic remark even though I waited another full minute to hear from him. Finally I decided he must be serious, gathered my things, and vacated the restaurant as quickly and as invisibly as possible. For a half-blind girl, that meant I ran into a wall jutting out from the right side, near the entrance. Who put walls in places like that?

I exited, rubbing my right shoulder where there would definitely be a bruise forming.

Ben was at the car. As soon as he saw me, he pushed off the car, and hurried over to wrap his arms around me. "I am such an idiot!" he repeated.

"For?"

He pulled his phone from his pocket. "I asked you where you wanted to eat, and you said anywhere *but* sushi, but I was so excited to be going out with you, I skimmed the text and read it as you wanted sushi. I hate sushi, but figured if you liked it, we could do whatever you wanted. When I went to the bathroom and read through the text again, I realized my mistake. I'm so sorry."

"You were reading texts while using the bathroom?" I asked, laughing at him.

He rolled his eyes at me and bumped my shoulder, which was not appreciated, since it was still sore from the run-in with the wall. "I wasn't using the bathroom. I was doing research."

"In the bathroom?" I hurried to scoot back, in case he decided to shoulder bump me again.

"Stop making it sound weird! I was trying to text a few of my sushi-eating buddies for advice on what might actually be edible."

I let out a low chuckle. Being with Ben was way more fun than any other man I'd ever dated. This was absolutely the beginning of a great relationship. "So, we've committed the great edit caper, parked in no-parking zones on two separate occasions, and did the restaurant equivalent of doorbell ditching. We really are criminals."

"Sadly, we're not very good criminals, or we wouldn't have been caught on the illegal parking. We better go before the waiter comes out and finds us. So what would you actually like to eat, Miss Bradshaw?"

"There should be an In-N-Out not too far from here." I put up my hand, seeing the protest on his lips before he likely knew he was forming one. "And don't you dare disparage my choice. Sometimes a simple burger is the best thing life has to offer."

We went to In-N-Out and ate our burgers with the profound reverence of those whose taste buds were not refined enough for food that looked like slugs.

"They had seaweed salad," I said once my burger, fries, and strawberry shake were gone.

"Tasty," Ben said. He still had a few fries left. The fact that I didn't take them made me a true friend. "They also had tom yum soup."

"Poor Tom." I took one of Ben's fries after all, if only to clean up the rest of the ketchup on my plate.

He dropped his head in his hands and gave a low groan. "I cannot believe I misread your text. I never skim communications. I feel incredibly stupid. Please say you forgive me."

"Are you still apologizing? We've already established that we're both bad at communicating. And being with you right now makes up for anything." I paused, fiddling with my paper napkin. "I've really missed you since I left Mid-Scene."

"You've missed me?"

"So much. It's nice to have someone who gets me. I've missed everything. Like playing movie quotes. I've missed that," I said.

"What? No one else will play?" he asked, leaning his elbows on the table.

"Honestly, I haven't got enough friends in my life to play games with. Emma and I play a similar game with Jane Austen quotes, but I always get tripped up trying to remember which ones came from the actual books and which ones came from the movies. Emma knows more about Jane Austen than anyone on the planet."

"You do, too, don't you? I seem to remember something about you going to a Jane Austen ball or something."

I laughed. "I did do that. It was so much fun. It's too bad—" I cut off since I was going to say "It's too bad I hadn't taken you with me." We weren't working together when I went to the ball, so I could have invited him. Why hadn't I thought to invite Ben? "Anyway," I continued, "though I am definitely a fan of all things Austen, I love the movies more than the books, which would be a sacrilege to Emma. You can't ever tell her. I don't think she'd ever forgive me."

Ben drew an X over his heart; he was the only person I

knew in the whole world who literally crossed his heart when making a promise.

"So, what's the worst line in all of movie history, in your opinion?" Ben asked.

"Easy. 'I truly, deeply love you.' Padme to Anakin. Episode Two. I feel like throwing up just thinking about it."

"Lines like that are done in other movies all the time. Do you hate it in all of them, or just in that one?"

"What other movies?" I'd forgotten how good he was at our game.

He laughed, nudging the tray of food wrappers to the side so he could cross his arms on the table in front of him. The restaurant had filled up while we'd been eating, and the static buzz of dozens of conversations around us required us to speak louder. "Well, there's the movie with the actual title *Truly Madly Deeply.*"

"I don't think I know that one."

Ben looked surprised. "Really? It had Alan Rickman in it and won several awards. I think you'd like it."

I gave him the benefit of the doubt. "Maybe it wasn't the line, maybe it was the fact that Padme and Anakin had zero on-screen chemistry. I just didn't believe she really loved him. And I definitely don't believe he loved her. The line probably would have been fine if it had been a couple who really seemed in love. What about you? What's the worst movie line you've ever heard?"

"In *Man of Steel,* when Lois Lane says to Superman, 'They say it's all downhill after the first kiss.' And then Superman says, 'I'm pretty sure that only counts when you're kissing a human.' I hate that one."

I thought about it for several moments before shaking my head. "I think it's kind of cute. Why do you hate that one?"

"It's an insult to all male members of the human race. It's saying that a woman has to kiss an alien in order to have a long-lasting and meaningful relationship because not one human man is up to the task."

His point was not lost on me. "I see. It's another way society makes men into bumbling, inadequate idiots. But it can also be looked at as an insult to women. I'm sure the writers didn't mean it that way, but in that particular situation, Lois Lane is the human. So, wouldn't it be all downhill for him because *he* kissed a human?"

Ben grinned. "I kinda like that—the great equalizer where *all* humans are inadequate, not just half the population. But since we both know the writers did not mean it like that, it stays on my least-favorite list."

Point accepted. I glanced at our empty food tray with a degree of disappointment. When was the last time my appetite had actually worked to remind me I was hungry? Since starting at Portal Pictures, I'd been too nervous or busy to eat, so my appetite abandoned me, likely realizing I planned on ignoring it anyway, but now that calm and peace had settled over me, my body felt ravenous.

"What else?" I asked. "On your least-favorite list, I mean?"

He thought a moment. "*Sixth Sense*: 'I see dead people.' But it's also on my list of best lines because there is so much awesome about it. The problem is that, out of context, it's incredibly corny. In context, it's creepy. It's also a great hint at the twist ending, since Haley Joel Osment looks right at

Bruce Willis's character when he says it the first time. I guess that makes it count as a best and a worst."

He looked at the tray with what might have been disappointment, too. I told him to hang on a moment and went and ordered us another basket of fries to share. When I got back, he shook his head and said, "What would you say if I told you that it makes me uncomfortable that you bought that?"

"Why would it make you uncomfortable?"

"Because I am taking you on a date."

"I'd probably give you a lecture regarding my independence and tell you to get with the century. But I would also tell you that it's nice to see a man who takes respect seriously and that it's nice knowing you aren't a failure-to-launch guy living in his mom's basement playing video games all night with his online-only friends and sleeping all day."

"Ah. Good thing I didn't mention anything so that we avoided an awkward conversation where I'd wonder if you'd judge me for living in my parents' house until I was through all of film school and that I spent a lot of time playing video games during that period in my life. It's also a good thing we avoided the conversation so you didn't get the misconception that it was a failure-to-launch thing, since it was more of a delayed launch. I'd hate for my self-image to be damaged in any way."

"I don't know. You seem pretty confident to me. I doubt your self-image has ever been shaken by a dumb girl."

He wiped his hands together to brush off the salt. "You're right. But an intelligent woman has the ability to do some very real damage."

I didn't bother to pretend that his words didn't have an effect on me because I could see the very real vulnerability in his eyes as he said them.

The delivery counted as smooth. And sweet. I'd never thought of Ben as smooth before. Sweet, yes, but smooth was a new side of Ben. A side I found incredibly attractive. The open honesty was also attractive. But talking about him in the context of other women made me curious. Ben and I had spent hours talking about everything while we'd worked together, but we'd never talked much about our dating lives at all.

So we talked about our experiences dating other people. He told me all about the time a very pretty girl had invited him over to meet her entire family because she'd told them he was her boyfriend—except it was only their first date. I told him about the time a guy who wore a prosthetic asked me to prom by sending me a box with a wooden leg inside it that had belonged to him when he was little. The note said, "Would you be willing to dance your legs off with me?"

I told Ben about how I answered the guy with one of my fake eyes from when I was younger and a note that said, "Eye would love to!" Ben about choked on his laughter when he found out the guy hadn't known I had a fake eye.

Ben and I spent another hour sitting in those hard chairs discussing everything that came to our minds, telling each other stories about our childhood or other jobs or other dates. The awkwardness of our first real date had ended with the failed sushi attempt, and everything from that moment on had been comfortable and easy. The easiness of the conversation was not lost on me. I thought of how Emma said that friends made the best boyfriends and decided she might really be onto something.

When Ben finally took me home, it was accompanied by apologies for getting sidetracked by his restaurant gaffe, and for lingering over dinner so long we had to forgo his other plans because it was simply too late.

He never mentioned what his other plans might have been, but no amount of over-priced entertainment could have replaced the simple, tranquil peace I'd found in a night of easy companionship.

Ben walked me to the door with his brow furrowed deep. "Really," he said. "I am much cooler than tonight would lead you to believe. This was just an off-night for me. Please let me have another chance."

"I don't know, Ben . . ."

At his stricken look, I realized this was not a time for teasing. Maybe later—because the way things felt at that exact moment, I was certain there would be a later. Likely even a *much* later.

I stared at Ben with open wonder when I turned to face him. We stood close enough, the smell of him made me want to flutter my eyes closed and simply breathe him in. Who knew such a citrusy, musky scent could be so incredibly masculine?

"How about tomorrow? Is tomorrow too soon to try again?" he asked.

"I'm helping my grandma tomorrow night."

"Oh." The hope in his eyes snuffed out like a candle at bedtime. "What are you doing?"

"It's a charity thing. The real kind with manual labor this

time. She's been acting so strangely lately, though, we could be doing anything, really."

"Volunteering is considered strange behavior?" He leaned against my porch railing.

Why wasn't I inviting him in? Why was I not unlocking my door and asking him to come in and sit down on my couch so we could continue talking?

I didn't know. So I pushed on with the conversation at hand while not reaching for my keys or opening my doors or asking him inside.

"Volunteering is fine. It's just that she's made a lot of changes all at once, and it's hard to keep track. Her behavior patterns have all shifted, and I'm still trying to figure it out. I mean, she has a boyfriend I didn't even know about until last night."

"What time are you going to help her?"

"Five tomorrow evening."

He looked up and to the side like he did when he was trying to visualize something. "Why don't I pick you up at 4:30, and we can help your grandma together?"

I gave him a doubtful look. "You want to hang out with my geriatric grandmother on your Sunday afternoon off?" Grandma would not love how I'd phrased that.

"Sure," Ben said. He pulled himself up onto the banister and perched there. "Why wouldn't I? It's with you."

Yep. Smooth Ben was definitely worth knowing. I maintained eye contact to be certain he genuinely had no objections. I moved toward him, carefully, slowly. "So, I've been meaning to ask you about a certain picture on your fridge . . ."

A grin curved his lips. "You saw that, huh?"

I nodded.

"I'm torn between being glad that you saw it and embarrassed."

I put my hands on either side of him on the banister, knowing the move was forward, but also knowing I would have to be forward because Ben, smooth or otherwise, was always Nice Ben. We were close, painfully close. Yet, painfully too far away, as well.

"Why am I on your fridge? And why did you take me down again?"

He didn't blink, didn't flinch away from the question like most people would have. He owned it outright. "Because I've been in love with you since your first month at Mid-Scene when you stomped into Stan's office and yelled at him for changing your work on the Valentine project. To see you stand up for yourself like that was very attractive. Most people are afraid to demand respect like that. It made you stand out. That's why it bothered me to think Dean Thomas was strangling out the woman I'd fallen for."

"He wasn't strangling me, at least he's not as much anymore—"

"Silvia?" He interrupted me by placing his hands on my shoulders and pulling me closer, enough to feel the warmth radiating off him. His closeness, his warmth, made me forget what we were talking about.

"Hmm?"

"You're missing the most important part of all that."

"What part?"

"The part where I told you I love you . . . twice."

"Oh." Just oh. As in, *Oh my stars, how did I get to this wonderful place?*

He smiled wider, his eyes scanning my face as if memorizing me. "It would be great to know how you felt about me in return."

"Right. How I feel . . . about that . . ." No sense in delaying any further. I tilted up on my tiptoes and pressed my lips softly against his. A kiss with a question in it. *Do you really love me? Really?*

His answer was to pull me in the rest of the way. One of his hands reached behind my neck; his fingers threaded through my hair. His other hand moved to the small of my back and tightened around me until no space existed between us. The soft kiss became more urgent. One kiss became two and three as years of unrequited love received its just reward.

I pulled away, cradling his face in my hands, and said, "Does that answer your question?"

"I'd ask you to say the words out loud, but I get that this is pretty new for you, even if I've felt this way for a long time. I can accept this for now."

"For now?"

"I've dated lots of women between knowing how I felt about you and right now. Enough to know that my feelings for you are the real deal. I need to know your feelings for me are also the real deal. So when you're ready, let me know."

He was right. While I felt all the stirrings and knew the potential of what we had, he'd been thinking about it for far longer than I had been. "Deal." It was as close as my heart could give him.

We kissed on it.

Chapter Seventeen

"If people loved each other more, they'd shoot each other less."
—Ariane, played by Audrey Hepburn in Love in the Afternoon

The next evening, Ben and I spent time helping Grandma and Walt do inventory. Walt and Ben had become fast friends and lobbed jokes back and forth to each other the entire night. Walt even laughed at Ben's mention of the chances of dying while skydiving. A double date with grandparents might have been weird with anyone else, but with Ben, it was nothing short of perfect.

If Ben and I had been in a movie, I might have awoken Monday morning to find a hundred flowers on my doorstep, but we weren't a movie, and I expected nothing like that. What I did wake up to was flowers on my phone. A GIF of fragile, pink cherry blossom petals being blown out of the open palms of someone's hands showed up in my text messages from Ben. Could life be any more flawless?

The short answer was yes. My glorious weekend received

a small extension, since I allowed myself to sleep in and be a teensy bit late to work. This meant I arrived in the office to a buzz and flurry of activity by people who usually weren't in the office until much later. It startled me to see them all. After shaking down a few people for information, I pieced together the reason for the busyness: the success of the press junket and a few particular reviews had essentially guaranteed *Sliver of Midnight*'s recognition by the Academy. Every review so far had declared the film as "one to watch," "the darling of the year," a film that would "sweep the Academy Awards." But some new reviews had just come in from some of the more renowned outlets that were the equivalent of an iron-clad contract with the Academy.

The buzz had inspired the executive team of Portal Pictures to visit our side of the building, an occurrence that definitely could be filed under hardly-ever-happens. The pride they felt over the success of *Sliver of Midnight* had our entire department striding around the office with more swagger than usual.

Adam happened to come into work early on the day the executives planned to show up, which made me wonder if he'd known they were coming and kept that knowledge to himself. "Today's the day," he whispered to me. "Today's the day I'm going to be noticed. I need to meet these guys, be introduced, have them like me, and invite me to audition for *Gray Skies*. At this point, I don't even care if they give me a part as the janitor. Today, Silvia. Dean promised."

I gave him a thumbs-up, hoping it would turn out like he wanted. We worked in such a fickle business where decisions were as much luck as anything. It didn't help that Dean's promises weren't anything that could be taken to the bank.

Adam knocked on Dean's door, which had been closed since I'd arrived that morning. He didn't invite Adam to enter, but he seldom did, so without waiting, Adam smiled brightly and opened the door. "Do you need anything befo—" Adam broke off mid-word.

I poked my head around the corner and peeked into Dean's office.

Dean had on his angry eyes, the ones that were rimmed red from hours of drinking, the ones that meant it would be hard working with him. Today, of all days. The big question was whether Dean was still drunk or just hungover. Hungover meant he needed us to help clean him up. Still drunk meant we'd be better off closing the door, telling the execs that he'd gone out, and praying he didn't exit his office to reveal us as liars.

"Dean?" I said.

"She moved," he said, his eyes unfocused, as if seeing something beyond the room, beyond us, beyond his control.

Not exactly the comment I was expecting, and also not enough to base a determination of sobriety. "Dean? Are you okay?"

"What?" He finally looked at us and actually saw us and not whatever it was he'd been talking about. "I'm fine."

He didn't look fine.

Adam and I shared a glance that encompassed a whole conversation.

We debated our possibilities and finally settled on Adam getting Dean the lemon water/energy drink/apple cider vinegar concoction that had worked so well before. Adam scurried off, leaving me alone with my boss.

"Dean. Executive staff is coming today. Bronson, the sound editor, is already waiting in the reception area. They'll be here any minute. What can I do to help you get ready?"

"I'm ready." He shifted his shoulders and lifted his chin. "I am!" he insisted when I raised my eyebrows at him.

Adam raced in with the water and nearly spilled it trying to hand it off to Dean.

"I hate this stuff," Dean said, but he knocked it back, swallowing in deep gulps, likely so he could avoid it being on his taste buds for longer than necessary. He stood. "I'm ready."

He didn't look any more ready than he had a moment before, but film editors had to work with the messes we were given. Even if it was a walking, talking mess like Dean Thomas.

When we arrived in the reception area, everyone else was already waiting. I sighed, the lone woman in a pool of suits and ties. Other women worked in the business, but I didn't get the pleasure of working with them often.

With Dean busy being broken, I felt guilty, like I hadn't been babysitting him closely enough, like the responsibility of his bad behavior somehow fell on me. I hated that.

Danny and Christopher came in with the executives and immediately lit up when they saw me. Danny embraced me and then turned, with his arm still around me, and said to the CEO, "Silvia here is a keeper. Her name better be listed above the line for editing because when *Sliver of Midnight* wins an Academy Award for best film editor, I expect her to be recognized for her work on it."

Dean, who had been all but ignored as we entered the

area, bristled. He apparently felt a compliment to me was a slap in the face, or rather a punch in the gut, to him.

We stood around making small talk before the executives said they wanted to see samples of the projects we were currently working on. We moved to the editing suites—the place where the magic happened.

Bronson had his personal suite, and Graham, the SFX editor, had his own suite as well, though the special effects needed for *Sliver of Midnight* had been so minimal, I oversaw and signed off on the work Graham did for the film. Graham was still a pretty new employee, and I doubted Dean knew Graham worked for the company.

The executives and production staff mingled and talked as we made our way to my editing suite. Technically Dean claimed it as his, though he hardly did any of the work there. He turned on the systems and sat in the chair like he knew what was going on. When he looked at the screen to open the files of a current project, he lost some of his credibility. He didn't know what the files were called or where they were stored on the servers.

"Actually," Dean said, "let's have our assistant do some assisting. You guys all know Silvia Bradshaw, right? She's our new assistant film editor."

"New?" Danny snorted. "She's been with the studio six months."

"Yes, well," Dean shot back, "considering I've been here for decades, she seems new to me."

Calling attention to his time with the company was old arsenal. He used it with me all the time, but it seemed to do the trick with everyone else, because no one said anything more while I slid into the seat next to him and took control of the editing board. I opened files and explained where we were with two of our current productions. Dean took over a few times to point out a few things he'd personally worked on, like a petulant child demanding attention.

Danny spooned praise over me and none at all over Dean. Dean obviously noticed because he kept bringing the attention back to himself and the previous movies he had worked on and the awards he had won.

It was awkward, and I felt incredibly grateful when it was all over. Bronson was all too happy to take the wheel and guide them to the sound studio.

In Bronson's lair, he showed the executives how he had created one of the most disturbing sounds I'd ever heard by slowing down a dog's howl. At the lower speeds, the mournful noise became horrible, painful, agonizing.

The executives all laughed, enjoying the moment of cringing that they all displayed. They'd done a good job hiring Bronson; he knew his stuff. We visited several other suites to talk to various directors and editors, all doing their part.

We went to Graham's editing suite last. He brought up some work on the car crash scene he was doing for *Gray Skies*.

Adam, who had yet to be introduced to anyone on the executive staff, and who had been a mix of both hope and fury since Dean seemed to have purposely left him out, must have found his courage because he stepped forward.

"*Gray Skies*," he said. "Funny you should mention that. I'm a huge fan of the series, and I've been meaning to talk to you guys because my resume—"

"Not now." Dean's face and neck blotched red in fury that

Adam would dare attempt such a leap for an audition when it was supposed to be all about Dean's great work on *Sliver of Midnight*. He turned to Adam and muttered low, "This is hardly the time or the place for you to make a power grab."

"Power grab?" Adam look wounded, but if his trembling limbs and curled lip were any indicator, he was also enraged. "And not the time? When is the time, Dean? Because you promised me for months now—almost a *year* now—to get me an audition for a part in that series. I've watched parts come and go to actors with half my skill for almost a year! When is there going to be a better time?"

"Well, this certainly isn't it. And if you're going to pull that kind of attitude in my studio, you might as well empty out your desk. You can go find employment elsewhere. I don't have time for an assistant who doesn't know how to keep his place."

Adam's face went bright red, matching the color of his hair—and Dean's face. Adam's trembling limbs became positively spastic. He stuttered a few times before finding strength in his voice. "What kind of assistant is it that you want?" He snapped his fingers. "Oh, I know. You want one like Silvia. You want an assistant who will do all your work for you. You want an assistant who is willing to do whatever it takes to get the job done, even when it means bringing in help from another production studio to do *your* job because *you're* so stupid drunk that you're passed out on the company couch while another editor put together your Academy Award–winning movie. That's right!"

He clapped his hands to call everyone's attention even though he already had it. "Here's how hard your editor is working: *Sliver of Midnight* was not done by Dean. You guys keep talking about a best picture and even a best film editor award, but the only award he should get is the studio's best drunk! He didn't do any of the work. He didn't do anything on that movie. Silvia did most of the work. And then, on the night before it was due, when she needed somebody to sign off on all the details, she enlisted the help of an editor from a competing studio to get the work done."

I leapt forward in an attempt to—I didn't know . . . stop him? Put my hand over his mouth? Punch him in the trachea to prevent him from saying anything else?

"What is he talking about?" Christopher demanded. His quiet request sounded like a shout in the silence that followed Adam's outburst.

"It's a lie!" Dean shrilled. His face had shifted from the angry red to a sickly yellow color, like a dying leaf on a diseased tree.

I was caught between fleeing, fighting, and freezing. I forced my muscles to relax, uncurled my fingers from the fists they had formed, and shifted my body so my stance was casual. For a moment, I considered calling Adam a liar and denying everything. But if I had to lie to be where I was, then it wasn't worth being there.

"What is he talking about?" Christopher asked again.

The entire staff had their eyes on me, except Dean, who had his eyes fixed on the ground. In a matter of moments, Dean Thomas had become a beaten man. Gone was the playground bully. The only thing left was the child.

"I . . . I can explain."

And so I did.

Chapter Eighteen

"Now . . . the first thing we have to do is stay calm."

—Susy Hendrix, played by Audrey Hepburn in Wait Until Dark

When the clamor and chaos died down and everyone re-treated to their own corners to figure out what to do with the mess they'd been handed, I followed Adam to his desk.

"What were you thinking?" I whisper-yelled at him. "How could you do that to me?"

He grunted and flopped down in his chair. "This isn't about you. This is about me sticking it to the man."

"Are you kidding? It's about all of us! You didn't stick anything to anyone except to Dean and me and you."

"How do you figure that? This can only help me. They're going to notice me, now. They're auditioning for a new part—Merrill—and I'm going to be there. They'll remember me. I finally got my chance to stand out."

"As a stool pigeon!" I wanted to use him as a punching bag. He really didn't understand the ramifications of his actions, the consequences that should have been obvious to anyone with sense.

"You have no idea what I've been through to try to make it in this business. I've been waiting for a long time for this chance—"

I interrupted him before he could make himself look like the victim of the hour. "Chance to what? Ruin the prospects of everyone present—yourself included?"

"Why do you keep saying that? This doesn't affect me at all."

I stared at him in disbelief. "Because this is a good old boys' club, and you just proved you aren't one of them. If you can't play nice in the sandbox, then they kick sand in your face and send you packing. No one is giving you an audition after this."

His face was impassive. He didn't believe me. But it didn't make me less right.

I tossed a look of sheer fury at Adam. "Did you not hear them? They actually talked about lawsuits! Lawsuits, Adam!"

His face paled. I'd finally gotten his attention. "I didn't mean to make things hard on you—I was just so mad. He's been promising for so long. It just came out. I didn't plan on doing any of that."

But he *had* planned on it. Every action from him proved he had intended to be noticed, either because Dean pointed him out or because he pointed himself out. Standing here, arguing with Adam, was not helping me. I had to call Ben. I had to warn him. Because it would be awful if he found out about this mess via his boss instead of me. I didn't know how long it would take for the executives at Portal Pictures to contact the executives at Mid-Scene Films, but chances of them delaying were slim. Portal Pictures would meet with their own lawyers first, then they would contact Janice at Mid-Scene.

I didn't know what would happen then. Maybe everything would be fine and we'd all laugh about this tomorrow and say what a great joke it had all been. But nothing seemed further from likely than the joke scenario.

"Hold my calls," I directed Adam. "Don't let anyone into my office. Tell them I'm very busy and can't be disturbed." In my panic, I forgot that Adam was Dean's administrative assistant, not mine. But I sincerely doubted that he would be doing anything for Dean anytime soon. Not after what had happened. Not only would Adam refuse to take orders from Dean, it was unlikely Dean would want Adam anywhere near him.

Adam shot me a look that declared his doubt in my sanity, but I didn't care; I was too busy pulling out my phone and hurrying to the safety of my office.

I dialed Ben's number before my office door could skim closed. It rang three times, then went to voice mail. "Call as soon as you can, Ben. It's urgent. Life-and-death urgent!" No reason to sugarcoat the truth. A panicked message was all I had to offer.

I waited a full minute, then tried again. "Please pick up," I begged with each ring. As soon as it went to voice mail, I hung up and tried again.

My next seven calls went to voice mail. I didn't leave another message. What could be said beyond that first pleading?

I tried to contact Ben with fervent desperation via all social media direct messages, email, and phone to no avail.

I paced my office.

Maybe they'd already contacted Mid-Scene. Maybe Ben couldn't answer because he was cleaning out his office and placing his Superman action figure into a box alongside the book of puns I gave him for April Fools' Day. Maybe he'd been yanked into the office of Mid-Scene's lawyer. I'd always thought of Janice as the nicest woman I knew, but that was because I'd never been on the opposite side of her lawyer temper. I'd seen her get feisty. The thought of her glaring at Ben over the top of her glasses made me shudder. She'd chew him up.

That decided it.

I had to go to him. I had to see him physically, in person, right now.

He needed to know how sorry I was. He needed to know how I never meant for any of this to happen. He needed to know I was on his side—whatever that side might be. And I needed to see him to make sure he didn't hate me over this debacle that was entirely my fault.

Ben not hating me was the most important thing because now that I knew he loved me, I didn't want it any other way.

I grabbed my keys, my phone, and my purse and flung the door to my office open wide.

On the other side stood a man with his hand raised, poised to knock.

Owen Theodore Carlson, Esq., offered a polite but coldly professional smile. "Miss Bradshaw. We need to talk."

Candace, the HR representative for Portal Pictures, stood behind him. She looked like she might faint if anyone spoke too loudly in her direction. She hated confrontation, and if her wide eyes and pale face of abject terror offered any insight, the meeting with Owen the lawyer wasn't going to be a friendly chitchat.

My head bobbled, though I hardly understood what I was trying to communicate, as I stepped to the side and allowed them entrance into my personal space within the company.

The door swung closed, but I managed to catch a glimpse of Adam's horrified face just before it clicked shut. So much for him guarding my door.

I resolutely turned toward the two people the company had sent to deal with me. Any words now could only be used for self-defense.

The shakedown from Owen the lawyer and Candace the HR representative could be described as nothing less than hostile. Owen, as if he knew of my weakness, sat on the chair to my right. He scooted it back and to the side enough that I could not see both of them at the same time and had to turn my head back and forth as they spoke.

They'd scoured me mentally and emotionally before they were done. They'd pried hard, trying to gain access to all the personal details of my life.

There were questions I didn't mind answering: How many man-hours had I put into the film? What was my work ethic? Could I show them any notes or records I'd kept regarding my processes during postproduction? I'd already given a lot of this information to the executives when I explained everything to them, but Owen wanted all the little details. How long had I worked for Mid-Scene Films? How long had I known Ben? What kind of person was he? What was *his* work ethic? How much work did he do on the film? How many actual man-hours were spent?

There were questions I didn't love answering but felt obligated to, since the security cameras would confirm or deny my words: What time did Ben arrive at the studio the night before the preview? To which rooms was he given access? Were there any other projects he was allowed to either view or access? Where was Dean during the time Ben and I worked on the film? How much of the film was Dean's work? Once Dean was sober again, did he have any recollection of there being an interloper in our offices?

That was what they called Ben: *the interloper*. Had I been seeing Ben on a personal level prior to the incident?

That was what they called our night of collaboration: *the incident*.

Who else had I allowed to access Portal Pictures files? Was I aware of the egregious breach of contract? Was I aware that the charges currently against me were enough for full termination? What did I have to say in my defense?

Finally came the questions I refused to answer: How long had I been seeing Ben socially? Were we intimate? Was intimacy the reason I'd jeopardized the security of Portal Pictures? Would I be willing to stop seeing Ben?

It took a full twenty minutes after they'd gone for me to be able to stand on shaking legs and, once again, gather my things to make my retreat. I had to get to Ben. The drive to his house was a blur. I blinked and found myself standing on his porch and knocking on his door.

"Why aren't you answering your phone?" I asked as soon as he appeared. His arms had been opening as if to embrace me, but upon seeing my distress and likely hearing it in my voice, too, he dropped his arms and asked what was going on.

"Has anyone from Mid-Scene Films talked to you today about *Sliver of Midnight*?"

His whole body tensed. His studio and my movie said in the same sentence only meant one thing. "How did they find out? Oh. Adam." He answered his own question before I could open my mouth to spit the word out.

I nodded.

"Well, that's unfortunate." He opened his door wider and ushered me into his house.

He led me straight to the kitchen and fetched me a glass from the cupboard. It was the same Kylo Ren glass I'd used before. Or maybe he had a collection of them. I smiled to see my picture back on the fridge where it belonged. As I filled the glass with ice water, he leaned against his counter and tilted his head. He rubbed the back of his knuckles over his chin. "Mid-Scene hasn't contacted me, yet. How long has Portal Pictures known?"

"Since this morning. Adam had a breakdown and has been declared mentally incompetent."

"Who made the declaration?"

"I did."

Ben's fingers tapped at the counter. The familiar pattern of three quick, two slow meant he was processing. "I'm imagining the studio is in some sort of damage-control mode, right?"

I nodded. "They're afraid you'll claim ownership of the intellectual property rights."

His fingers stopped tapping, and he rolled his eyes. "Of course I'm not claiming ownership. All I did was watch it and make a few suggestions. It's basically what every single person who ever watches a movie does: they watch it and comment on it. This isn't earth-shattering here. Why would I assume that meant ownership?"

I smiled at him, feeling comfort just being in his presence. "I told them you were an honorable guy and wouldn't make a claim for anything, but let's be honest, Ben. You did more than just make suggestions. You pressed the buttons, used the sliders—you did the work."

His eyes went wide, and he straightened from his slouch. "Did you tell them that?"

"No, but there are cameras in all the suites." I set the Kylo Ren glass in the sink.

Ben took hold of my wrist and pulled me into an embrace. "Let's go sit down, and you can tell me everything." He pressed a kiss to my forehead.

I leaned into him and rose up on my tiptoes to drop a quick kiss on his cheek. He turned fast enough to make certain that the tail end of the kiss caught his mouth, too.

Sneaky Ben.

Sweet, smooth, sneaky Ben.

Sneaky Ben turned out to be worth knowing as well.

Ben settled on the couch, and I sat next to him. We turned so we could face each other and talk more easily. It was hard not to think about how I'd fallen asleep on that exact couch, or that my picture was back on his fridge. It was hard not to think of how incredibly safe I felt with Ben. I forced myself to put all of that out of my mind and told him everything that had happened with Portal Pictures.

He listened with full attention, not showing any signs of emotion, the way he did when he reviewed a new film project. When I was done, he tightened his lips together for a fraction of a second before saying, "Best film editor, huh? The execs were there because they think you're going to get an Academy Award? That's some high praise, Silvia! I'm really proud of you."

"Seriously, Ben? That's what you got out of this conversation? We're in a lot of trouble here. Both of us, and it's all my fault."

"It's not your fault. I'm an adult. I make my own choices. And I don't think we're in that much trouble. I'll assure them that I have no intentions of seeking redress for intellectual property rights. I'll sign papers that say they own their own intellectual property, and it'll be over. Easy."

"Easy?" I repeated. I needed reassurance because my life that had been going so well now felt like a train wreck.

His fingers tapped out his thinking rhythm. When they stopped, he said, "Yes. It's easy. Sure, it seems like it's a big deal to them right now, but once they look at the entire situation, they'll calm down, and everything will be fine. You'll see."

I hoped he was right.

He made me dinner, and we played Zombicide, a board game where it was us against zombies. The zombies won. Ben pulled out his pocket watch and tsked when he saw the time. He walked me to my car to give me a "proper kiss good night."

"I love it when you call things proper," I said.

He leaned against my car, neither of us in any hurry to say goodbye and mean it.

His eyes stayed steadily on mine, sincere, intense, a fire burning in them. "I love you." He lowered his forehead to mine. "You cannot know what a relief it is to say the words out loud."

I didn't give him a chance to say them again. I pushed up on my toes and pressed my lips firmly against his. His arm curled around my waist, and he hooked a finger into my belt loop to tug me up higher, closing the distance between us.

His other hand was at the nape of my neck, his fingers twined in my hair. I was grateful he had such a strong hold on me because I was caught somewhere between collapsing to the ground with weak-kneed love sickness and floating off from the sheer exhilaration of joy. His lips traced over my cheekbone and to my ear where he whispered, "We need to say good night for real. We both work early tomorrow."

Work.

That word had never sounded like such a foul obscenity before.

"We could both quit," I said, but conceded the point and backed away.

"Given the current climate of your company, that actually doesn't sound half bad. Too bad we're both responsible adults."

I groaned softly. "Well, when you put it like that . . . Good night, Ben."

"Good night, Silvia."

He kissed me again, a gentle featherlight press of his lips before he stepped aside so I could get into my car.

I hated driving away.

My phone rang just as I turned onto the Five and caught up to freeway speeds. "Hello?" I said after pushing the answer button on my steering wheel.

Ben's voice called to me, a slow seductive siren call through my car speakers. "Oh, Silvia?"

He'd hit the right tone.

"Yes, Mickey?" I answered.

"How do you call your lover boy?"

I smiled and bit my lip. Chills up my spine forced a shudder from me before I answered, "Come here, lover boy!" in the huskiest impersonation of the real Silvia Vanderpool that I could get.

"And if he doesn't answer?" Ben asked.

"Oh, lover boy . . ." I crooned.

"And if he *still* doesn't answer?"

We sang the whole song together as I drove back to my house. He told me he wouldn't hang up until I was safely in my house with my dead bolt locked because he didn't want me messing with the odds.

"What are the odds?" I asked.

"There are too many variables on violent crimes. A lot has to do with location and what activities you've engaged in. Right now your odds of becoming a victim are low. But hanging out on your porch in the dark waiting for trouble to come find you could definitely raise those chances. So go inside and bolt your door."

I did as told, and he hung up. I missed him immediately.

I texted Emma, "I think you'd approve . . ."

She texted back after a moment when she must have realized I was waiting for her to respond. "Tell me it's Ben."

"Take all the fun out of it by guessing right away."

"Squeals over here! He is such a nice guy!"

"Yes, he is." I both texted this and said it aloud. No matter what happened at work, I had Ben.

Chapter Nineteen

"I'm here to make a simple delivery and find myself being pillaged and plundered."

—Jo Stockton, played by Audrey Hepburn in Funny Face

The next morning, Nathaniel had gate duty. As I flashed my badge at him, he smiled, waited until I'd opened my window, then offered me some fatherly advice. "If you want to keep that badge of yours working at this particular gate, you need to make sure you keep your nose clean. The execs are going crazy with what they're supposed to do with you."

Maybe Ben wasn't right, after all. "What have you heard?"

Nathaniel shook his head. "I haven't heard anything, not anything that would be useful, anyway. Just don't be bringing anybody else on the property, at least not for a while. And you showing up here early to work certainly doesn't hurt your case. You should keep that up."

I usually came in early, but this time, I'd definitely done it by design to prove my value to the company. Nathaniel let me through the gate, and the sound of the Dodgers game blasting from his booth faded into background static. No memorandums littered my desk or filled my inbox. No security guard waited at my door to watch me pack up my things and escort me from the premises. No executive or lawyer or HR representative stood in my office with their arms folded over their chests and their toes tapping impatiently for me to show up so they could give me bad news.

At every turn, I expected something. But nothing happened.

Maybe Ben was right. Maybe this wasn't a big deal after all. Maybe he could just sign a paper saying he relinquished any claim to intellectual property and the whole thing would be over and done with.

I answered my emails, and then opened my door to head to the editing suite. That was when the thing-I-was-expecting finally happened. Only not exactly, because instead of a lawyer or a timid HR rep, Dean Thomas stood outside my door. He'd apparently been waiting for me to come out of my office rather than knocking on my door like a grown-up.

Dean pressed his palm against my door and slowly swung it open wider. He took agonizingly deliberate steps into my office.

Once he was inside, he closed the door behind him so that we were alone and unwatchable. Not that we were really watchable anyway. I had come in early enough that few other employees had shown up yet.

"I spent a whole day wondering if you'd been planning the incident yesterday all along in an attempt to get me in trouble." He appeared unsteady. Unsteady but calm in the craziest way possible.

"I don't know what you're talking about." I thought about the sorts of doodles he drew in his notebook. Shooters and stabbers. I sidestepped away from him. "I wasn't planning anything. I'm not the one who told. I had no intentions of ever mentioning anything to anyone."

My legs felt like they'd turned to water. I moved behind my desk, anxious to keep something between us in case he lunged for me. My purse was within reach. What would he do if I made a grab for it and ran?

"I wondered how you got Adam to agree. Did you pay him to bring it up if he didn't get what he wanted with the audition? Was it some sort of bribery situation? Or maybe it was something else. You two have been awfully chummy lately. Maybe you two were just really good friends and decided to turn against me at the same time—a company mutiny."

His words made me furious. Didn't he realize that Adam's words had hurt me and my reputation the most? Dean might look bad, but I was the one the lawsuit would name. I was ready to tell him he was a lot nicer drunk than hungover, but I stopped and tilted my head and really looked at him.

The emotions coming from him were anger, sure, but also . . . pain. Hurt. He was hurt. He didn't come in here to actually accuse me of any of that. He'd come in to explain his thoughts over the last twenty-four hours. I swallowed my insult and closed my mouth, prepared to see all of this from his point of view.

He took a step forward and breathed a heavy, deep sigh. He sat in one of the chairs across from my desk.

Even with my determination to give him the benefit of the doubt, I still slid my purse off the desk as if clearing the space so we could talk. I reached into the side pocket and palmed the pepper spray before tucking the purse into the bottom drawer of my desk. Being reasonable didn't mean I had to be stupid. I sat down because I realized my legs weren't going to hold me up for very much longer. I really needed chocolate, a good movie, some popcorn, probably some donuts, and my best friend. I settled for the sturdiness of a solid chair.

With both of us sitting and me armed, I said, "What did they say to you?"

He ran a shaky hand over his haggard, unshaven face. "They didn't fire me, if that's what you're asking. I guess you'll have to wait a while longer for any promotions. Of course, the chances of you getting fired are just as good as the chances of me getting fired, so there's that."

"What did they *say*?" I asked again.

He shook his head. "They asked me where I was when you needed help. If you expected me to take the blame for you being stupid enough to go to another studio for help, then I really haven't taught you anything. I told them you were an independent woman who liked your space and who liked working alone. I told them I gave you a lot of leash because I thought you could handle it creatively and because you didn't take creative direction well. They said I'd hung myself on the extra length of leash I'd given you."

Sucker punch.

"Can't take direction?" I asked, feeling angry heat surge to all my extremities.

"I know. I know. You can't take what you weren't given."

The unexpected admission silenced me.

"I came in here because this incident isn't your fault."

The lawyer must have gotten ahold of him if Dean was referring to what happened as *the incident*.

He leaned in, resting his hand on my desk. "Up until yesterday morning, they were calling this film the next Academy Award–winning best picture. You did that. Not me. Not the kid from the other studio. You. They'll try to take that away from you now, but I wanted you to know that even if they manage to legalese it out of your grasp, it still belongs to you. You earned it. The only thing that's your fault here is the creation of a great film, and that's something to be proud of."

Dean complimenting me on anything had not been on the list of things I'd imagined to be possible.

He shook his head. "I told myself I never should have hired you. Every time I saw you, I thought to myself that I should have hired a man. Hired a man who was hungry and desperate for work. Not some idealistic female."

"Why *did* you hire me?" I'd asked him the question before, but he'd never given me a proper answer.

He lumbered to his feet; it appeared he wasn't going to give me a proper answer now, either. He walked to the door and opened it, but before he stepped over the threshold, he turned and said, "I came in here to let you know that this is Hollywood. Not the starry-eyed Hollywood, but the steel-and-flint kind. Steel and flint make fire. The next question you've gotta ask yourself is important: Is that fire going to burn you up, or is it going to light up the dark? Also, be careful who you trust. Even your little friend from the other studio might not be what you think he is. Smart people in this business don't trust anybody. Are you a smart person, Silvia?"

I didn't know how to answer that.

He left without another word. That man was a mystery; it was impossible for me to know how to feel about him. I stayed at my desk long enough to get my bearings and bring my heart rate back to normal. Then I headed to the editing suite. Once there, I tried to shake off the general feeling of unease that came from the drama of my actions.

I worked through lunch and into the afternoon, only getting up for a bathroom break and a walk around the building to get my blood moving again. I lingered over the walk, allowing the sun to soak into my skin and warm me up. The editing suite was kept cold to protect the equipment, but there was very little to protect the poor soul who had to deal with that cold. When I reentered the building, I went back to work.

Ben had been right. Aside from Dean's weird visit, nothing else really happened. People whispered more than usual and avoided me even more than that, but a little whispering never hurt anyone, and people avoiding me meant I had more time to get work done.

Ben and I spent time together nearly every night that week, aside from Wednesday night when he'd gone to hang out with Walt for a guys' night out. I had a girls' night with Emma and Grandma where we got pedicures and smoothies. Grandma got tired halfway through our night, so Emma and I took her home and played a round of Scrabble with her. I tried not to let the gray pallor of her skin or her raspy breathing make me nervous. She'd tell me if something was really wrong.

Ben and I met after work on Thursday at El Matador to go snorkeling. The drive up the Pacific Coast Highway was a much-needed mental break. Glad for the good weather, I waited patiently for a parking place to pop up in the paid lot at El Matador, and I let my arm dangle out my window to soak up the sun. Ben's text message popped up on my phone. "I'm standing in a vacant parking spot at the far end. I'm saving it for you!"

I put my car in gear and raced to get the spot.

Once we were parked and situated with fold-up camp chairs and a full-on cooler backpack strapped over Ben's shoulders, we began the trek down the stairs to the shore.

Because it was a Thursday evening, the beach was pretty vacant, with only a few families and couples scattered by the shore. A bride with her photography crew staked a claim along the sand.

Ben and I moved closer to the rock formations and set up our chairs so we could watch the sunset once we were done snorkeling. Ben made sure the chairs were placed as close to each other as physics permitted while allowing them to remain functional.

Ben pulled out a snorkel mask from his bag. "Ready?"

I answered by stripping down to my swimsuit and shimmying into a shorty wet suit. I put on the new mask my mom had sent to me and snapped a selfie of me in it to send to her. He put on fins, but I left my feet bare. When Ben looked at my feet, he smirked at me. "I thought you said all feet grossed you out."

"Not my own because I'm OCD about proper hygiene."

"Is there proper hygiene on a beach?"

I shrugged. "When in Rome and all that."

He offered the fins a second time with a pointed look. "When in Rome?"

I shook my head. "You know my irrational fear of crowds

because they make me feel trapped? Well, I have an irrational fear of fins as well. They make me feel like my feet are trapped. I don't swim as fast without them, but speed is an acceptable loss to me."

"Completely understood." He slid his mask over his face. He really did understand all my irrational fears: my fear of cancer, my fear of crowds, my loathing of feet, my fear of fins, and so much more. It was quite a list of things to put up with.

My stomach fluttered while holding his gaze. Even if he did look absurd in his mask, he also looked pretty amazing even with his bare feet, which I made a point to keep out of my line of vision entirely. I should have tried to keep all of him out of my line of vision, but as much I tried not to stare, it was hard not to notice that Ben had been hiding some seriously sculpted muscles underneath all those punny, nerdy T-shirts. Who knew?

I put on my own mask to keep myself from ogling. "No wet suit for you? This isn't the South Pacific, you know."

"My body tends to run hot."

"You can say that again," I muttered.

"What?"

"Nothing." I zipped up my wet suit jacket. "Let's avoid the sharks."

"Your chances of dying in a shark attack are one in three point seven million. I think we're safe."

"You say that, but how many of those three point seven million are going in the water? Is that a statistic of everyone or just of those who venture into the sharks' neighborhood?"

His answer was to put in his snorkel and wade out into the waves before diving beneath them. I followed his lead.

We were lucky that the ocean had been calm for a while, no major storms or winds to stir the water to froth. This made the water clear enough to allow for an interesting swim. Starfish to admire and sea urchins to avoid. I even saw a sea lion, and I was glad he was far away and swimming in the other direction. Sea lions were notoriously not nice, and they made shark bait out of snorkelers. I didn't want to be the unlucky one in Ben's pseudo-reassuring statistic.

When we were done snorkeling and back lounging in our chairs, sand and salt drying on our skin in the fading sun, I peeked at him, glad he had his eyes closed and his face lifted to the light. Studying him while he wasn't aware allowed me to consider all the things I thought about him and felt for him.

"Love." The word slipped from the safety of my wandering thoughts to the out-loud danger of the real world.

Ben turned his face to me. "Hmm?" The sound came out lazy, a buzz above consciousness.

"Oh. Just wondering what your favorite line from a romantic comedy was."

He squinted one eye open as he grinned. "Feeling romantic, Silvia?"

"Just curious."

"My favorite line is from *Love Actually* when Sam says to his stepdad, 'Worse than the total agony of being in love?' And his stepdad responds, 'Oh. No, you're right. Yeah, total agony.'"

I laughed. "Love is total agony? That's your favorite romantic quote?"

He didn't laugh. "Love someone for over three years without being able to say anything about it, and you'll agree with me."

That was a naked truth I hadn't been prepared for.

"I'm sorry," I said, not knowing what else could be said.

"Don't be. The agony of loving you is worth it every time." He took my hand and rolled a slow kiss over my knuckles. Droplets of water shook down from his hair and onto his lips and the back of my hand.

I almost said the words back, told him I loved him, too, but I wanted to be sure that when I told someone I loved him that the words were real.

Attraction wasn't enough. I loved to kiss him. Loved to look at him. Loved to talk to him and work alongside him. But did I love *him*? I didn't know. For all the movies I'd seen in my life, for all the romantic comedies that made me smile and sigh at the end, I thought I'd be better prepared to understand myself when it came to love. Of course I would know what it felt like because all the women on the screen knew. None of them seemed to be wishy-washy about it. I didn't want to be wishy-washy either. I didn't want to be the dog, Dug, from the Pixar movie *Up,* who said, "I have just met you, and I love you." Sure, Ben had been my friend for years. We hadn't just met. But he didn't deserve the trip and stumble of love that was the result of friendship and a few dates. He deserved the forever fall.

The peace of Thursday evening with Ben was enough to have me still smiling when I went into the studio on Friday morning.

The smile dropped when I saw Owen the lawyer and Candace from HR waiting for me at my office door.

Owen spoke first. "I left some things on your desk and wanted you to know that we, Candace and I, are available if you have questions." They stepped aside to allow me to pass, and then they nodded to each other before leaving. I didn't understand why they both had to come to deliver a message. They were like a human version of a sticky note. How long had they been standing there waiting for me?

In my office, I found a letter on my desk letting me know that all intellectual property regarding the film *Sliver of Midnight* belonged solely to Portal Pictures. The letter stated that the film *Sliver of Midnight* would be released on schedule as planned with no further additions to the film regarding payroll or credit acknowledgment. There was also an actual sticky note clinging to the side informing me that an identical letter had been sent to Mid-Scene Films.

A second memorandum was under the first. Only this one was far more personal in nature. It spelled out the details of my breach of contract as well as what Portal Pictures expected of me going forward. If I had ever believed that Mid-Scene Films had absurd control-your-life, nonnegotiable contracts, they were nothing compared to what Portal Pictures expected me to put my signature on at that moment.

They wanted me to sign an agreement that would sever any and all communications I had with Ben. They wanted Ben out of my life permanently.

Chapter Twenty

"How she must have loved him, to give up everything."

—Ariane as played by Audrey Hepburn in Love in the Afternoon

I swept up the memorandum and stomped down to the law offices of Owen Theodore Carlson, Esq.

"Absolutely not!" I said. "I will absolutely *not* sign this."

Without breaking eye contact, Owen tapped a button on his laptop before he smiled at me. "It's either sign the document or get fired. You know how this business works, Miss Bradshaw. If you are fired, chances of you finding a job in this town again are almost impossible. Not a very good way to work your way *up*, but a great way to work your way *out*."

I lifted my chin and crossed my arms over my chest, setting my feet as though bracing myself for impact. "There is no way this is legal."

"You're more than welcome to take Portal Pictures to court to find out." He leaned back in his chair, completely at ease. He knew my choices were small if I had any ambition in me at all.

The problem was, I had a lot of ambition. I didn't want to be just a film editor. I wanted to be a *great* film editor. And I wasn't stupid. I knew no one remembered the names of film editors no matter how popular or amazing the movie was. Few people knew who edited *Star Wars* or the Harry Potter films. Sure they knew the director and sometimes even the producer. They almost always knew the production studio. But the film editor was negligible, one of those silent partners in filmmaking.

So my ambition was not for the fame necessarily. It wasn't even for any kind of glory. Sure, I wanted the awards—I wanted them very much—and sure, I would love a star on the Hollywood Walk of Fame. But what I really wanted was the *knowing*. I wanted to know that I had created, or had a hand in creating, films that would stand the test of time. I needed to be in a bigger studio in order to make that happen. If I got blackballed now, there would be no chance later.

I narrowed my eye at him, glaring hard enough, I hoped, to make him feel like he was being shoved into the wall. "My edit on that film was flawless, and you know it. If Portal Pictures loses me, they lose a valuable asset."

Owen steepled his fingers together—a miniature tower of apathy. "We don't *want* to lose you. But we all decided that it would be better if you had a shorter leash. If you had a shred of ambition, you'd take this peace offering for the gift that it is."

A leash. Dean had mentioned a leash as well. Was that how they all saw me? Like I was a dog? A creature to control?

A thing meant to serve but to never be equal to them. My mother would have slapped the smirk right off Owen the lawyer's face. She would have hit him over the head with her women's rights protest sign.

I took a step back. His words *shred of ambition* kept replaying in my head. How many shreds of ambition did I have? Just one? A dozen? Was I a warehouse full of ambitious shreds? Was I willing to give that up for my dignity? Did I want to make advertisements for pet apparel like Alison did?

I took another step back. With each step, I felt the loss of *something*. What did I want? What would this contract cost me to sign?

"I need to talk to my lawyer."

"You don't have a lawyer, Silvia."

"I guess I'll need to get one on my way home tonight."

"Remember the confidentiality clause in the contract you signed when you were employed by Portal Pictures. Though that does not prevent you from seeking legal representation, it does prevent you from taking anything you've heard, seen, said, or done at this company to the press or anyone else. There's also the matter of you already being in breach of contract with our company, which means we are within our rights to file suit against you. At this time, we don't see the value of doing such a thing, but if pressed, well . . ."

He didn't need to finish the statement for me to understand.

"I won't sign this." I lifted my chin and took a step forward, finally finding my dignity. I shoved the crumpled paper into my sweater pocket as if to prove to him I had no intentions of giving in to his bullying.

Candace came in at that moment. She was accompanied by Dean and a couple of the executives.

"You're late," Owen said.

Those who'd entered didn't acknowledge his admonishment but instead sat in the chairs against the wall off to my right. They had, once again, split my vision, putting me at a disadvantage they had to know existed.

Owen nodded to the chair opposite his desk. Apparently we were going to be there a while. I didn't sit. He shrugged and leaned back in his black leather executive chair. "You really should rethink your actions, Miss Bradshaw, since your *guileless* friend from Mid-Scene Films, the one you assured us did not expect any kind of compensation or recognition, is suing." Owen sniffed and ran a hand under his nose. His eyes stayed on me.

"Excuse me?" I asked, sure I'd heard him wrong.

"Mid-Scene Films is suing." He dropped a stack of papers on his desk in front of me.

"That's not possible," I insisted in spite of the stack that evidently stated otherwise or else he wouldn't have been so smug.

"We were served a few hours ago. Only one day after we sent them notice of our stance regarding the matter. The demand for recognition and compensation for the intellectual property of *Sliver of Midnight* makes it pretty clear that this impossible thing you speak of is, in fact, possible."

The word *no* thundered in my head while I picked up the stack and skimmed through the pages. Underneath all the legalese was the basic gist. They were suing. Ben was a pivotal part of the suit.

Did Ben know?

No.

Of course not.

Ben already assured me that he would not arm wrestle Portal Pictures for rights. He didn't want anything to do with a lawsuit. This was all Mid-Scene ownership making a grab for gold that didn't belong to them.

Owen pounced on my shock by sliding another paper under my nose. It was a duplicate of the one I'd crumpled and shoved into my pocket. The one that stated I would not collude, conspire, or fraternize with the competition until the lawsuit was settled and that I was never, ever to even consider bringing any known employee of any studio that was not Portal Pictures onto Portal Pictures properties. How many copies of this menacing document did Owen have? Would there be one on my car windshield when I left to go home?

I wanted to look at Candace, Dean, and the suits, to gauge their reactions, but Owen ruled this room, and I needed to keep my eye on him. I put down the stack of papers and settled the unsigned document on top of it. I slid the whole stack toward him and lifted a shoulder. "This has nothing to do with me."

Owen rolled his eyes. "This has everything to do with you, Miss Bradshaw. You're the one who let the fox into the henhouse. You have been educated in this matter. You are aware of our requests, and we expect you to honor them. Anything less will be considered collusion and will lead to termination. The work you've done for Portal Pictures will remain the property of Portal Pictures, and your name, as it stands, is below the line. Dean will get full credit and be handed the award you worked so hard for. Is that what you want?"

Owen put a pen on top of the paper. "We know you want this job. We know you love the art. You're good at it. But we need to know we can count on you. We need to know that when *Sliver of Midnight* is called up for Best Film Editor and your name is listed, that when you, in your glittering gown of triumph, walk up to that podium to accept the award, it's Portal Pictures you're thanking for the opportunity. We need to know you're loyal to us. And if you are, well then, there will likely be many awards, many acceptance speeches."

"And if I don't sign this?"

Noise pulled my attention to the people on my right. I turned my head to look. The suits shifted. Dean hung his head and stared at the carpet.

"Then we won't be sure of anything, will we? And if we're not sure about you, then *you* can be sure there won't be awards. There won't be speeches. You know how it is. We're family here in Hollywood. If you hurt one of us, you hurt all of us. You won't find work in this town ever again. It's really quite simple."

"Just sign the paper," Candace urged.

Owen was right. I did love the work and the art; I wanted the awards. I picked up the pen. My balance swirled with the motion as oxygen seemed to be strangling itself in my chest and not making it to my brain.

Owen had also called the act of signing quite simple.

Simple?

I stared down the line of suits who all met my gaze evenly. I let my gaze settle on Dean. Dean, who had sold his soul to these people. What had that cost him? What would it cost me?

I thought of Ben, who smiled at me from the crowded dance floor and made me feel free, of the way he saw my trouble and jumped in, no questions asked, how he coaxed Dean into the car. I thought of the way he viewed art, how he felt the rhythm of timing and the rise and fall of each scene. How he laughed with my grandmother whenever they were together, how he'd asked her to dance at the ball, and how she seemed to sparkle when he brought her back to the table. How he pointed out a pair of torpedo rays while we were snorkeling to make sure I didn't miss them.

This was the guy who initiated water fights with me at work, laughed at my jokes, fixed my car when it broke down in the parking lot at Mid-Scene. The guy who had whispered peace to my panicked heart in a crowded elevator that had been stuck between floors.

This was Ben.

And I knew. No more wishy-washiness. This was the fall. And I was willing to fall. No matter what it cost my career.

"I'm not signing anything." I put the pen down.

Dean's head shot up, surprise evident in his red-rimmed eyes. Candace let out a noise of exasperation. Owen sat in his chair and shook his head and tsked at me as if I were a small child caught doing something naughty. The suits didn't move at all.

"It was nice working with you, Miss Bradshaw. You are hereby suspended from your duties."

"You're not firing me?"

"Not yet. We'll wait and see what transpires with the

lawsuit. Nathaniel will help you clean out your desk of any of your things that you might need during the interim."

I stood. "I'll need all of my things—because I quit."

I glanced down the row of people brought in to intimidate me and caught a satisfied smile play across Dean Thomas's lips.

I smiled, too, because it was time.

Time to tell Ben I loved him.

The convenient part of my decision was that Ben and I already had plans to see each other that night. The work we'd done for the Audrey Hepburn Society had been so inspiring that we'd decided to keep going. Tonight's job included the gritty warehouse work of loading boxes for a UNICEF shipment leaving for Bolivia in a few days.

The drive to the warehouse where I'd planned to meet Ben was the worst twenty-seven minutes of my life, as I contemplated all the implications of Mid-Scene Films suing Portal Pictures.

I saw Ben's car already parked, and I slid into a space as near to his as possible. I got out and spotted him near the trucks, wearing his UNICEF shirt and nodding his head at something the volunteer coordinator was saying to him.

He didn't know. He could not have known that his company was suing mine and still be so relaxed.

Which meant the unfortunate task of telling him fell to me.

I crossed the lot and wove around several other volunteers, one of whom handed me a UNICEF shirt.

Ben saw me but didn't smile.

He didn't smile.

Which meant he knew after all. My heart stuttered in my chest. How much? How much did he know?

I didn't break eye contact, even though he tried to look toward where the truck waited. "Mid-Scene is suing Portal Pictures." The words spilled out as soon as I was within earshot.

Well, that was one way to drop the news on him. Not that the information was wrong, but the delivery lacked any kind of delicacy.

Ben frowned. "I know."

His knowing filled me with an irrational anger. I had *so* wanted him to be completely uninvolved. Stupid Dean had made me insecure with his whole "trust no one" speech. Though I didn't like admitting it, a teensy tiny part of me worried that Ben had known, worried he'd been involved, worried about what it meant for us as a couple.

My worries didn't like being confirmed.

I wanted to wrap my arms around him and use his strength to refill my own, but instead I stepped back as he fixed me with his serious, cool-blue eyes.

"Spill," I said. "What exactly do you know?"

The woman in charge of the volunteers called everyone's attention to her as she read from her clipboard, giving us our assignments and specific directions. I tried to keep Ben's attention on me, to continue our conversation, but he faced her and focused on her every word as if there would be a test later. We no longer had the opportunity to talk—at least not one he would take. Not then, and not for the next three hours it took to load the stuff from the warehouse into the truck.

By the time we were released from our duties, my arms were as sore and as shaky as they'd been when I'd helped Grandma unpack her house. The work had been good for me, though. If nothing else, the physical rhythm of the labor calmed me down enough to be ready for the conversation that waited for us when we were done.

Ben walked me to my car, where I pulled out the wrinkled contract and handed it to him.

He read through it, nodding as if it somehow was familiar to him. "It's not signed," he said, his voice flat, a muscle twitching under his eye.

I kept my eye on him, searching for signs of something beyond this cold exterior. "Should it be? What's going on, Ben?"

His jaw flexed. "I received a similar document today."

I closed my eyes, feeling my heart plummet to my toes. "I'm sorry, Ben. What happened? I didn't mean to get you in trouble. Is everything okay? Did they . . . ?"

"No. They didn't fire me. But they will if anyone sees us here together. I need to go."

"If anyone sees us? Who's going to care if we're together? We're not doing anything wrong. I didn't sign their stupid agreement."

He took a shuddering breath and settled his blue gaze on me, making me feel suddenly cold. "No. You didn't. But I did."

Chapter Twenty-One

"I'll stay out of your files, and you stay out of my icebox."
—Ariane as played by Audrey Hepburn in Love in the Afternoon

I listened in stunned silence as he explained we could have no further contact, as he told me it was for the best for both of our careers, as he told me that the only reason he'd shown up tonight was because he'd already signed up to volunteer, and he never backed out where his word was concerned.

He stopped talking, likely expecting me to say something, but I had no words. I could only stare. A dull ache throbbed in the socket behind my glass eye, but I couldn't even lift my hand to adjust anything to make the pain stop. I couldn't do anything to make the pain stop anywhere.

"Aren't you going to say anything?" he asked.

"What do you want me to say? Do you want me to make you feel better for selling out our friendship? Because I'm not going to. And since you're now in violation of your contract, you should probably leave. It wouldn't look good for anyone to see you with me, since you're so big on keeping your word and all."

He flinched. His jaw worked. And he nodded grimly. He handed me back my unsigned document, told me to sign it, got in his car, and drove away.

Only then did I allow the sob to escape me.

Ben, the one who always said that he would be there for me, that this wasn't a big deal and would all blow over quickly. How could he, at the first sign of trouble from Mid-Scene Films, sign the agreement? The very same agreement I refused to sign.

My discovery of my genuine love for Ben came because I refused to put my name on that document. I knew it was love, real love, because losing my career was far less important than losing him. That was how I knew. Ben, who insisted he'd loved me for years, was the one who'd signed a paper that kept him from me. He caved at the first test of that love.

To find your heart and have it broken in the same hour was probably the worst thing that could happen to a novice at love. I paced around my car as everything Ben had said over the last twenty minutes crashed through my memory.

I stopped pacing.

Fine.

Just fine. If he was willing to write me off in exchange for his career, he could have it. Ben wanted me to leave him alone so no one saw us together? Fine. He would be alone. Forever, for all I cared.

I didn't need him. I jerked open my car door, got in, and slammed it closed.

I pounded on my steering wheel, making my car alarm go off. I must have accidentally pressed the panic button on the key fob in my fist. I reset the buttons and shouted, "He is *so* not needed!"

Except he was needed. I needed him very much. The splintered pieces of my heart cut my soul, and all the trust and security I'd placed in him bled out.

No. I'd lived my whole life without him and would be fine continuing to do so. What I needed was my grandma. I started driving.

Driving while crying is hard for anyone. Driving while crying when you only have one eye to begin with made it a miracle I arrived safely.

No one was home when I got there, which was probably better. I needed time to pull myself together before she arrived on the scene. I sat in the dark on my grandma's living room floor and did all the breathing exercises Emma had taught me from her yoga classes at the gym.

The deep breathing only made me feel like I was hyperventilating. Since that wasn't working, I went to Grandma's movie collection and picked out a drama about independence and strength with no romantic subplot anywhere. But when I went to put it in her player, the movie that was already there was *Breakfast at Tiffany's*.

I put the drama back on the shelf. I closed the tray and hit play.

The opening music and the sight of a young Audrey Hepburn meandering around the Tiffany's building while eating a pastry calmed me more than I would have imagined. Against all rationale, the fast-talking Holly Golightly also calmed me, enough that by the time noise from the general direction of the doorway alerted me that Grandma and Walt had returned, I felt like I could talk to another person without being a mess.

I gave them a moment in case they were kissing good night and wanted some privacy. Just because my love life had been vaporized didn't mean hers needed to be. But the noises coming from the entryway didn't sound like making out. It sounded like a struggle. Frowning, I went out to meet them at the door but stopped short when my eye landed on Grandma. She was slumped against Walt as he pulled the key from the doorknob. When she lurched forward, Walt hurried to hand her something that looked like a long, white paper bag. Grandma used the bag to throw up.

Walt smoothed back her hair, which was basically pasted against her head as if she had slept on it for several days in a row.

"What's going on?" I asked.

They both looked up, so preoccupied by what they'd been doing that my sudden presence startled them. Grandma looked like she might say my name. Instead, she threw up again.

I rushed to help get her inside.

"Thanks, Silvia." Walt gave me a relieved smile.

"It's not a problem. I'm glad I was here." I guided Grandma to the couch and barely got the bag under her before she threw up a third time.

Walt went to dispose of the bag and to fetch a container that would be better able to handle the vomit, while I propped up Grandma's feet, took off her shoes, and tucked a throw blanket over her. She shivered with cold even though her face was shiny with sweat.

"There's no need to fuss," Grandma said. "I'm fine." But her eyes closed as soon as her head touched the pillow.

"You're not fine," I said.

Walt returned with an ice bucket—rather fancy but certainly functional. He also brought back a warm, wet dishcloth and used it to wipe at her mouth.

She lifted her hand as if to shoo us both away, but apparently decided she didn't have the energy and dropped it to her side again.

"Should we call her doctor?" I asked.

Walt shook his head. "No. He knows she's having problems and says that it's normal enough, considering her age and predispositions."

"Problems? What problems is she having? Did she eat something that didn't agree with her?"

Grandma's eyes fluttered like she might answer, but Walt shook his head again. "I doubt a chemo cocktail agrees with anyone. The anti-nausea medication doesn't seem to help. Her doctor said it's probably because she has such big problems with motion sickness. She's just predisposed to the acute sickness."

I barely heard him over the roaring in my ears after his first sentence. "Chemo?" I knew that word. A girl with a cancer phobia knew all the words associated with it.

It was then that I noticed what she wore. She had on loose, baggy clothing: drawstring pajama bottoms, a blousy shirt, an old pair of slip-on Toms. This was definitely not something she'd worn on a date. This was the outfit a person wore when they were going to the hospital to spend a day in treatment.

The hole in my heart that had seemed cavernous before now felt like the vacuum of space.

"Grandma? You have cancer?"

The way Walt's eyebrows shot up over his eyes proved he was ignorant of my ignorance. "You said you were going to tell her."

"I was," Grandma said between raspy breaths. "Waiting for the right time."

Now was not the right time, not with my heart broken and my career destroyed, but would there ever be a right time? No. I could have just won the lottery, and it still would not have been the right time. Which meant she should have told me immediately—the very moment she found out.

"How long?" I asked, surprised at the high-pitched keen of my voice. "How long have you known?"

She passed a hand over her eyes. "I don't know. I just finished my fifteenth week of chemo. I probably knew a few weeks before that. They wanted to shrink the tumor before they removed it."

I did some quick math. At least four months. Maybe five. She'd known all that time and didn't tell me. I stepped forward. I stepped back.

Walt finally took me by the elbow and said, "Why don't you sit down, Silvia?"

I didn't want to sit. I wanted to run away from that old enemy that had stolen my eye all those years ago. The enemy was back and working on stealing my grandmother. Walt edged me to the love seat, where my legs buckled involuntarily.

The day had been awful, and they were tired of trying to hold me up. Walt sat across from me on the armchair and filled me in on all the details I had missed because I'd been too blinded by my career and love life to see them.

Walt shared the details, not her. She had fallen asleep, exhausted by the treatment and the sickness that came with it. After he'd answered all the questions that spilled out of me, Walt finally stood. "I'll go, since she has you here tonight."

"Do you usually stay?" I asked.

"Only when she's sick. I'd never leave her if it was my choice, but once she found out about the cancer, she wouldn't talk about getting married. She said she didn't want to burden me with a broken old woman." He smoothed back her hair as he'd done in the doorway when I'd first seen them tonight. "She's not broken, though. Most days, she's the only thing holding me together." He looked up at me. "Don't be afraid, Silvia. She didn't want you to know because she said that, with your fear of cancer, the news would be the end of you. But she'll survive this. And so will you. A lump in the breast is not enough to take down someone as strong as your grandmother. She'll survive, so you don't need to be afraid."

He bent low and kissed Grandma's forehead, said good night, and showed himself out the door.

I readjusted a pillow under her head so she was more comfortable. I wanted to walk her to her bed, but her skin looked so gray, and her breathing seemed so shallow, it made me nervous to think of moving her.

How fragile was she *really*?

How had I missed the signs of her illness?

A lot made sense now: selling her house, moving to this

downgraded villa, spending so much money on causes that mattered to her. Her new habit of worrying over my love life. A pattern outlining the problem had been there; I just hadn't seen it. I'd been blind. Or half-blind, since I'd seen, just not understood. I laughed. Half-blind.

Funny.

The bad thing about losing Ben on the same day I found out my grandmother had cancer was that I couldn't tell Ben about Grandma, and I couldn't tell Grandma about Ben.

The TV screen made a slight electric fizz sound before turning itself off. I'd forgotten I'd left the movie on pause, and the TV must have decided it had been abandoned.

After fetching myself a blanket and a pillow, I snuggled up on the love seat and turned the movie back on to keep me company while I kept vigil over my grandmother.

And, like that night so many years ago when I was a little girl in a hospital, I thought of Audrey. In my mind, I pictured her, but instead of picturing a woman in long, white, glowing robes like I had as a child, I imagined her as she was in the movie playing on Grandma's TV.

Audrey wasn't the fancy, black-dress-wearing Holly Golightly. She was the casual Holly Golightly wearing a sweatshirt and pants, sitting at her window, and staring out over a city. Instead of a sword and a shield, I gave her a guitar and imagined her at the foot of the couch, keeping watch over my grandmother while singing "Moon River." The ghost of Audrey conjured by my imagination battled the cancer lurking in my grandmother's chest with the hope found in a song. She'd fought death back for me once, and I trusted her to win that fight again.

Only then, with this picture of this woman guarding my grandmother firmly fixed in my mind, did I finally go to sleep.

I woke up on the floor, probably having rolled off the love seat in the night because my legs needed to stretch out. The TV was off again. Grandma still slept, but her rest seemed more peaceful now than it had before.

I'd obviously slept badly because Audrey-the-eye felt gummy enough to aggravate the back of my eyelid. I took her out and stuffed her in my pocket.

I hated how much I wanted to call Ben, to tell him everything, to have him hold me and whisper in my ear that everything was going to be all right.

Because everything wasn't going to be all right. How could anything be considered all right when I couldn't talk to him to tell him my grandma had cancer? *Cancer!* On top of that, my career was over. Maybe I could meet up with Alison. Making film advertisements for pet clothes couldn't be all bad, could it? She and I could start an ex-girlfriends-of-Ben club. I sat up, tucking my legs into my chest, and leaned against the love seat.

Ben.

Faithful, loyal, untrustworthy, betrayer Ben. My heart rolled through all the things Ben was, but couldn't see the part of him he showed me last night. I'd known Ben for years. Last night, he was a stranger.

I didn't want to call the stranger. I wanted to call the friend. But even if Friend Ben still existed, he couldn't be contacted because he signed the agreement.

He chose his career over me. He chose Hollywood.

There had been a time I might have made that same choice, but not now. Grandma's reel-to-reel movies in antique tins showed a glittering Hollywood that no longer existed—if it ever had. My career had been important, but not so important that I would allow it to turn me into someone like Dean or Adam.

What sort of person would Ben become after making the choice he did? Would he be a Dean in another decade? I wrapped my arms around my legs and squeezed hard, as if I could squeeze out all the ache, and looked at Grandma. She had survived losing my grandfather. She would know what to do for me. But even with her in the same room, she was unreachable in her current state.

I might be losing her, too. *That* ache was unbearable.

Being left alone with all my emotions would kill me. I needed someone. I needed Emma. The ghost and the cyclops. One thing this cyclops knew was that she could always count on the ghost.

Chapter Twenty-Two

"I don't know how to say goodbye.
I can't think of any words."

—Princess Ann, played by Audrey Hepburn in Roman Holiday

Emma texted me to let me know she was outside Grandma's door. She didn't want to ring the doorbell in case it would wake up my grandma. Grandma was sleeping so soundly, I wasn't sure anything would wake her.

When I opened the door, Emma wrapped me up in the tightest, most supportive embrace I'd ever received. When she pulled away, her eyes echoed the depths of worry within my own heart. The question in them needed answering, so I led her to the kitchen where we could talk without bothering Grandma.

I gave her the quick details. Breast cancer, chemo to shrink the tumor, surgery soon, and, according to Walt, she was stable and holding her own. Every time I used the word *cancer*, I felt myself flinching as if it hurt me physically, like a burn across my tongue.

I made us both a cup of hot chocolate. It was a cool morning, and a cup of comfort was definitely in order. I made enough so Grandma could have one, too, but was hot chocolate good for her? Would it make her sicker?

"Walt said nearly ninety percent of all breast cancer patients survive at least five years," I told Emma. I hated how repeating such a statistic reminded me of Ben.

"And your grandma is a fighter. She'll double that at least," Emma said. "In the meantime, we should be thinking of her diet and exercise. I have a few experts at Kinetics who can recommend a menu of foods that create apoptosis."

"Apop-whatsis?"

"It's programmed cell death. In this case, it's cancer-cell death. It's basically the same thing the chemo is doing, only this way it's by eating whole foods."

"How do you even know that?"

"It's my job to know. I've heard curcumin is a great, natural way to stimulate apoptosis in cancer cells, but I'll find out more. While a good meal plan doesn't replace good medical care, working together, they can often result in a healthy patient."

I nodded, numbly agreeing, desperate to try anything.

"Walt's the name of Grandma's new guy, huh? That's so adorable, I don't have words to describe how cute I think that is. Do you and Hottie Ben double-date with them?"

Her question led to the discussion of all my other life grievances. My emotions were so frayed and raw, getting all the words out proved to be an effort.

Emma quietly listened to the entire sad tale with the

compassion of a woman who knew what it was to become a casualty on love's battlefield.

I ended with, "I hope Ben chokes on the pen he signed that contract with." My voice was thick with anger and ache.

Emma's mouth twitched at the corner. "Wow," she said, trying not to smile. "I think that's the least reasonable thing I've ever heard come out of your mouth."

I laughed quietly and picked at the frayed knees of my jeans. "I'll be reasonable tomorrow. Or maybe next week . . . or maybe next month."

"You don't have to make a hasty return to reasonableness on my account. It's actually good and healthy to give in to the irrational every now and again."

I felt more calm and less broken having said everything out loud.

"What happens now?" Emma asked. "I mean, what do the lawyers say happens now regarding the intellectual property? Are you being sued personally?"

"I don't think so. The lawsuits are between the companies. Portal Pictures already owns every creative effort I made while I worked there, so they have no reason to sue me, and I don't have anything Mid-Scene would want, so they have no reason either. I'm just jobless, now, which is awesome."

"And by awesome, we mean . . ."

"Catastrophic. I'd move in with Grandma except, with her new boyfriend, I might cramp her bachelorette style. Plus, this is assisted-living housing, meaning I'm not old enough to qualify for residence. Plus, she's sick . . . so there's that."

Emma ignored my sarcastic rant and went straight to the

meat of the problem. "Do you have savings you can live on for a while?"

"Enough to last me a few months," I admitted.

"Good, because otherwise Grandma would—"

"Kill me. I know." My grandma had encouraged both Emma and me to save ten percent of our incomes anytime we were paid for anything. She said the savings would act as a gift that we give to our future selves. Even when times were lean, I tried to keep a savings account active. I said a mental thank you to my past self. Past-Silvia really did me a solid by not getting frivolous when the pay rate went up when I moved to Portal Pictures.

Emma sucked in a deep breath, which meant she was about to say something I didn't want to hear. When she started her sentence by saying, "I know this isn't what you want to hear, but . . ." I allowed myself a private chuckle. "We can always use good film editors at Kinetics. If things get tight, you always have a job with me. I'd hire you knowing full well you would be looking for employment elsewhere, and there wouldn't be any hard feelings regarding you quitting when you got the job you wanted."

"Thanks, Emma. I hope it won't come to that, but it's nice knowing I'm not lost." We both knew it was an option I would take only in the most desperate circumstances. I wanted to make films for entertainment, not films to peddle a product. Not that Emma's profession morally assaulted my ideals. It just wasn't what I wanted for myself.

"What is your legal recourse?" Emma brought me back from wandering into thoughts of Ben. "Does your intellectual property still get credited to you, or does the studio take ownership of it because of anything fraudulent that might have happened with it?"

These were good questions. Questions I probably should have asked when Owen the lawyer was reading me the riot act over my poor behavior and bad decisions. Or maybe it was good that I hadn't asked, since asking would be treating them like they were there for me. The problem with corporate lawyers was that they were there for the corporation. The Portal Pictures lawyer could have only one interest—the studio.

"Do you think I should get my own lawyer?" I asked Emma. It might not be my name announced at the Academy Awards, but I wanted, and expected, my name to be in the credits. They couldn't pull that from me, could they?

"Maybe. A consultation might not hurt. An intellectual property rights lawyer could help you see where you stand legally, and you know how much I like knowing where I stand on things."

I nodded, and then groaned and threw myself back against the couch. "I feel stupid about this whole thing, like a kid getting caught stealing candy at the grocery store, but really, Emma, what choice did Dean give me?"

Emma proved her worth as a friend by not answering. Her business-savvy mind had probably already come up with ten different solutions that would not have played out like this one had, but she didn't give me answers that were too late to be of any use. She wasn't stupid enough to live in the would-have, could-have, should-have world. Emma was too practical for that. At least, she was when it wasn't her own love life on the line. Emma had a harder time seeing the forest through the trees when she was tromping through her own forest.

But I guessed we were all like that.

"Thanks for giving me advice on what to do now instead of lecturing me on what I should have done," I said, wanting to make sure she knew how good she was for my soul.

"It's what you do for me," she said. "Besides, now is the only thing that matters. The past is old news. The end." She gave me the names of several intellectual property lawyers, people she'd worked with specifically on several product lines in her gyms. She trusted them completely.

"What else?" she asked me.

We'd danced around the elephant in the room for long enough. Emma was apparently ready to talk about it whether I was or not. "What else?" I asked. "You mean besides the lawyer at Mid-Scene making Ben sign a contract that prevents him from seeing me anymore? Is that the 'what else?' you mean?"

"Are we talking about the lawyer you think dabbles in the dark arts and possibly sacrifices kittens for her own evil purposes?"

"Yes. That one. But it's not just about her. This is about Ben. He signed the Hollywood equivalent of a restraining order. Why would he do that?"

"I don't have a good answer for that. Ben doesn't strike me as a fall-in-line-behind-the-company kind of guy. Perhaps the dark-arts dabbler spiked the company water cooler?" she suggested, only half joking.

"No." I rolled my head to stretch out my neck muscles. "He wasn't compelled to do this. No one can make Ben do anything he doesn't want to do. He just doesn't . . ."

"Don't finish that thought," Emma said. Her eyes dropped to where my fingers had started pulling the fringe threads out of the knees of my jeans, but she didn't say anything, and she didn't try to stop the microcompulsive behavior.

"You don't know what I was going to say," I insisted.

She gave me a look—the one we both knew how to do because we'd spent years being on the business end of that look from Grandma. "You were going to say he doesn't love you after all."

The bad thing about a friend who knew you well enough to finish your sentences was that she knew you well enough to finish your sentences.

Emma got up from the chair at the kitchen table and headed for the counter. "You're the woman who is logical and levelheaded about everything." She pulled an apple from the fruit bowl and set it to the side of the sink, then she pulled out a tub of rolled oats from the pantry. From the fridge, she found a package of blueberries as well as some apple juice. She added them to her stuff on the counter. She used the juice in place of half the water and began cooking the oats.

"What is that supposed to mean?" I said.

"It means, don't throw the baby out with the bathwater. He might have had a good reason. Maybe you should text him and find out what that good reason is." She chopped up the apple and added it to the oatmeal.

"No. Absolutely not. He already told me I'm not allowed to contact him. It's like being grounded from your boyfriend *by* your boyfriend. The whole thing is ridiculous. And if he thinks I'm going to crawl to him and beg and plead, he's wrong. He chose this. He gets to live with it." I sniffed and winced at the throb in my head, right behind my eyes. "Why do I always get headaches when I cry? Isn't it enough for me to feel emotional pain? I have to be in physical pain as well?"

A chuckle of commiseration came from the pantry. "Call it nature's way of kicking you while you're down."

"Yeah, well, nature's got a mean streak, doesn't she?"

Emma reappeared from the pantry with Grandma's hot-air popcorn popper. She was probably the one who bought the appliance for Grandma. Emma didn't use microwave popcorn after she'd read an article that said chemicals inside the popcorn bag were endocrine disrupters. I didn't even know what an endocrine was, let alone that they could be disrupted. I tried telling her that since I wasn't planning on licking the bag, the chemicals wouldn't hurt me. In response, she bought me a hot-air popper, too. Though I never admitted it, I liked the flavor and texture better in the hot-air popper. It was also nice to be able to season the popcorn my own way rather than the way that was meant for the masses.

She poured in the kernels and positioned a bowl to catch the popped corn. "Nature's a monster. Speaking of . . . did you lose Audrey again?"

I grunted, remembering how my eye had bothered me when I first woke up. "No, it's in my pocket." I tugged Audrey-the-eye from my pocket and used the kitchen sink to clean it off. Once it was dry, I put it back in my socket.

Emma sprinkled sea salt over the popcorn, along with a spritz of lime oil she'd found in the fridge, and placed the bowl on the table. She went back to check on the oatmeal, then took a deep breath. "Remember when Blake had been an idiot and was groveling for my forgiveness, and you said I would cave and he didn't deserve to get me back, so you took away my phone?"

I nodded. I pulled my phone from my back pocket and held it out for her to take—to return the favor.

But Emma didn't take the phone. She folded my fingers over it and said, "This isn't the same thing. Sometimes radio silence is the best option. With Blake, it absolutely was—"

"Because he was on a date with Trish the Fish."

Emma smirked. "We have to stop calling her that. She's going to be my sister-in-law."

"I don't have to stop calling her that. I'm no relation."

"The point is," Emma said, trying to bring the conversation back on track, "I think communication here would help, not hurt. You're the one who tries to always see the other point of view. Give Ben a chance to explain."

"What is there to explain? He chose a job over me. Romeo wouldn't have ever made such a choice."

"Romeo isn't real."

"Colin Firth wouldn't have done it. And don't try to tell me *he's* not real."

"He is real, but the character he played isn't. We have no idea what the real Colin Firth would do in a dating situation since it's unlikely either of us will ever date him."

I pouted. "Hitch wouldn't have done it."

Emma stared at me while I lifted my eyebrows and took a handful of popcorn to celebrate my victory. She blew out a breath of exasperation. "Fine. Though Hitch isn't real either, he probably wouldn't have done it, at least not unless he had a really good reason. Remember, Hitch was a master at other people's love lives, but he was a disaster with his own."

"The movie *Hitch* was inspired," I said around a mouthful of lime-flavored popcorn. "The dating scene really does require the help of a specialist because the love Hollywood has given us is a lie. Everything I know about love I've learned from Hollywood. I've learned if you've never been kissed, go undercover as a reporter in a high school. If your best friend is a guy who is marrying someone else, sabotage the wedding. If you're an overworked doctor who doesn't make time for love, you'll probably need to go into a coma to find the one meant for you. The hotel maid only needs to steal clothes from one of the rooms to get the politician's attention. The famous actress just needs to find the guy with a blue door in *Notting Hill*. I know all these stories backwards and forwards. Movies teach us how to fall in love, how to have a first kiss, how to have a good fight and then make up afterwards. And because of Hollywood, I know how to break up."

"Break up? Seriously? With the guy you were planning on declaring your love to less than twenty-four hours ago?" Emma actually looked worried.

Those words hit their mark, and I felt myself deflating. "I really was. I was going to use the *L* word." My barely audible whisper must have been heard because Emma squeezed my hand.

"That is some definite bad timing," she said.

"Yeah." I barked a short laugh. "I thought we'd be snuggling in front of the fake fireplace in my apartment, but it seems the only spooning I'll be doing is with Ben and Jerry's."

"Your grandma has some Chunky Monkey in the freezer," she said.

"Sounds perfect. We should definitely eat it so she isn't temped by it. Ice cream can't be good for h—"

"You eat my ice cream without sharing," Grandma called out, "and I'll be kicking you both out of here before you can say, 'Sorry, Grandma.'"

"What are you doing up? Do you want help getting back to your room?" I asked, rushing to her side.

"I would think me getting up in the morning is preferable to the alternative. I'm fine, Silvia. I'll likely take a long nap this afternoon because the treatment makes me tired, but I usually function okay the day after."

"I made us breakfast," Emma said, dishing up three bowls of apple oatmeal topped with blueberries and setting them on the table.

"This is probably a good way to get blueberries in my diet. I hate eating them plain, but the doctor said raw antioxidants were important, so I've been forcing them down. They hide better in oatmeal, don't they?"

Emma seemed glad to have had her offering accepted and even liked.

"Silvia called in the reinforcements over my little problem?" Grandma asked. "You really don't need to worry, either one of you. I'm going to be just fine. Plus the breast cancer ribbon is pink, and you both know I look great in pink."

Before I could answer, Emma said, "Oh, we know you don't need Silvia and me to help you. We know you've got this. It's Silvia we're worried about."

I widened my eyes and gave her a shake of my head while also giving her a kick to the leg. She ignored me and spilled my troubles out in their entirety to my grandmother.

This opened up a lengthy and heated breakfast argument as to whether or not I was wrong to not let Ben explain himself. When Walt showed up, he took their side. Three against one.

I decided I didn't like any of them.

When Walt saw Grandma was having a girls' day, he graciously bowed out, declaring that movie marathons weren't really his thing unless someone was in a spaceship or getting shot at. No wonder he got along so well with Ben.

Since I'd already watched *Breakfast at Tiffany's*, I asked to stay with the theme.

"Are you sure those are the movies you want right now?" Emma shot a meaningful look at my grandmother and lowered her voice. "Didn't you once tell me you avoided Audrey's movies because you didn't want to die like she died?"

I sent an apologetic look at Grandma, who shrugged and nodded in agreement. "That's not unreasonable. I don't want to die the way she died either."

"But," I added, "I think I might want to try to live like she lived."

Though I could tell Emma had been hoping for something with Colin Firth in it, she gave in to the Audrey Hepburn marathon.

At some point, I would have to find out if my mom and dad knew about Grandma's cancer, though I suspected they didn't have any idea. My parents loved Grandma Bradshaw. They deserved to know. But I decided to wait to call her out on her need for secrecy. She was still tired from her treatment. That argument could wait for another day.

Thinking of my parents made me cringe. The only

conversations we'd had recently were updates on the various grandparents we were in charge of. Mom did most of the talking since she lived in constant exhaustion due to dealing with two elderly people in varying stages of Alzheimer's. I had become good at not telling her my troubles because I didn't want to burden her with more things to worry about. All of yesterday's events definitely fell into the category of "more things to worry about." For that reason, the information had to be cautiously shared. They didn't need to know I'd quit my job since, of course, I would find another one. They didn't need to know that Ben had trampled my heart and reignited my daydream of running away to Peru. Did they need to know about the cancer?

I peeked at Grandma, who was laughing at the scene in *Charade* where various people were trying to determine whether the guy in the coffin was dead or not, and thought maybe I would wait until she was ready to tell them. She didn't look like the Grim Reaper was hovering over her any longer. Her color had mostly returned, and her spirits seemed pretty good even if her appetite was hit-and-miss. I would let her choose when to tell them as long as her choice *was* to tell them. If she didn't want to, well, then I would.

Grandma had all the Audrey Hepburn movies, and beginning with *Charade* was a good choice since Grandma spent the whole time sighing happily over Cary Grant. We watched *Sabrina*, which made Emma cringe, making me wonder if a story about two brothers as love interests for the same girl hit a little too close to home for her.

We ordered a pizza from Geppetto's—vegetarian, since Emma liked it that way, and because Grandma's health was on the line. Emma scowled at me when I used a knife and fork to eat my pizza. Like she could make fun of how I chose to eat my pizza when she would eat hers like a savage. She folded her pizza in half like it was a sandwich and didn't mind smearing sauce all over her mouth. Seriously. Savage.

After lunch, we were watching *Love in the Afternoon* when Emma hit pause on the movie. "What does she see in him? He's grandpa-old! No, even that's not right. He's great-grandpa-old. No. Not even that. He's *Night of the Living Dead, Tales from the Crypt* old. There is no way any beautiful young woman with any kind of self-respect would even look his direction."

"I think he's handsome," Grandma said.

Emma stuck to her guns. "No offense, Grandma, but your opinion might be biased. He's definitely too old for her."

I laughed, relieved that it could happen when my stomach had knotted so badly it would require a merit badge on knots to undo it.

"And he's morally reprehensible," Emma said. "She has to pretend to be a player for him to even have a moment of interest? She needs to cut and run."

I loved it when Emma got ranty. Working in Hollywood, I expected people to be jaded and things to be marbled gray through the blacks and the whites of morality. Emma's idealistic line of work was all about putting the *kind* back into humankind with their namaste lifestyle. When things were skewed, Emma sounded her war cry of indignity.

I almost didn't need TV when Emma was around. I let her carry on about the ridiculous age gap before speaking up. "You do know that Mr. Knightly is sixteen years Emma's senior, right?"

Emma stopped mid-rant. I'd apparently poked at a sore spot. "That's different," she sputtered. "Knightly wasn't exhibiting predatory behaviors like the guy in this movie. They were friends; this guy is a player. She's going to get her heart broken when he gets bored and ditches her."

"Did you know that more than thirty people jump from the Brooklyn Bridge every year due to heartbreak?"

Grandma and Emma both frowned; obviously neither of them liked that comment. "Should we be glad there isn't a bridge anywhere nearby?" Grandma asked at the same time Emma said, "Where would you even hear something like that?"

I lifted a shoulder. "A movie, a long time ago. Don't worry, guys. I'm not suicidal. I don't plan on jumping from any bridges anytime soon. I'm fine." And I meant it. I wasn't going to jump off a bridge. But I kept touching my sternum as though it was bruised. There obviously was no real bruise, but it hurt just the same. Heartache might not be listed on the death certificate, not enough for it to count on one of Ben's mortality statistics, but I wondered how many people died of a broken heart.

Emma viewed me a moment longer before saying, "Promise me that when we say something is a bridge-jump moment, it will always only mean that it's a moment to take chances on good things, not a moment to try to end everything."

I nodded, which seemed to satisfy her. Years ago, we'd decided that some things weren't meant to be overthought; they were just meant to be done with a leap and a shout. So we'd gone bungee-jumping. I must have really rattled her by bringing up the movie quote about bridges.

Emma eventually had to go home. She'd taken the day off work to spend it with me, and though we didn't solve any world problems in our time together, her presence had been the bandage keeping my heart from bleeding out on the floor.

"Call Ben!" Emma texted me almost as soon as she'd left. "At least find out his reasons."

"If he wanted me to know them, he would have told me already," I texted back.

"Who cares if he wants you to know? This isn't about what makes him comfortable. You need to know. Find out so we'll know if we should hire a hit man or not."

I laughed but sent her a scolding. "You shouldn't send stuff like that over a text. If Ben mysteriously dies tonight, they're going to pin the murder on us."

"No jury could convict us. Dead people creep me out more than feet creep you out." She sent a GIF of a woman's face turning into a demon that screams into the camera.

I set aside my phone and watched *Funny Face* and *My Fair Lady* with Grandma.

The happily-ever-after endings in the movies I watched irritated me because, in my own life, I didn't see how that would work. With Ben agreeing to solitary confinement, we couldn't even have a happily *right now,* let alone a happily ever after.

Grandma went to bed—her actual bed and not the couch. I put in *Charade* and watched it again. Something about it appealed to me, though I couldn't say what or why.

The moment in the movie when Audrey Hepburn declared, "You mean you're a thief!" to Cary Grant, I thought of myself. I thought about the word *charade.* The act of being one thing while doing something else entirely. Had I done that? Was Ben doing that? Emma said he might have a good reason for his actions. But if he did, what could that reason be?

The job mattered. Of course the job mattered. I felt the pull, ache, and need to work in that industry as strong as anyone, but I'd managed to choose being myself instead of living in their second-rate morality.

Why couldn't Ben have loved me enough to choose the same?

I wanted to see him, to talk to him. What if, tomorrow, I happened to bump into him during his morning breakfast at his favorite diner? No one could fault me if we both went to the same place to eat. Just because it was his favorite restaurant really had nothing to do with me at all.

Or what if I went grocery shopping next Saturday at the exact same place he usually went grocery shopping? How could I be faulted? The farmers market was for everyone, and they had the very best price on bananas. Or maybe it was oranges. Or honey. Regardless, it remained a public place.

I groaned and put my head in my hands. What would Ben say to me breaking his contract and getting him into trouble? Was Ben a villain or just playing the villain?

The male lead of *How to Steal a Million* was also pretending to be a thief and a bad guy in general, but in reality, he was a good guy doing the best he could with his circumstances. These characters were good guys doing good-guy things even if they had the appearance of bad-guy things.

What was Ben?

I stiffened and sucked in a deep breath. I would not go to Ben's favorite breakfast haunt. I would not go to the farmers market. Because when it came right down to it, I wasn't playing the good-guy-pretending-to-be-a-bad-guy lead in a movie. I was playing me.

Emma sent me one last text telling me to stop being so dramatic all the time and to give Ben a chance—at least a response. But it was Grandma who changed my mind. There was a picture of her and Walt on her mantel. A picture I'd never seen before. It was from the night of the ball. Here was a woman who had the disease that scared me more than anything, and yet she was still living, still taking chances. Shouldn't I be taking chances, too?

"Fine," I said to the house. I would carry out my original plan to tell Ben I loved him. I would just do it with a movie-quote clue. I pulled out my phone and tapped out three words.

I rewound the movie so I could see Audrey Hepburn get her hero's kiss with Cary Grant. I smiled. Audrey would have approved of my decision to be good and not force Ben to see me and explain himself. Audrey would likely also approve of my decision to be bad if Ben took too long to sort out the mess.

I glanced at my phone, verifying it had sent the message, and nodded with satisfaction at the three words on the screen.

"As you wish."

Chapter Twenty-Three

"I told you, anything you do for yourself is a waste of spirit."
—Hap, played by Audrey Hepburn *in* Always

I spent the next couple of days at Grandma's house. Why not? It's not like I had to get to work. We went to the library and checked out several of Audrey Hepburn's documentaries, one done by A&E, which Emma would have approved of since she adored A&E's version of *Pride and Prejudice*. We stopped at the grocery store. I tried to stick to the list Emma sent me regarding the healthy foods cancer patients should be eating, and I had to argue with Grandma when she wanted to buy orange soda and chips.

"Crushing a can of creamsicle-flavored soda is not the same as freshly squeezed orange juice," I complained when she told me she *was* eating healthy. She harrumphed, but we eventually agreed that if she ate everything I made her for dinner, then she could snack on whatever she wanted.

When she grumbled, "Who would have guessed you'd

turn out to be the prison warden over food?" everything seemed right with the world.

Except, not everything. Ben never wrote back.

He never wrote back the next day either.

Or the day after that.

Ben didn't write.

On Friday, I returned home to water my plants and to remind myself that I was an unemployed member of society. So, naturally, instead of sending out resumes, I went surfing.

Ben didn't write.

I surfed on Saturday as well.

Ben still didn't write.

I visited Grandma and organized her spice racks. Her expression made me wonder if she was happy I'd done it or irritated that I'd messed up her system.

I finally called my mom and told her about the job and Ben. She praised me for sticking to my morals and for working to change the world for the better so that opportunities for women were available in Hollywood. I didn't admit that my actions hadn't stemmed from an ideological desire to further the cause of women's rights, but instead because I'd fallen for a guy who was apparently unworthy of that fall. I did not tell Mom about Grandma since Grandma promised she would tell her herself after her last chemo treatment next week. She would be going in for surgery shortly after that.

In all that time, Ben still hadn't responded, which made me furious. He knew the quote. He knew what it had to mean. "As you wish" was code for "I love you." Buttercup and Westley—*The Princess Bride. Everyone* knew that!

I told him I loved him, and he ignored it.

I spent the rest of Sunday applying at various studios.

By Monday morning, I realized Ben had no intention of trying to make a reconciliation.

Which was fine. I didn't care. I'd lived my life this long without him, which, okay, wasn't technically true, since he'd been a part of my life in some capacity or another for several years, but I had been independent for a long time. I could continue to be independent.

Sliver of Midnight media was everywhere. The premiere was scheduled at Grauman's Chinese Theatre. Would I be invited?

I didn't know, but it seemed unlikely.

Thinking about how I'd told Ben I'd take him as my date and how none of it was possible now—not me going, not going with Ben at my side—made me furious. He still hadn't called, hadn't texted, hadn't anything. It had been a week, and he hadn't said anything. Emma told me he needed a chance to explain. I'd given him that chance, hadn't I?

I picked up my phone to call Emma to ask for her advice but put it down again. No. Emma had made her position clear. This was a bridge-jump moment—the kind where you leapt without asking for advice or thinking too hard. You just jumped.

I grabbed my purse, stuffed my feet into my shoes, and yelled "Geronimo" as I started up my car.

Like it or not, Ben was going to talk to me.

Finding Ben wasn't a problem because he was a creature of habit. He ate at the same restaurants he'd eaten at when we'd worked together. It was just before eight, which meant he would be headed to Tiffany's Cafe—a throwback to the all-American diner. Ben insisted they made the most amazing stuffed French toast in the entire world, and he went there for breakfast before work every Monday.

I found him sitting alone at a table with his phone in one hand and a fork full of raspberry-sauced French toast in the other. He appeared to be reading something on his phone, or maybe he was watching a movie. Either way, he was about to be disrupted.

"This seat taken? No? Great." I sat without allowing him to even register what was happening.

When it finally clicked in his mind that I had just joined him for breakfast, his mouth opened in shock. "Silvia! You can't be he—"

I cut him off. "Don't you dare say something we'll both regret. And before I decide that you aren't worth the mental energy I've been giving you, I wanted to give you a chance to explain yourself. Emma and my grandmother have both told me that I'm being unforgiving by not allowing you a chance to share your side of the story. Even Walt believes I owe you a chance. So here I am. What gives?" Then I went silent, waiting for his answer.

His answer was to look around to see who might have noticed that I'd joined him.

Really?

To alleviate his blatant need for secrecy, I stood up and yelled, "Hello, everyone! I'd just like it known that I, Silvia Bradshaw, am spending the breakfast hour with Benjamin Armstrong. It's no big deal. We are not conspiring to topple film studios. We're actually discussing whether or not we have a future together. Stay tuned, folks. Breakfast at Tiffany's just got interesting!" I sat again. "There. No secrets. No reason to flinch because it's all in the open."

"You're insane." This was the first thing he had to say to me after not seeing me for so long, after signing the world's stupidest agreement, and after not responding to me telling him I loved him.

Not a great beginning.

"Hey." I snapped my fingers at him. "You told me you loved me, and then you signed the paper version of keep-away. Who's insane here? Because anyone who really cared about another person wouldn't have let a piece of corporate pulp come between them."

"Pulp?"

"Paper!" I said, probably louder than necessary.

Ben put down his phone and his fork, wiped his mouth with his napkin, and fixed me with a stare that was infuriatingly Ben. "Did you really show up here to accuse me of not caring?"

"You signed the paper! The same paper I hadn't signed. The one I wouldn't ever sign because it was manipulative and controlling and unfair, and worse than all of that, it made it so we couldn't be together, but *you* signed it!" Stinging burned at the back of my eyes, twice as bad behind the prosthetic. I didn't cry, not over things like this, never over things like this, but I hadn't ever been in love before either.

"Of course I signed it! What did you think I was going to do? Let you get fired?"

"They didn't fire me—"

Ben cut me off this time. "Of course they didn't, because

I signed the agreement like Adam told me to!" Ben was yelling too, now.

I held up my hands to stop him, not only because what he was saying confused me but because it unnerved me to hear Ben shouting. "What does Adam have to do with any of this?"

"I ran into him at the movies." Ben's volume dropped to normal again. He glanced around as if only just noticing that the diner patrons I'd called to attention were still paying attention. His nostrils flared, but he kept his voice low. "He said they were going to fire you if you didn't sign the agreement."

"Did he also tell you that he's a snake who is trying to impress some executives just so he can get a crummy bit part in a TV series?" Had Ben really signed those papers to save me from being fired? Had Emma, Grandma, and Walt all been right about his motivations? I picked up Ben's abandoned fork and speared a piece of French toast. After stuffing it in my mouth, I pointed the fork at him. "Anyway, this isn't about me getting fired. We'd already talked about that. And even if they did fire me, so what?"

Ben raked his fingers through his hair in frustration. "So what? So it's just your whole career that means more to you than anything, that's what."

"Not more than anything. Not more than you. I loved you enough to not sign the papers. I was hoping for the same level of commitment from you. Not that I wanted you to get in trouble with your work—of course I didn't want that, *don't* want that—it just felt—"

"Stop!" Ben commanded.

I did, but only because his shout after he'd been so careful to keep his voice down startled me.

"Did you just say you loved me?"

That set me off again. "Yeah, act all surprised like you didn't know that. Whatever, Ben."

"I didn't know that. How would I know that?" Ben shoved his plate aside and leaned in, his ice-blue eyes mystified.

"I told you already, in a text, after, may I add, you told me you'd shoved our relationship into oncoming traffic."

"No, you didn't tell me that."

"Yes, I did."

"I would definitely remember you using those words."

"Well, I didn't use those words exactly. But you knew what I meant!" I had to take a breath to keep my volume from rising again.

"The last thing you said to me was 'As you wish'!" Ben whisper-yelled. "That sounded like you were writing me off."

"So help me, Ben, this is the least funny thing you've ever done. You know what those words mean!" I was whisper-yelling, too.

His blank look made me pause.

"*The Princess Bride*?" I prompted.

A faint understanding dawned in his eyes, like sunlight on an extremely cloudy day. "A movie?"

"Seriously, Ben? You've never seen *The Princess Bride*? Westley to Buttercup? Only one of the best movies for one-liners on love ever created?"

No recognition flashed in his eyes.

I speared another piece of French toast and pretty much

swallowed it without chewing. I needed to think. After nearly his entire breakfast had disappeared from Ben's plate, he pointed at the remaining bite. "Do you need me to get you your own?"

I dared to look up at him. He was smiling. For the first time since my showing up to disrupt his breakfast, Ben looked relaxed.

"What are you smiling about? There is nothing to smile about with this entire conversation."

"You love me. Why wouldn't I be smiling?" Then it disappeared from his face with his sharp intake of breath. "But that doesn't solve the problem of the lawsuit. We still signed an agreement."

"Speak for yourself. I didn't sign anything."

Ben frowned. "How did you keep your job without signing?"

"I didn't." Since the French toast was gone, I dug into his hash browns.

He fell back heavily in his chair. "They fired you."

"Nope," I said around the food, wishing Ben had used Tabasco sauce to season them. "I quit."

"You quit?"

"Is there an echo in here? Yes. I quit."

Ben sat silent, processing in the way that Ben did, not responding until all the pieces had clicked into places that made sense to him.

I finished off his meal. Who knew confessions and confrontations could make a person so ravenous?

"So that paper I signed that said I was not to fraternize with anyone in the employ of Portal Pictures?"

"Probably means you and Dean shouldn't date, but it doesn't apply to me." I dropped his fork to his plate with a clatter and crossed my arms on the table, offering my first real smile in days.

Ben stood slowly and rounded the table, maintaining eye contact. "You love me."

"I know."

It was close enough to a Han and Leia moment, but when Ben pulled me to my feet and cradled my face in his hands while he stared at me with awe and wonder, I knew this moment was better than anything Hollywood could have produced.

"I'd love to hear you say it," he whispered as he bent toward me until there was nothing but a breath between us.

"I love you."

His smile and his kiss happened at the same moment that he wrapped his arms around me with the gentle reverence of a man who knew what it was to love and to wait for that love to be returned. I don't know how long we stood there together, breathing and existing as one person, one sigh, but it wasn't long enough. Was this what it meant to love? To need and want and dream and hope all in one frantic heartbeat after another?

A few people from our audience whistled and clapped.

Geronimo, indeed.

Chapter Twenty-Four

*"If I'm honest, I have to tell you I still read
fairy tales, and I like them best of all."*

—Audrey Hepburn, played by Audrey Hepburn in real life

Ben didn't feel inclined to go to work that day, not after everything the two studios had put us through. We ordered another round of breakfasts since I'd pretty much eaten his and still managed to feel hungry. We filled each other in on everything that had happened over the week.

I told him about Grandma, her sickness, how she was handling everything, and how Walt had been such a loyal and good companion during the entire ordeal.

His eyes were wide with horror. "You didn't call me?" He actually sounded furious that I dared leave him out of such important news.

"Well, you did kinda dump me, so I feel like my lack of communication had just cause."

"But you had to go through that alone." His eyes brimmed

with apologies and sadness for my suffering. "You should have called. I would've come right over."

"Even though you signed your name to a paper saying you wouldn't?" I couldn't help but tease him a little.

Ben narrowed his eyes at me. "I thought I was helping you. If I'd known you were in trouble, I would have come. I'd never leave you alone."

I thought of Emma and Walt and Grandma. I also thought of Audrey and the haunting words to the song "Moon River." Audrey had been with me. She'd been with me since that first night in the hospital when I was five years. "I wasn't alone," I said finally.

"I'll send Emma a thank-you card," he said, not understanding what I meant.

Sure, Emma had been there and had been an immense source of comfort, but that first night, it had been Audrey.

Ben told me how Mid-Scene had said that if he didn't sign, it would pretty much guarantee my death in the Hollywood dream, and when Adam confirmed how much trouble I was in, he felt like he couldn't allow that to happen to me. Ben had not been the villain in the story. He'd tried to be the hero. The good guy. He'd just confused what I wanted for what I actually needed.

"I get what happened to us through all this," I told him, deciding to explain it in a way we could both understand and both forgive so we could move on in our relationship. "We were making jump cuts when we should have been making cross-fades. But the great thing is that we're masters at splicing." I laced my fingers in his. "I'm calling this a final cut, the perfect edit: seamless."

We talked through breakfast and into lunch. His hand held mine for a good portion of that time, his fingers tangling up in mine like we were in high school and just discovering the art of hand-holding. The waitress kept our drinks full and never once complained that we tied up a table for four hours. Ben left her a healthy tip to thank her for her kindness, even though he was about to join me in the unemployment line.

Because when Ben did go in to work that day, it was to quit.

"Are you sure?" I asked him for the seventh time since leaving the diner. We'd arrived at the gate where Ben showed his badge to get onto the studio property. I recognized the guard as Lee Taylor. If I recognized him, he had to know me as well. That fact made me suddenly very nervous. "Are you really, really, absolutely, not lying about it, *sure* that this is what you want to do?"

"Why are you trying to talk me out of this?" he asked as Lee went back into the guard shack to get the visitor pass Ben requested.

"You signed those papers because you didn't want me to lose my job. And now we're here, getting a pass for *me*. I'm just wondering if you understand the consequences. You're quitting your job. The chances of finding another one aren't awesome. No job means no income. No income means not paying your bills, not to mention possible starvation and homelessness."

"Not homelessness or starvation," he said as Lee returned with the pass.

"How do you figure?"

"My mom has a sweet basement, and she's an amazing cook." He laughed as I glowered.

Lee must not have recognized me because he smiled and waved us through.

"I'm serious," I said once we were through.

"I'm a grown-up, Silvia. One of the responsible variety. If I have to take an interim job while I search for one that actually suits me, I will."

I still worried because an interim job for people like Ben and me usually meant we'd have to do something that didn't fill our well creatively. I did not want that for him. But the alternative was for us to not be together. Neither of us wanted that option.

Ben quitting turned out to be the best thing for everyone, because, as our attorney later informed us, quitting released Ben from any legal tie to Mid-Scene Films that wasn't directly dealing with the specific projects he did for them. He also signed a statement for Portal Pictures that he'd offered advice to a peer but had done no actual work on *Sliver of Midnight*, voiding Mid-Scene's lawsuit.

We sent a copy of the letter to Mid-Scene.

The squabble between the studios was over, and Hollywood settled down into business as usual, minus two specific film editors. Mid-Scene hired Alison to replace Ben, and Ben actually seemed pleased that she was finally getting her shot. He held no malice at the fact that Mid-Scene had been out of line in the entire situation, or that Alison had swooped in when she saw her chance to break into the business. I was glad for her, too. She got the job, but I got the guy. I was calling us even.

The day of Grandma's surgery, Ben sat with Walt, my dad—who'd flown in for the surgery—and me in the waiting room. I stared at him with wonder.

"You doing okay? What are you thinking?" Ben asked.

"I am okay. I'm actually thinking about the movie *Sabrina*. The original one with Audrey Hepburn. There's a scene where she says something about learning to live, how to be *in* the world and *of* the world, and not just standing aside and watching. I used to feel like I was standing to the side and watching all the time, but I don't anymore. I feel like I'm living."

"I understand completely." Ben wrapped his hand around mine.

I gave a low laugh. "You know, when I was little and not getting along with my parents, I used to threaten to run away to Peru. I've always had a tendency to run from things. *Sabrina* ends with Audrey promising she would never again run away from life. Or from love, either. You know, I almost did that."

"Promised to never run from life or love? Should I be worried as to where all this is going?"

"No. You shouldn't be worried, not any more. Because I almost did run away from you, from the possibility of us, and if it weren't for that cute little lady in the surgery room right now, I probably would've done it."

"I guess I owe her flowers then," Ben said with a smile.

"Yes. You probably do."

The doctor came out about two hours later to tell us the operation had been a success. The chemo had shrunk the tumor by fifty percent, which made it much easier for them to get everything when they cut it out.

Dad and I both stayed with Grandma after the surgery. When Dad left me alone with my sleeping grandmother to hit the vending machines for something to eat, I closed my eyes and listened to the beeps and hums of the monitors. I remembered those noises from a long time ago when I pictured a woman with a flowing gown and a sword saving me from cancer.

I imagined her now sheathing her sword and offering me a salute and a smile.

"Thank you," I whispered to the ghostly image in my mind. She'd stayed with me all this time, but now the haunting was over.

Ben came with roses the next day, not for me but for Grandma. "How are you feeling?" he asked her.

"Well," she said, her voice still thick with all she'd been through, "I've decided to call myself the uniboober." Walt laughed. Dad was horrified. And I smiled. She was going to be just fine.

A few days after Grandma's surgery, I headed back home. The plants were likely all dead from neglect, and the mail was likely flowing out of my box and irritating the postal carrier who had to stuff everything in to make it all fit.

Tucked between the bills and junk mail, there was an envelope gilded with silver foil. My mouth fell open. "No way!" I breathed and tore it open. Inside was a ticket admitting me and a plus-one to the premiere of *Sliver of Midnight*.

Tears sprang to my eyes. I was invited. *Invited*. I hadn't realized how important such an invitation was to me until it was there in my hands.

It came with a note from Danny.

Dean gave me your address since Portal Pictures refused to release it to me. He said it was the least he could do after botching things up. I want you there to see the movie we made together.

In case you hadn't heard, Christopher and I are putting together a team for a movie we're funding on our own. I know the rule in Hollywood is to always let the studio pay and never use your own money on any project, but since Christopher and I don't much care for Hollywood's rules, we're funding this ourselves. We need a good editor, and we know one when we see her.

I've included my business card with all my contact information. Call me. Let's go to lunch and discuss the details. Bring your boyfriend along. Christopher and I spent some time studying the work you two have done together and like what we're seeing. We'll want a strong team that can work well together.

Keep in touch, Little Audrey.

All my best,

Danny

The night of the premiere, Ben and I wore the formal wear Grandma had picked out for us for the Audrey Hepburn Society ball. I didn't have my hair done like Holly Golightly or wear any jewelry, but I wanted to wear the gown. It only seemed right to give a nod of appreciation to Audrey when she had been such a big part of leading me down this path into Hollywood.

"Are you ready?" Ben asked. He'd tucked my hand into his to keep me from picking at the ends of my gloves.

"I thought I was until now."

The limo Danny had sent to pick up Ben and me stopped at the red carpet.

"I feel like I've been waiting my whole life for this." I bit my lip.

"Me too." But Ben wasn't looking out the window toward the crowd or at the attendant stepping up to open the door. He was looking at me. I stopped biting my lip and leaned in to kiss him.

"Me too," I echoed. I closed my eyes and whispered another silent thank you to Audrey.

It was not to say that I'd been cured from the irrational fear of the disease that took her, but I could say that, by getting to know her through her films and biographies, I'd come to respect her and love her and to be grateful for the path in Hollywood she'd shown me.

She was the one woman to teach other women how to be, my grandmother had once said. Grandma was right about that. Audrey taught me about love. She taught me to be a woman. She taught me to follow my passion as a film editor, a friend, and an advocate.

Ben exited the car, grinned at me from the red carpet, and held out his hand. I placed my own gloved hand in his and saw clearly, for the first time, how Audrey had taught me to be myself.

Acknowledgments

I used to work in Hollywood . . . well, not *in* Hollywood, but for various production studios out of Hollywood doing basic film work in Utah. I finished writing my first book by hand in a spiral-ring notebook while doing photo double, stand-in, and featured-extra work for *Touched by An Angel*. My claim to fame is that Ewan McGregor kissed me at a wrap party.

Writing about Hollywood is like visiting an old, dear friend. Being able to pay homage to a much-loved actress in that world of film made writing this book even better. So it is that I must give credit to Audrey Hepburn and all that she was and all that she stood for within the acting community. She genuinely was a woman who taught other women how to be. She stayed true to her heart in raising her family, in spite of a glittery world that would have told her to put her career first. And when her own children had grown, she looked to the children of the world. Thank you, Audrey, for being such a shining example to follow. You were a beautiful actress, but you were a brilliant human.

Writing the character Silvia could not have been done without the real Sylvia. My dear, sweet, hilarious friend, thank you for letting me write a fictionalized you into this novel. You have greater vision and better sight with your one eye than most of us do with our two. Thanks for laughing with me, not caring that I snore when we have to share cabin rooms and tents together, and for answering, "Yes, Mickey?" whenever I call out, "Oh, Sylvia?"

And I can never state enough how much I appreciate the love, support, and friendship of Heather Moore, Josi Kilpack, Jeff and Jen Savage, and James Dashner in my life. They are some of the greatest blessings to have come from my venture into literature.

The team at Shadow Mountain is amazing. Heidi Taylor, the more I get to know you, the more I love you. There's a long list of all the reasons why I am grateful to have you in my life. Thank you for everything! Lisa Mangum, you are magic as an editor. You see all those wrong and awkward places and understand exactly how to place the Band-Aid so those places heal properly. You're an amazing editor. You are an amazing writer. You are an amazing friend. To Chris Schoebinger, Jill Schaugaard, Sarah Cobabe, Malina Grigg, and Richard Erickson—you guys rock your jobs. Thanks for all you do! You cannot know how much I appreciate all of you.

And thank you, Sara Crowe, for all that you do for me as my agent. I so appreciate you. I know I told you that you were the agent I would sever a limb for, but I'm so glad you didn't require limbs. Whew!

Last, but never least, I am so grateful for my family: my parents, my children, and my own Mr. Wright. My happily ever after. The best dad any three kids could ever have a right to. I've thought a lot about my family while writing this book, about the sacrifices that must be made when a career mom is involved. We found a good balance that allowed us all to grow and become our best selves, but we couldn't have done it without each other. Thank you, dear family, all of you, for being my balance. Scott, I'm so glad that our lives, if written down, could be called a kissing book. I'm never going to get tired of that. As You Wish.

Discussion Questions

1. How does the title work with the themes of the book?
2. How has Audrey Hepburn's role as an advocate inspired others to use their voices and platforms for good?
3. As an actress, Audrey had to play many different characters and parts in her life. Silvia also played many different roles in her life, except she wasn't acting, she was surviving. In what ways do we change ourselves for the various audiences in our lives, and how do we stay true to the real us?
4. Hollywood is a place still under the control of men, but that fact is changing. In what ways can women outside of Hollywood affect those changes to quicken the process?
5. Were there any particular quotes that stood out to you, and why?
6. Silvia is at a disadvantage with the loss of her eye, but— like the real woman her character is based on—she works

around her disability. In what ways does Silvia see more clearly than people with two functioning eyes?

7. In what ways does Silvia choose not to see? And how are we blind to truths in our own lives because we might be afraid of putting ourselves in situations where we might get hurt?

8. How can disabilities, both real and perceived, strengthen us and weaken us? How can we stand up to those challenges?

9. How many Audrey Hepburn movies have you seen? Which is your favorite, and why?

About the Author

JULIE WRIGHT wrote her first book when she was fifteen and has since written twenty-three novels. Her novel *Cross My Heart* won the 2010 Whitney Award for best romance, and her novels *Eyes Like Mine* and *Death Thieves* were both Whitney Award finalists. She won the Crown Heart Award for *The Fortune Café*. She has one husband, three kids, one dog, and a varying number of fish, frogs, and salamanders (depending on attrition). She loves writing, reading, traveling, speaking at schools, hiking, playing with her kids, and watching her husband make dinner.